THE B

Dick Hardesty Mystery Series

THE BAR WATCHER

Dick Hardesty Mystery Series

Novel by

Dorien Grey

GLB Publishers   San Francisco

Published in the United States by
GLB Publishers
P.O. Box 78212, San Francisco, CA 94107 USA

Cover by GLB Publishers

ISBN 1-879194-79-1

Library of Congress Control Number:

20010944415

2001

To those who not only
hear the different drummer
within themselves, but dare to
march to his beat.

CHAPTER 1

One of the reasons I became a private investigator was because I like puzzles, and every case is like working a jigsaw puzzle without the picture on the box. Of course, the bulk of any private investigator's cases are like the puzzles you see for kids on the little table in dentists' office waiting rooms—five pieces and there's the bunny. But every now and then you get one that is more like one of those 1,500-piece reproductions of a Bosch or Breughel painting—a real challenge. They drive me crazy sometimes, but when I finally put the last couple of pieces together, there's a sense of satisfaction that's hard to describe, or match.

And almost always the people you're looking for are right there in the picture, though you don't recognize them until the puzzle's completed. And from time to time, the picture you think you're working on isn't the one you end up seeing.

Now, take the case of the bar watcher....

* * *

It's what I refer to now as my "Slut Phase." My monogamous five year relationship with Chris had broken up some time ago, and I decided it was about time I let the other guys spend their time looking for "Mr. Right"—I'd concentrate on Mr. Right Now. Looking back, I'm glad I didn't whittle a notch in the bedpost after every trick, or I'd have ended up sleeping on a mound of wood shavings.

When I wasn't pursuing research for a book I thought about writing on "101 Fun Things to Do With a Penis," I was actually making some progress in that part of my life which did not involve lying down. I'd obtained my private investigator license late the year before, and was struggling to make ends meet.

Business was beginning to improve, though slowly, Thanks to a solid working relationship I had with members of the local gay Bar Guild, for whom I'd done a couple favors prior to taking out my license. Referrals from Guild members were in fact the source of much of my business. And the fact that there weren't exactly a lot of gay private investigators to choose from also helped, I'm sure. I'd rented a small office in one of the city's older commercial buildings, with an address far more impressive than the building itself.

If I'd started out with any illusions that being a private investigator might be a pretty exciting job, reality kicked me in the ass in short order. Lots and lots of checking on possibly (and too often definitely) wandering lovers, one or two incidences of blackmail, a case of embezzlement involving the business manager of a gay resort—that sort of thing; and lots of sitting around waiting for the next client.

Oh, yeah...and I'd given up smoking. Cold turkey. That was a hell of a lot harder than any case I'd had, or was likely ever to have. So I was relieved when the phone rang just as I was trying to figure out a 10-letter word for "reclusive or brutish person" in the paper's crossword puzzle (don't bother: it's "troglodyte").

"Hardesty Investigations," I said, in my professional, half-octave-lower-than-normal voice.

"Hardesty: this is Barry Comstock. Jay Mason of the Bar Guild referred you to me."

"Well, Thanks for calling, Mr. Comstock," I said, making a mental note to Thank Jay as well. "How can I help you?"

"I own Rage...you're familiar with it?"

Rage was the city's hottest bathhouse. I knew it.

"Of course," I said, then waited for him to continue.

"We've got ourselves a problem, and while I think it's a bunch of bullshit, they tell me you might be able to help resolve it."

"Is it anything you can mention on the phone, or...?" I

asked.

"No; definitely not."

"I understand," I said—but of course I didn't. "Did you want to come to my office, or..."

"No, you come over here. I've got a business to run and I can't just be taking off."

Like I *wasn't* busy. Well, okay, I wasn't, but I didn't like his 'busier than thou' attitude.

"No problem," I said. "I could be there in around an hour, if that would be all right. I have a client coming in a little later this afternoon." I lied, but he didn't have to know that.

"Good," he said. "I don't see your name on our members list, but I might have missed it."

Actually, he hadn't—I wasn't a member. Baths are fine, but they're not my thing. I like to have a few words come out of my mouth before putting something in, and the baths aren't exactly the place guys go for complex conversations like "Hi. My name is...."

"I know how to find it," I said. "I'll see you in an hour, then."

He hung up without saying "goodbye."

Though I'd never met Barry Comstock, I'd seen him at a distance a couple of times in the more trendy bars and discos, always accompanied by two or three different good-looking guys whom he seemed to enjoy treating like dirt. He had a reputation as a wheeler-dealer in the rapidly growing gay business community. A former porn star, he'd opened Rage about eight months earlier. He was noted for having a monumental schlong, and an ego to match. I'd seen some of his movies—I think I still have a copy of one of his better ones: "Comstock's Load." He was also rumored to have the first nickel he ever made, so I imagined he would not be calling on me unless it was something pretty important.

* * *

Rage was located in what local gays were beginning to refer to as The Central—sort of an homage to San Francisco's Castro district—and about a half a block off Beech, the main gay thoroughfare. No ground floor windows; just a dark blue canopy with "Rage" in white script, over a matching blue entry door. Just as I reached for the handle, the door swung open and a drop-dead gorgeous hunk exited carrying his gym bag and a satisfied smile. Our eyes locked for a moment, and he gave me a broad wink. "Have fun," he said.

Before I had a chance to reconsider my opinion of baths, I was inside the small lobby.

A blond Adonis stood behind the registration window wearing a "Rage" tee shirt so tight I thought at first it had been spray painted on his bare chest. *Yeah*, I thought, *maybe I should reconsider....*

"Your card?" the blond said.

"I'm not a member," I said. "I've got an appointment with Barry Comstock. The name's Hardesty."

The blond picked up a phone out of sight below the window, said something I couldn't hear, then hung up the phone and nodded toward the only door leading to the interior from the lobby. "First door to your left," he said, and pressed an unseen buzzer which opened the lobby inner door.

"Thanks," I said, and passed through it into a short hallway. The first door on the left said simply "Private" and I knocked.

"Come in," a voice said, and I did.

The room was large and windowless, paneled in what appeared to be dark oak. It apparently couldn't decide whether its function was to impress or to be a working office, and therefore didn't quite fit either category. There were several small framed photos on one wall, apparently of Comstock with various celebrities, a large painting of a nude male torso—undoubtedly Comstock himself—on a side wall next to a door, a couple file cabinets, a worktable with a copy machine and a typewriter, a couple of comfortable and expensive looking leather chairs and a large, equally expensive looking desk, behind which sat Barry Comstock, slitting open a stack of mail with a very wicked looking letter opener.

I mentioned that Barry Comstock had been a porn star, but it was obvious that he was no longer in his 20s—or, despite valiant efforts on his part, even his 30s. His face had that stretched-too-tight look that indicated a plastic surgeon's handiwork. In some odd way, he was rather like the room itself. He'd have been considerably more attractive if he'd just left himself alone.

He did not get up and so I deliberately walked over to the desk and extended my hand, which he had to put down the letter opener and lean forward to take.

"Dick Hardesty, Mr. Comstock." I said. "What can I do for you?"

He motioned me to a chair and resumed opening the mail, shifting his glance back and forth between the mail and me.

"We've had some…well, what my partners consider to be threats. I think they're bullshit, but they insisted I look into it. Frankly, I don't have the time, which is why I called you."

"What kind of threats?" I asked.

Comstock finished opening the mail, set the opener aside again, and leaned back in his chair. "Oh, we've been getting bitch letters since we opened…most of them have tapered off lately."

"What kind of 'bitch letters?'" I asked.

Comstock gave a slight sneer. "About our membership policy," he said.

"And your membership policy is…?" I asked. Actually, I had a pretty good idea from what I'd been hearing on the street, but I wanted to hear him spell it out. He looked at me with a mixture of disdain and surprise.

"Which is that this is a place where hot young guys come to meet other hot young guys. We don't let fats or old farts in. If you're fat, or bald, or old, or ugly you can go someplace else."

So much for my buying stock in the Barry Comstock School of Charm, I thought. This guy was really starting to piss me off.

"So what made this letter different…and did you keep it?" I asked.

"Nah," Comstock said with a shrug. "I pitch them all. But I remembered this one—it came in maybe four, five months ago—because the asshole made it up to look like a ransom note…you know, all cut-out words pasted together. It said that if we didn't change our membership policy we'd be hearing from him again. Fuckin' blackmail's what it boils down to, pure and simple. And I'm not the kind of guy you want to try to blackmail." He unconsciously hunched his shoulders forward as if flexing his muscles.

We sat silent for a moment, until I said: "And I gather you did hear from him again?"

Comstock gave a contemptuous snort and reached into the bottom drawer of his desk, pulling out what appeared to be a shoe box. "This came in the mail, addressed to me." He pushed it across the desk, and I leaned forward to take it. The box had no marking of any kind, and I lifted the lid to find it stuffed with tissue paper. Moving the tissue paper aside I found a 3x5 card on which someone had pasted a panel from what I assume was a comic book. It was a picture of a fireball over which was the word: "*BOOM!*" Turning it over, words cut from obviously various sources, in assorted sizes and typefaces said: "Last chance. Everyone plays or YOU pay." Kind of melodramatic, I thought, but it made it's point.

I put the card back, closed the lid, and pushed the box back across the desk.

"Did you save the wrapper it came in?"

"What the fuck for? I've got enough garbage around here as it is."

If he was too stupid to entertain the idea that a return address or postmark might have come in handy, I wasn't about to spell it out for him.

"It's probably just somebody with a grudge and an active imagination," I said. "But you never know; this guy could be

serious. I guess you didn't consider contacting the police?"
Comstock shook his head scornfully. "Are you out of your
fucking mind? I let the cops come in here scaring off the
customers and I might as well shut the place down. I told you
it's fucking blackmail. And I told you I don't pay blackmail."
*Yeah, I heard you the first time, and I wasn't impressed
then, either,* I thought. Though I didn't say anything, it struck
me that for anyone out to settle a grievance, real or imagined,
with Rage, it would only take a couple of "concerned citizen"
or "they're selling drugs" calls to the cops to effectively shut
the place down. The police would love any excuse for a raid,
and no gay man in his right mind would willingly put himself
in a gay bath house that was subject to frequent raids.
Obviously, something else was going on here.

"Exactly who determines who gets in and who doesn't?"
I asked.

Comstock leaned forward, putting his elbows on the desk,
one hand wrapped around the other lightly clenched fist. "I'm
the boss. *I* decide. The desk men are told in no uncertain terms
who gets in and who doesn't; they do the sorting out," he said.
"If there's any doubt, they buzz me. But usually it's pretty cut
and dried. Ugly's ugly. Fat's fat; old is old."

"And how do they handle it when an undesirable comes
in?" I used the word "undesirable" deliberately.

"The ones we want as members are given membership cards
to fill out. The others are told that memberships are closed."

"And if somebody is filling out a membership card when
a non-desirable comes in?" I asked. "Or worse, if somebody's
getting the 'closed membership' spiel and somebody worthy
of belonging comes in?"

"Same thing. They get the message pretty fast. And you can
cut the fucking sarcasm. I'm running a business here, not a
bleeding hearts social club. There are lots of other baths around.
Let the creeps go there."

That's it, Comstock, I thought; *you're definitely off my
Christmas card list.*

He stared at me and then said: "Well, do you want the job or not?"

"I can certainly try," I said, "but you realize there aren't any guarantees." And then I told him my rates and he leaned quickly back in his chair as if a cobra had suddenly appeared on his desk. "That's pretty damned steep for no guarantees," he said. "I'll tell you what I'll do, though. You do a little preliminary checking around first—you know, in exchange for a year's membership, say—then we could talk about officially hiring you when you had a better idea of whether you think you can find the guy."

Now it was my turn to see the imaginary cobra, but I didn't move a muscle. I wanted to tell this sorry excuse for a cheap bastard what he could do with his year's membership, but I managed to keep my cool.

"Sorry, my rates aren't negotiable. Why don't you think this over for a day or so," I said, getting up from my chair, "and if you decide to hire me, give me a call."

I wondered whether I should offer to shake hands with this walking prick or not. I was surprised when he also got up and extended his hand. "I'll let you know," he said as we shook hands. Then he sat back down in his chair and I turned and left the room.

"Rage" was a good name for the place, I decided.

* * *

On my way back to the office, though I tried to concentrate on other things, my mind kept going back to Comstock and Rage. There's a definite difference between having a big prick and being one, but in Comstock's case he qualified in both. Rage's membership policy was, without a doubt, reprehensible and insulting to anyone who did not meet Comstock's standards of what was or was not "hot." I could well imagine the humiliation and…well, yes, rage… anyone so blatantly and obviously refused entry to the bath might well feel. Perhaps whoever it was who sent the letter and the box was overreacting just a little, but then again, if it had happened to me....But, hey, *I'm* okay: I got offered a full year's membership! Big fucking deal. I wondered whether it ever occurred to the guys who got in how the guys who didn't must feel?

Okay, Hardesty, I told myself, *take your heart off your sleeve and put it back in your chest, now.*

* * *

On my way home after work, I stopped in at Bob Allen's bar, Ramón's, for their happy hour, and to see if I could talk to Bob. I wanted to find out a little more about Barry Comstock and his "partners," and Bob was in as good a position to know as anyone.

I didn't see Bob around, but Jimmy, the bartender, was at the far end of the bar signing for a beer delivery from a guy whose talents were definitely wasted in pushing dollies full of beer all over town. He stood about 6'3" and was wearing a short-sleeved uniform shirt. I've seen oak trees with trunks smaller around than that guy's biceps. And when he turned to face in my direction, I saw that the rest of him matched. Short-cropped hair, a nice, square jaw, a huge expanse of chest with perfectly curved pecs the shirt couldn't hide, a V-shaped torso and a bulge down the left leg of his pants that ran halfway to his knees. Definitely my kind of guy.

Normally, I'd have taken the first stool I came to, but something—care to guess what?—drew me to the far end of the bar. The delivery man looked up at me as I was about halfway there, and when our eyes met, I felt like that 3x5 card in the box at Rage said, *"BOOM."*

"Hi, Jimmy," I said, taking a stool next to where the delivery man was standing.

"Hi, Dick," Jimmy said.

"Yeah, hi, Dick," the delivery man said giving me a First Class Cruise smile. Then, eyes still on me, he half turned toward

Jimmy and said, in a tone that didn't leave much doubt as to who he was really talking to: "Yeah, Jimmy, like I was saying, this is my last stop for the day, so I'm not sure what I'll be doing after I take the truck back." Again the grin.

"Open for suggestions?" I heard myself ask.

"Got one?" he asked.

Oh, I had one, all right! I had a suggestion, too, as a matter of fact.

"Earth to Dick," I heard Jimmy say, snapping his fingers: "Earth to Dick; order, please."

I pulled my eyes away from the delivery man long enough to look quickly at Jimmy. "Yeah, give me a whiskey old fashioned, sweet." *And a bucket of ice water to pour over my head,* I thought. "Can I buy you one?" I asked the delivery man.

"Thanks," he said, "but not until I get off work. Will the offer still be good then?"

"Sure," I said. "About how long?"

If he said 'About 11 inches' I think I'd have fallen off my stool. Luckily, he didn't.

"Maybe 20 minutes," he said. "You still be here?"

Silly question. "Count on it," I said.

Without another word, the delivery man got his dolly, waved at Jimmy, who waved back, and left through the rear door.

Jimmy brought my drink, going through his standard flourish routine with the napkin. "Thank God he's gone," Jimmy said, shaking his head, face serious.

"Why?" I asked, a little startled.

"I was afraid I was going to have to turn the fire hose on you two," he said. "I know Jared works fast, but this set an all-time record, even for him."

"His name's Jared?" I asked, realizing he hadn't mentioned it.

Jimmy nodded. "Jared Martinson. And, honey, I don't know what you're going to do with that boy!"

"What do you mean?" I asked.

Jimmy looked up and down the bar for anyone needing immediate service and, seeing no one who did, he leaned across the bar toward me. "I went home with him right after he started delivering here," Jimmy said, his voice lowered though there was no one within two stools of us in either direction.

"And...?" I prompted.

Jimmy stood back from the bar and spread his two hands apart like a fisherman demonstrating the size of the one that got away. Impressive, to say the least.

"Lordy," he said, "all I could do was throw my arms around it and cry! Actually, I kind of feel sorry for him—not one guy in ten that I know could accommodate that ramrod!"

Someone at the far end of the bar signaled for another drink, and Jimmy pushed himself away from the bar, saying "'Scuse me," and moved toward the waiting customer.

Jared Martinson, eh? He sounded like a real challenge in more ways than one.

* * *

I was about halfway through my second old fashioned, having learned that Bob had said he wouldn't be in at all that night, when I felt a strong hand on my shoulder. I turned to look up into the incredibly handsome face of Jared Martinson.

"Offer still good?" he asked, smiling.

"One among many," I replied, signaling to Jimmy, who waved and nodded.

"That was quick," I said as Jared took the stool next to me. He'd changed clothes, into a short-sleeved pullover sport shirt that outlined every curve, indent, and nipple.

"I don't waste time when I'm after something," he said. I hoped he meant me.

Jimmy brought up a drink and set it in front of Jared with a wink. Apparently Jimmy knew quite a bit about Jared Martinson.

"So how long have you been driving delivery trucks?" I asked, after we'd done a silent glass-click toast.

Jared took a slow drink before answering. "Since I got into town, about six months ago," he said. "I like it. Gives me plenty of time to think, and helps keep the muscles in shape."

"So I noticed," I said. "You always been in this line of work?"

Jared smiled and shook his head. "Not really. I taught for a while."

"Really?" I said. "What level? What subject?"

"College," he said casually. "Russian Literature."

"You're shitting me," I said.

He shook his head and smiled. "Nope. I've got a Masters in it. Working on my Ph.D. now."

"Why did you quit teaching?" I asked, really curious.

"Because I wasn't much older than my students, and some of them were just too damned tempting. So I set it aside for a while to work on my Ph.D.. By the time I finish it I'll be ready to go back. And I really like what I'm doing now. No pressure."

I was really impressed, and it probably showed.

"How about you?" he asked. "What do you do for a living?"

"Nothing quite so exotic as a teaching Russian Literature, I'm afraid," I said. "I'm a private investigator."

"No shit?" He grinned. "Working on anything interesting?"

"Not at the moment," I said. "I might have one coming up, but I'm not sure yet."

We each took a sip of our drinks, and I said: "You ever go to Rage?" *Hey, that was subtle*, I thought.

Jared smiled. "Not any more. I sort of lost my membership."

"How'd that happen?" I asked.

"A long story—I'll tell you about it sometime."

I was curious, but let it drop for now.

"You know the owner?" I asked, trying another tack.

Jared nodded. "Oh, yeah. A lot more than I want to, I'm sorry to say. He's an arrogant asshole who thinks the word 'no' doesn't apply to him. He rubbed me the wrong way since the night I joined."

"How so?" I asked.

Jared turned toward me, his knee bumping against my thigh. I instinctively moved my leg out of the way, but he reached down and pulled it back against his knee. "It was not too long after I moved here...maybe four or five months ago," he said, giving me a smile and continuing to move his knee slowly back and forth against my thigh, subtly but definitely. "I'd just filled out this membership card they give you, paid my membership fee, and was waiting for my official entry card when these two guys came in. One was a real humper; his friend was average looking but kind of overweight, looked like a nice guy. They went up to the window and said they wanted to join. The clerk looked really confused and stammered something I couldn't hear. Then he picked up a phone, and a minute later this Comstock guy comes into the room behind the glass—I recognized him from some old porn movies I had.

"Anyway, I tried to pretend I wasn't paying attention, but I heard Comstock say to the good-looking guy that he was welcome to join, but that his friend couldn't. His friend didn't say a word, but the good looking one wanted to know why. 'We have strict standards,' this Comstock bastard says. Jesus, you should have seen the look on that poor kid. It was like someone had spit in his face! I think if Comstock had been in the lobby rather than behind the glass, the good looking one would have decked him. Hell, *I* would have decked him!

"But instead, the humper just turned around, grabbed his friend by the arm, and they left. If I hadn't already paid my money, I'd have walked out, too. And this Comstock bastard just walks away, unconcerned as all shit. What a fucking asshole!"

We'd about finished our drinks by then, and Jimmy came by to see if we wanted a refill. We shook our heads in unison and looked at each other.

"You ready for a little action?" Jared asked.

Oh, yeah!

We paid our tab and left.

* * *

Jimmy had not been exaggerating when he talked about Jared's physical attributes. It *was* a real challenge, but I love a challenge, and it was more than worth it. And Jared had a few special techniques of his own that he amply demonstrated to my delight and ultimate total exhaustion.

"Well. *that* sure beat the shit out of Mr. Toad's Magic Ride," Jared said as he plumped up his pillow and put it behind his head.

"Ditto," I observed.

We just sort of lay there for a few minutes, until Jared said, staring at the ceiling: "You need any help?"

I turned to look at him. "Well, after this, I might need a little help standing up," I said.

He grinned. "Not that kind of help. I mean, like in your work. You know, finding out stuff, getting information—that kind of thing. I like keeping my mind active, and I'm in just about every bar in town and I always keep my ears open. I hear a lot of stuff—I never repeat it, but I hear it. And I'm pretty friendly with most of the bartenders. And I…uh…get around a lot, too."

"That's really nice of you, Jared," I said. "But I'm not in a position right now to…"

He looked at me quickly and shook his head. "I wasn't talking about money," he said. "I just think it would be kind of fun. Give me something to do while I'm hauling those beer cases around."

"That would be great!" I said, though I wasn't quite sure how I might be able to use his services. "But I'd have to have some way of repaying you."

"Hell, no," he said. "I'd have to be most of those places anyway. Maybe I could just take it out in trade." He grinned.

"Now there's a deal," I said, and meant it. I thought for a second, then said: "You know, I could use another pair of ears when it comes to Rage. I'd appreciate knowing more about

Comstock. And particularly anything anyone might be saying about their membership policies."

"You mean other than that they suck? Sure," Jared said.

We were quiet for another moment, and Jared said: "Maybe I shouldn't even bring this up, but I hope we might be running into one another more often, and I think I should tell you right off that I'm not looking for a relationship right now—not that I thought you were, but...."

I reached out and laid my hand on his washboard stomach. "Not to worry," I said. "I'm not exactly out baiting the traps yet. Besides, I'm having too much fun right now; I'm like a kid at Halloween, and it's trick or treat time."

"Ready for another treat?" Jared asked, with a wicked grin.

I looked at him in amazement. "You wouldn't happen to be a Scorpio, would you?" I asked.

"Yeah," he said. "How'd you know?"

"Figures," I said.

* * *

The phone was ringing as I walked into the office the next morning. I ran across the room to grab it. "Hardesty Investigations," I said.

"I've drawn up a contract for you," the voice said, not bothering to identify himself. Fortunately I recognized it as Barry Comstock. "How soon can you be here?"

"I've got a client coming in in about 10 minutes," I lied, but I wasn't about to start jumping through Barry Comstock's hoop. "I can probably be there by 11."

"The sooner the better," he said, and hung up.

* * *

I timed it so that I arrived at Rage at exactly 11 o'clock. The same blond was behind the lobby window, and he must have recognized me, because he nodded his head toward the door and pushed the buzzer before I had a chance to say anything.

I knocked on Comstock's office door, and heard him say...well, it was more of a bark: "Come on in."

He wasn't seated behind the desk this time. He was pacing back and forth between the desk and the worktable, obviously agitated.

He didn't wait for me to say anything. "The fucking bastard!" he almost yelled. "He's screwing with the wrong guy! I'm going to have his balls in a jar!"

I just stood there until he finally shut up.

"Mind telling me what's going on?" I asked.

His face was flushed with anger, and he forced himself to march to his desk and plop down in the chair. "My brand new, $49,000, just off the fucking showroom floor convertible is what's the matter!" he spewed. "That motherfucking bastard slashed the top and all four tires!"

"And you think it's the guy behind the threats?" He hadn't offered me a seat and I deliberately remained standing. He obviously didn't care.

"*Think?*" he fumed, pushing a piece of paper across the desk at me. "He left this on the front seat." It contained two words, cut from newspaper headlines: "You Lose!"

I looked at the paper, then at Comstock. "Are you sure you don't want to take this to the police? This guy can really mean business."

Comstock leaned forward in his chair, waving his finger back and forth like a windshield wiper. "God damn it, I told you *no*! No police. Are you a fucking detective or not?"

Some of his anger was rubbing off on me. "Yes, I'm a detective. But I'm also not stupid. I know when it's time to bring the police in."

"No," he said emphatically. "No police. Now do you want the fucking job or don't you?"

"Well, I..."

He picked up a thick envelope and pushed it across the desk

with such force that I caught it just as it flew off the edge and started its fall to the floor. "Here's the contract," he said. It was sealed, and I started to slip my finger under the end to open it. Comstock shook his head in disgust and picked up his letter opener. "Here, use this," he said and tossed it to me. I instinctively grabbed for it and was vastly relieved to catch it by the handle rather than by the blade. *What an asshole.*

I opened the envelope, very carefully laid the opener back on the desk, and stood there looking quickly over the contract while Comstock sat staring at me.

"This says half my regular fee, the other half to be paid *if* I catch the guy." I noted.

"More than fair," Comstock said. "I'm not paying full price with no guarantees. If you find the guy, you'll get the rest. If you don't, then I've just thrown good money out the window."

I carefully replaced the contract inside the envelope and slid it back across the desk.

"Then I think you'd better find yourself a detective who'll be willing to agree to this. I won't."

"Fucking loser!" Comstock spat. "You turn this down, I'll ruin you."

I literally bit my lower lip to keep myself from saying what I wanted to say. Instead, I just turned and walked out of his office, not closing the door behind me.

As I entered the lobby, the blond Adonis just stood there, eyes moving from me to the office, from which Comstock's voice yelled out: "Fucking loser!"

* * *

Needless to say, I didn't get much done for the rest of the day. I did some paperwork, made a few phone calls, then headed home. But my anger was still there, and I decided to stop in at Ramón's for their happy hour. If anybody needed a happy hour, it was me.

I was downing my fourth old fashioned and was pretty well

on my way to being blotzed when Bob Allen came in. Jimmy went over to talk to him, and they both looked over toward me. Bob nodded and came over.

"How's it going, Dick?" he asked.

"Like shit, Thanks," I said.

"Oh, oh," Bob said, grinning. "Why don't you and I go get something to eat, and we can talk about it?"

Now, I don't usually let things get to me, but Comstock had somehow managed to push all the right buttons, and I was as pissed at myself for allowing it to happen as I was at him for causing it. And I also tend to keep my private problems private. But Bob was a good friend and we'd been through some pretty rough times together. Him I could talk to. And I did.

After a couple cups of black coffee at the bar, Bob and I went down the street to a little Armenian restaurant run by some friends of his. We sat around talking for a good three hours. I kept telling Bob he had a business to run and he should get back to it, but he just shrugged it off, and it was nearly 10:30 when I walked Bob back to Ramón's and came on home.

I'd just gotten to sleep when there was a knock at my door. I put my robe on and went to see who it was. When I looked through the peephole, I saw a police badge.

I opened it, wondering what the hell was going on.

Two plainclothes detectives and a uniformed cop were standing in the hall directly in front of my apartment. I wondered how they'd gotten into the building without ringing.

"Dick Hardesty?" the one with the badge said.

"Yeah?" I saw the uniformed cop reach for his handcuffs.

"Dick Hardesty, you are under arrest for the murder of Barry Comstock. Anything you say…."

CHAPTER 2

Ever been arrested for murder? I don't recommend it. I was able to determine, between the time the handcuffs were put on (I was allowed to get dressed first, at least) and the point after booking that Barry Comstock had been murdered in his office at approximately 9:20 p.m. He had...you guessed it...been stabbed with his letter opener, which of course had my fingerprints all over it. (The real killer was obviously smart enough to wear gloves.) The blond Adonis clerk, who was working a double shift that day, had found Comstock's body and of course reported our falling out. They were able to trace my fingerprints quickly because they were on record as part of the paperwork for my private investigator's license. When I was allowed to make my one phone call, at just about 1:45 a.m., I of course called Ramón's, where Bob Allen was still doing the office work he'd not been able to do while sobering me up and having dinner with me.

Never, ever underestimate the value of friendship! Bob came immediately to the station, verified my alibi (providing the home phone of the restaurant's owners for extra confirmation of my whereabouts at the time of the murder). I was released on bond—which Bob put up—pending a court hearing.

Barry Comstock had been a first-class jerk, but murder is not an acceptable solution to any problem under any circumstances. It was pretty clear to me, if not to the police, to whom I had explained my brief dealings with Comstock, that it was the guy behind the threats—and, by some convoluted extension, Rage's membership policy—that had led to Comstock's death.

I wasn't paranoid enough to even think that someone had tried to set me up; my prints on the letter opener were pure chance, and any killer with an ounce of brains would have made sure *his* weren't on it —which, since they *weren't*, of course led to the obvious conclusion that this hadn't been a spontaneous act by one of the members unhappy over having gotten a dirty towel.

Under normal circumstances, I probably would have felt obligated to look more deeply into the murder on my own since I was, however peripherally, involved. But Comstock was a bastard and I didn't have the financial luxury of just running around working on cases without any money coming in. And besides, this particular case had gone beyond private investigator stage and was now firmly in the hands of the police where it belonged.

But, being me, I knew that once I want to know something, a little thing like something's being none of my business wouldn't stand in the way. And while I told myself that if Barry Comstock were still alive, I wouldn't piss on him if he was on fire, I couldn't help but be intrigued as to exactly what was going on.

I was therefore more than a little surprised when, on going to my office the morning after my arrest and release, my answering service told me I had had a call from Glen O'Banyon's office. O'Banyon was one of the city's most successful, wealthy, and therefore most powerful lawyers. He was also well known to be gay, though he played the closet game quite well. He traveled in the upper circles of the city's social elite, always accompanied by one beautiful woman or another, and at gay functions always had some incredibly hot number with him. I found it interesting that he was so rich that the young men he had with him were never referred to as, or thought to be, hustlers—just ambitious young men who enjoyed the reflected celebrity.

I returned the call immediately, pretty much at a loss as to why he might have called, other than the extremely unlikely possibility that perhaps he wanted to represent me in this murder thing. When I identified myself to his secretary, I was told he was with a client, but would return my call as soon as he was free. I thanked her and hung up.

A few minutes later, as I was trying—unsuccessfully, as usual—to balance my checkbook, the phone rang.

"Hardesty Investigations" I said, allowing it to ring twice before answering.

"Mr. Hardesty," a warm, very professional-sounding voice said, "this is Glen O'Banyon. I was wondering if we might get together for a talk. Would you by any chance be free at..." there was a pause and the sound of pages being turned "...three fifteen today, at my office? I realize this is short notice, but it's quite important."

"Three fifteen will be fine, Mr. O'Banyon," I said, hoping I sounded appropriately casual yet businesslike. "I'll see you then."

"I appreciate that. I'll look forward to seeing you."

We hung up, and it occurred to me that I hadn't even considered asking what it was all about—with men as rich and powerful as Glen O'Banyon, you knew there had to be a good reason. I also had the sudden suspicion that I might know what the reason was—O'Banyon might very well be one of Comstock's partners in Rage. I just hoped that if that were the case, O'Banyon wouldn't turn out to be an asshole like Comstock. And considering that if he were one of the partners, O'Banyon would be very well aware that Comstock and I hadn't exactly hit it off—and that I'd actually if briefly been considered a suspect in his murder, I couldn't imagine what O'Banyon might want from me.

* * *

The law offices of O'Banyon, Brown, & Stern were located on the top floor of one of the city's newest high-rise office complexes, where the rent per-square-foot was probably three times what I paid for my entire office. I checked in at the security-guard desk in the marble lobby for verification that I was expected, then made my way to the double bank of elevators discreetly watched over by surveillance cameras and a building employee in a blue blazer.

I checked my watch as I got on the elevator. It was 3:14. When the elevator doors opened on O'Banyon's floor, I noted that his offices were not merely *on* the top floor, they *were* the top floor. A receptionist's desk faced the elevators. On the marble wall just behind the desk, and just over the receptionist's head, were the words "O'Banyon, Brown, & Stern" in discretely elegant raised brass letters. To either side of the wall were brass-framed glass double doors, flanked by more floor-to-ceiling brass framed glass, ending in richly wallpapered walls which formed the box of the reception area. I announced myself to the receptionist, who smiled and pressed a button on her intercom. "Mr. Hardesty to see Mr. O'Banyon," she said, and less than twenty seconds later an attractive dressed-for-success young woman I assumed to be O'Banyon's secretary appeared at one of the glass doors, which opened automatically and silently.

"Right this way, Mr. Hardesty," she said, smiling, and I followed her down a rather long corridor to another small, more intimate-appearing reception area with a desk, a comfortable looking sofa and two large, overstuffed chairs. She knocked at the large oak door in the wall to the left of the desk, opened it, and said "Mr. Hardesty is here, Mr. O'Banyon," then turned to me and, with one hand on the door handle, stepped slightly aside to let me pass, though the door was wide enough that an armored personnel carrier could have gotten through with no problem.

As I entered the room, Glen O'Banyon got up from the leather chair behind his desk and came across the room to greet me. I'd seen him in person a couple times at community events of one sort or another, but never really up close. He was considerably shorter than I'd remembered. About 45, slim, with greying hair. His handshake was firm and warm.

"Mr. Hardesty: right on time, I see. A good sign." Of what, I had no idea and he did not elaborate. But he motioned me to a seat in front of his desk and moved around it to sit down himself. "Would you like some coffee?"

"No, Thanks," I said, and he looked to his secretary, who was still at the door. "Thank you, Donna," he said, and she left, pulling the door closed behind her.

"What can I do for you, Mr. O'Banyon?" I asked, getting right to the point.

O'Banyon smiled and leaned back in his chair. "Before I start," he said, "I'd like to say I'm sorry for the inconvenience the police put you through last night." *So he knew about that,* I mused. *Word travels fast.*

"Understandable mistake," I said, then decided to go with my suspicion. "I gather you were Mr. Comstock's partner in Rage?"

O'Banyon smiled again and nodded. "Very perceptive," he said. "I was one of them, yes."

"Then you undoubtedly know that we didn't exactly hit it off," I said.

"Yes, I heard. You wouldn't sign the contract."

"You know about the contract, then?" I asked.

O'Banyon nodded with another smile. "I drew it up for him, though he was the one who insisted on the terms. I told him you'd be a fool to accept it, and I'm glad to see you didn't. Barry never had a very high regard for the value of professionalism. He had his own way of doing things that frequently bordered on arrogance, and I wouldn't be surprised if that characteristic was one of the factors that contributed to his death."

I was still a little confused as to exactly what I was doing there, and said so.

"I've discussed this by phone with my other partner, who is currently in Europe on business, and we'd like to hire you to try to expedite the finding of Barry's killer."

"You don't think the police will be able to?" I asked.

"Possibly, eventually," he said. "But as you know, even though Chief Rourke's recent retirement has brought some welcome changes in the police department's dealings with the community, the element of homophobia is still quite strong, and crimes involving gays are still dealt with as something less than first-class priorities—even with such prominent members of the gay community as Barry Comstock. And in any event, the police tend to view a murder as 'a murder' and don't spend too much time contemplating peripheral factors such as motives."

He was silent for a moment, just looking at me impassively. I'm not sure what he was looking *for*, if anything, but it didn't make me particularly uncomfortable. I just waited for him to continue.

"To be honest with you, I'm not being totally altruistic here," he said at last. "While my participation in Rage is not general knowledge, it's not a secret, either, so I cannot overlook the possibility, however remote, that if the murderer's anger was directed at Rage, it might extend beyond Barry to include me." He gave a small smile and matching shrug.

"And, finally," he continued, "there is the simple fact that someone from the community would be much better qualified to work with and within it than the vast majority of the police, who don't have a clue, and certainly very little interest, about how the gay world operates. A gay private investigator would be more likely to know what questions to ask, and of whom."

He had a point, of course. Gays would be much more willing to talk and cooperate with another gay than with the police.

"But," I said, "I don't think the police would take too kindly to someone meddling in what they see as their affairs."

O'Banyon gave a subtle shrug. "Understandable," he said, "but I see this as more of a supplemental investigation and I trust you to be discreet enough not to draw their undue attention. Should you find out anything that would benefit the police in their apprehension of the murderer, all the better—though I would expect to act as intermediary for you in relaying any such information."

He was silent for a moment, watching me, and then added: "Do you have any questions?"

I did, as a matter of fact.

"Well, for starters, maybe you could tell me a little more

about Barry Comstock. I gather I wasn't the only one to think he was never up for a 'Mr. Congeniality' award."

O'Banyon smiled. "No, I'm sure you're not. Not that it is any excuse, but in his heyday as a porn star, he could have anything and anyone he wanted. The fame rather went to his head, I'm afraid—not an uncommon thing. He and I were not exactly what you'd call 'close.' But he was shrewd with money, and knew how to make it. Rage was his idea, actually, and I and our other partner were more financial backers than directly involved in the operation. Barry had, I understand, other business ventures that he ran in conjunction with Rage, but since they did not interfere with Rage's success, I never considered it much of my concern."

"Ventures such as…?" I asked.

"I understand Barry still had his hand in the porn industry," he said. "And Rage certainly provided a wealth of potential artistic talent for it."

He leaned back in his chair and folded his hands across his lap. "So… do you think you'd like the job?"

"I'll give it my best," I said.

"Good." O'Banyon reached forward to press a button on his intercom. "Would you bring the contract in, please, Donna?" He smiled yet again. "I hope you'll excuse my presumption in assuming you'd agree. But I'm also sure you'd hardly be surprised to know I checked you out quite carefully," he said. "I know the role you played in Chief Rourke's early retirement, for which the entire gay community owes you a debt of gratitude, and I've spoken with various members of the Bar Guild, who think quite highly of you."

"I really appreciate that," I said, as the secretary knocked softly and entered, carrying a leather-bound folder. "But as I told Mr. Comstock, there are no guarantees."

"None are expected." O'Banyon nodded and the secretary opened the folder containing the contract and placed it and a pen on the desk in front of me. He then got up from his chair and followed his secretary out of the room, saying: "I'll give you a moment in private to look over the contract. You'll note it is for a period of two months, with the possibility of extension should circumstances warrant." Then they left, closing the door behind them.

I picked up the contract and went through it carefully, noting with considerable relief that my fee had no stipulations or qualifications attached. The contract specified that I was to investigate the circumstances behind the threats that had led to Comstock's death, and to follow "other possible connections" which might arise from my investigation of it. It gave me a pretty wide field, though it did request the exclusivity of my time during the period of the contract—a logical request, and I wondered if O'Banyon also knew I was not working on anything at the moment anyway. I was to file weekly reports with O'Banyon on the progress of the investigation.

O'Banyon and his secretary re-entered the room just as I'd finished. "All in order?" he asked as he moved around the desk to his chair and sat down.

"It looks fine," I said. His secretary watched as first I and then O'Banyon signed both copies of the contract, then added her own signature as witness. She then picked up the folder and left.

"So much for the formalities," O'Banyon said, smiling. Suddenly, he reached into his inside suit jacket pocket and extracted a large wallet, from which he removed a business card and wrote something on the back, which he then handed me. "This might be of some assistance to you," he said. I glanced at it briefly before putting it in my pocket. It said "Your cooperation with Mr. Hardesty will be appreciated. Glen O'Banyon."

Replacing his wallet in his pocket, O'Banyon rose from his chair to walk around the desk toward me. "I'm afraid I have clients waiting, and I know you'll want to get right to work. I've had Donna draft a small advance to cover your immediate expenses. She'll have it with your copy of the contract."

"I appreciate that," I said as I got up from my chair and took his extended hand. "It was a pleasure meeting you, Mr. O'Banyon," I said.

"Glen," he corrected. "Glen, please." He began to walk me toward the door.

"And it goes without saying that you have full access to Rage, it's staff, and its employees. Again, it may have been a bit presumptive of me, but they've been instructed to cooperate fully with you in any way they can."

We shook hands at the door. "Donna should have your copy of the contract ready," he said, smiling. "I look forward to your first report, and if there is anything you need in the interim, don't hesitate to call."

With that, he went back into his office, as the secretary rose from her desk, envelope in hand, and moved to close the office door before turning to me.

"Your copy," she said with a smile, handing me the envelope. "I'll walk you to the door," she said, and since I assumed that was standard procedure I didn't object.

When we reached the reception area, she again smiled as I passed through the glass doors, then turned to a well-dressed elderly couple seated in matching chairs against the wall on one side of the elevator. "Mr. & Mrs. Jacobs? Mr. O'Banyon is expecting you. If you'll follow me…"

She gave me another brief smile, which I returned, and then I pressed the button for the elevator.

* * *

My mind was already working overtime as the elevator doors closed behind me and the car began its soft-whoosh descent. Since the only way to gain entrance to Rage was to be a member and to check in at the lobby, it would seem pretty obvious that the roster of those in Rage the night of the murder should include the name of the murderer. And I'd be willing to bet that would be where the police would be concentrating first. But I also knew that the obvious is frequently wrong. I felt kind of sorry for the guys who had been there that night, because I knew the police would be harassing the hell out of them.

I'd go down and do some checking, of course, especially to find out how someone might get in without going through the lobby. The other obvious thing was that if the murderer was unhappy with Rage's membership policies, it was probably because he didn't meet Comstock's standards. But if that was the case, how would he have gotten in? Anybody less than a 7 on a 10-scale for "Hot Face/Hot Body" would stand out like a sore thumb in there. Still....

* * *

I decided to go home and change clothes into something a little more casual before going to Rage to see if the blond Adonis might be on duty, and maybe to nose around the place for a few minutes before the busy hours started around 9:30 or 10. Not, I knew, that it was likely to be busy tonight or for quite some time until the chance of the of the police dropping in on "official business" relating to Comstock's murder subsided.

I waited until I got home to open the envelope and take a look at the check O'Banyon had included. It was more than enough to cover any expenses I might incur short of a trip to Hong Kong. I decided I like working for rich people.

I'd showered that morning before going in to work but decided another wouldn't hurt. Besides, I tend to use showers like some people use Valium—and I do some of my best thinking in there. Chris used to say I should have been a fish, I spend so much time in the water.

After drying off, I rummaged through my clothes for something that I hoped would help me look like just another one of Rage's regulars.

* * *

When I approached the bathhouse, rather than going in immediately, I decided to take a walk around the block to check out the immediate area. I noticed at once that Rage sided onto a relatively wide alley, and that there were one or two cars parked close against the wall on the other side, under "Private Parking" signs. The two-story brick wall along the alley was broken on the ground floor by two doors...one, about a third of the way down from the front, was a single, inset door; near the rear of the building was a larger, flush-with-the-wall double metal door, obviously an emergency exit. On the second floor, about halfway down, was another double metal emergency door leading to a small fire escape with one of those suspended ladders which only came down when stepped on from the fire escape. No windows on the ground floor, and maybe four opaque-glass windows on the second.

It would be pretty hard to enter the building through the second floor fire escape door, which had no outside handle even if anyone could get to it, considering that the bottom rung of the ladder was about 12 feet off the ground in its suspended mode. And if the killer had tried to leave that way, the ladder would have stayed down and the police would certainly have seen it.

Walking down the alley, I noted that the first, slightly recessed door appeared to be more of a private entrance than an emergency exit. It was the only one of the three doorways to have a handle or a stoop. Directly across from the first door was another "Private Parking" sign with no car under it. As I walked up to have a closer look at the first door, I glanced down at the ground and saw a key lying beside the stoop. Curious, I picked it up and on a hunch put it in the door's lock. It didn't fit. Still, something told me this was a clue to something, so I put it in my pocket and resumed my circle tour.

Keeping my eyes on the ground as I walked along the side of Rage, I spotted another key about ten feet from the first door, at the edge of a small puddle of water in the center of the alley. A new key, like the kind you'd get with a nice, new car. I was definitely on to something but, as is so often the case, wasn't all too sure exactly what that something was.

I found nothing else of interest in the alley, and the rest of the block was pretty standard commercial buildings, with a number of gay-owned businesses: book store, vegetarian restaurant, clothing store, etc. Which brought me back to the entrance to Rage. I opened the door and entered the lobby.

Sure enough, the blond Adonis was on duty, every perfectly shaped muscle on prominent display beneath the Rage tee shirt. As I walked up to the window, he just stared at me, then gave a nod with his head toward the door, which buzzed to unlock as I reached for the handle.

To the left was the door to Comstock's office; to the right, an open door to the registration area where the blond stood by the counter, unsmiling.

"Hi," I said, stepping inside the room. "I'm Dick Hardesty."

"Yeah, I know," the blond said, notably unimpressed.

"And your name is…?" I asked, a little puzzled and mildly irked by his attitude.

"Brad," he said flatly, his face impassive.

"Well, Brad," I said, "I'd like to ask you a few questions, and it looks like you're not overly busy at the moment."

"I've got paperwork," he said, defensively.

"I'm sure you do," I said, trying to ignore what I was beginning to see as a blooming case of Major Attitude. "But I also assume you've been instructed to cooperate with me. Am I right?"

Brad shrugged.

"Good," I said. I noticed a tall stool by the counter and pulled it to me, straddling it to sit down. "Let's start with how long you've worked here?"

Brad leaned against the counter on one nicely muscled arm and crossed one ankle over the other. "Since it opened," he said.

I had one of my hunches and decided to follow up on it. "How well did you know Barry Comstock?" I asked, and noticed a brief look of anxiety cross his cover-model face.

"He was my boss," he said, but I got the definite feeling that wasn't exactly all.

"Just your boss, huh?" I asked, and Brad's face flushed and his eyes looked down at the floor.

"I don't know what you're talking about," he said. "He was my boss. I told the police all this shit anyway."

"Well," I said, "I'm not the police." Then, sensing that maybe I was being a little hard on the kid, I tried another tack. "Come on, Brad. Barry Comstock was murdered. I know you thought I was the one who killed him, but I didn't have anything to do with it. He was gay, you're gay, I'm gay—this is a family thing, here. Help me out."

Brad shifted his position slightly, uncrossing his ankles. Still looking at the floor he gave another small shrug. "Like how?" he asked.

"For starters, how did you happen to find Barry's body?"

Brad gave a huge, lung-emptying sigh, then began to speak. "He was here in the office with me, going over some receipts, and then he left to go back to his office. I had to run into the back for a minute. A few seconds after I got back here I heard Barry say something like, 'What the fuck?' and then a thud—probably Barry hitting the floor. I ran over there, and there he was on his back on the floor, with that letter opener sticking out of his chest."

"And no sign of anybody around?"

Brad shook his head. "Nope."

I pondered that bit of information for a moment, then said: "So tell me a little more about Barry Comstock...and you."

Brad sighed again and reached for a matching stool behind a file cabinet.

"Well," he said, some of the attitude missing from his voice, "I work here for Barry, and then I was sort of his assistant in his other business."

"The videos?" I asked.

Brad nodded. "Yeah. I was in some of them when we first started, but then Barry made me his assistant."

I leaned forward on my stool. "And what did you do as assistant?" I asked.

Brad shrugged, not looking directly at me. "Lots of things," he said. "Helping the cameraman, setting up props, working with the lighting, recruiting..."

I caught that one in mid air. "Recruiting?" I asked. "From Rage's membership?"

He nodded.

"How did that work?" I asked.

Brad's glance swept idly around the room, meeting my eyes for only a moment, then moving on, casually. "I get hit on a lot," he said, in what I'm sure was an understatement of classic proportions. "A guy comes in, we like each other, we talk a couple minutes, I call one of the attendants up front to watch the desk, and I take the guy to a room right next to Barry's office. I buzz Barry just as I'm on my way to the room, and Barry watches from a two-way mirror he's got hidden behind a picture on his wall. If he thinks the guy has talent, he comes out of his office just as me and the guy are leaving the room and invites the guy in for a talk. Then he holds his own audition, and if the guy passes and is willing to do porn, he gets a job."

I found myself oddly envious of Comstock. What a neat racket!

"And if the guy doesn't go along?" I asked.

Brad sat back, rotating his shoulders as if to relieve the tension.

"No problem," he said. "The guy's not interested, he's not interested. Although Barry could get a little...well, aggressive at times."

"Meaning?" I asked.

Brad hesitated, as if he didn't want to speak ill of his departed employer, then apparently realized that Comstock wouldn't be filing any objections, and continued.

"Meaning one guy punched him out one time."

"And how did Barry respond to that?" I asked.

"He yanked the guy's membership," Brad said.

At this point, the front door opened and two U.S.D.A. Choice specimens came into the lobby. Brad got up from his stool and moved to the window to greet them, check their membership cards, and have them sign in. That completed, he reached under the counter for the buzzer, and the two guys passed by the open doorway on their way to the locker room. We exchanged smiles and nods.

When they'd gone, I got up from the stool.

"Thanks, Brad," I said, extending my hand, which he took and, for the first time gave me a smile.

"Sorry if I was a little...whatever," he said. "Barry was really pretty damned good to me, and the last time I saw you he was yelling at you...and then he was dead."

"I understand," I said, and I did. " I think I'd like to look around the place for awhile."

"Sure," he said, then gave me another quick smile. "Too bad you're not a member," he said, and ran a spread-fingered hand across his chest, slowly.

"I just might join one of these days," I said, as I turned toward the door. "I'll see you a little later."

"I'll be here," Brad said.

* * *

I went first into Barry Comstock's office, and immediately to the large painting of the nude torso. Moving it slightly to one side, I saw the two-way mirror looking into a small room with a single bed and a night stand, upon which was an assortment of lubricants, a bottle of poppers, and a small bowl filled with condoms. There was one wooden chair in the corner with a stack of towels on the seat. Putting the picture back in place, I opened the door beside it and entered the room itself.

For so small a room, there were three doors: the one I'd just entered through on one side wall, and one at each end of the room. The one to my right undoubtedly led to the hallway; the one to the left, I knew automatically, was the doorway to the alley. It was my guess that the parking space directly across the alley was where Barry Comstock parked, and that he came and went through this side door—and I suspected, from the keys I'd found just outside the door, so did the killer. And without being seen by anyone. There was a dead-bolt lock, but I noted that it was not engaged.

Just as I was leaving Comstock's office, I was passed by yet another club member who'd just entered. He was built like a Clydesdale and from what I could see, hung like one, too. I really did have to reconsider joining....

The door to the registration office was closed, and I thought it advisable to knock rather than just barge in. Brad opened the door a crack and then, seeing it was me, opened it fully to let me enter. "That was fast," he said.

I nodded. "Yeah, I think I saw what I needed to. Tell me, is that door to the alley always locked?"

Brad nodded. "The police asked the same thing. I told them it was."

"And dead-bolted?" I asked.

He shook his head. "No; the dead bolt's broken. Barry was going to see about getting a new one, but he never did."

"Who else had a key to that door, other than Barry?" I asked.

"Nobody," Brad said. "Barry was the only one who ever used it." He was silent a moment, brows slightly knitted in thought. "But I know he had a spare set of keys somewhere—in his car, I think..."

"His car?" I asked.

"Well," Brad replied, looking at his reflection in the reception window and smoothing back a wayward lock of hair above his left ear with one hand, "one time he thought he lost his keys after an audition with one of the members, and he had to go somewhere. So he did. I guess the car was the only place they could have been."

Of course! I thought. "And where's the car now?" I asked.

"Still at the dealership, I guess," Brad said. "He had me call them right after that asshole slit his tires and top and they came and got it to fix it."

"Do you remember which dealership?"

Brad furrowed his brows briefly in thought. "Central Imports," he said.

I made a mental note to stop by the dealership in the morning. Chris, my ex, had one of those little magnetic key boxes he kept under the driver's side front wheel well. I was pretty sure Comstock had one too, but I'd be sure to find out.

"Hello?" I heard Brad say, and realized I'd been staring off into space again.

"Sorry," I said. "You said some guy had his membership yanked because he'd punched Comstock? Do you remember the guy's name, by any chance?"

"Sure," Brad said, leaning against the counter on one elbow. "A hunk like that isn't easy to forget. His name was Jared."

"Jared Martinson?" I asked, somehow not surprised—he had said his membership had been canceled, and he'd made it clear he had no particular love for Comstock.

"Yeah. What a body! And hung! Jeezus, I've seen horses with smaller dicks!"

Let me count the ways..., I thought.

"Do you know exactly what happened? Why Jared punched him?" I had a pretty good idea, but thought I'd better make sure.

Brad shook his head. "Barry wouldn't talk about it, but I could pretty well figure it out. As usual, he came out of his office just as Jared and I came into the hall. Barry asked Jared into his office, and Jared looked confused, but went in with him. A few minutes later I heard shouting—I'm pretty sure it was Jared—but couldn't make out the words. And a second or two after that there were a couple of thuds, and Jared comes steaming out of Barry's office looking really pissed and storms out the door, and Barry's standing there with blood pouring out of his nose and his fly open. I guess you don't fuck with Jared."

I'll try to remember that, I thought.

"And two more things," I said. "Can I have a list of everyone who was in Rage the night of the murder?"

"The cops took our registration book," Brad said, "but I always make a copy of who comes in on any given day. I'd just set it aside when Barry came in to go over the receipts. I can get it for you. Not more than twenty guys in the place, though—it was still early."

He opened a drawer and shuffled through some papers, coming up with a small notebook which he handed to me. "That's the members," he said. "I'll have to check for sure on just which employees were on duty."

"Great," I said. "I can pick that up later." Then, remembering the second loose key in my pocket, I said: "Do you have Comstock's address?"

"1101 Spruce," Brad said without having to stop to think of it.

"House or apartment?" I asked.

"A house. Big old Victorian. We used it for a lot of the videos."

Neither one of us spoke for a moment and our eyes met and locked, and I was once more convinced that ESP lives. I was also aware that it was suddenly very, very warm in that small office, and I decided I'd better get out while the going was good.

"Well, Thanks a lot for your time, Brad," I heard myself saying. "I appreciate it. I guess I'd better get going." But my feet didn't make any attempt to move.

"Did you see the room?" Brad asked, his free hand moving to his crotch.

"Yeah, I saw it," I said, staring at the growing bulge in his sprayed-on trousers.

"It's a slow night," he said. "You wanna see it again?"

Shit, yes! I thought. "You talked me into it," I said.

While Brad waited for someone to come up to watch the office, I went across the hall to make sure Comstock's office had a lock on the inside of the door. It did. I wasn't about to be distracted by wondering if someone were standing behind that two-way mirror. By the time I entered the little room from the office side door, Brad was already stripped, lying back on the bed in full display–and an impressive display it was. He watched me undress with a practiced eye.

"You ever think about doing porn?" he asked, as I kicked my shoes off.

"Not really," I said.

"You should," he said, tracing the outline of his lower lip with his tongue. When I took my pants off, Brad sat up on the edge of the bed, eyes glued to my crotch and said: "You know what my favorite job is on the porn set, when I'm not in the picture?"

"Uh, no..." I said, puzzled.

"I'm a great fluffer," he said. "You know what fluffers do, don't you, Dick?"

I knew, but looking down at myself, I said "I hardly think I need fluffing, do you?"

"Let's fake it," he said, scooting off the bed and onto his knees.

Action!

CHAPTER 3

I was able to pry myself out of bed the next morning in time to arrive at Central Imports when the service department opened at 8:00. I could tell the moment I walked in the door that this wasn't Joe's Neighborhood Garage—there were a number of exorbitantly expensive cars scattered around the large shop in various states of repair; some on hoists, some with hoods raised and hooked up to lots of expensive-looking machines that appeared as though they would be more comfortable in a hospital operating room, and the floor was clean enough to eat off of. I walked up to the Service Desk and asked the neatly-uniformed man behind it to see the manager.

He smiled and disappeared behind a rack of boxed parts, to return within seconds and say: "He'll be right with you."

A moment later, a tall, very good looking guy came around from behind the rack, and I recognized him immediately as a guy I'd tricked with out of Ramón's several weeks earlier—though I'd be damned if I could remember his name. Luckily, his starched, razor-crease uniform shirt had a name tag: "Sam". He smiled when he saw me and extended his hand across the desk, which I had to move forward slightly to take.

"Sam," I said: "I didn't know you worked here."

"Only for ten or twelve years," he said, grinning. "What can I do for you?" I got the definite impression he didn't remember my name, either, which made me feel a little less guilty.

"You have a car here belonging to Barry Comstock— brought in a couple days ago with four slashed tires and a slashed top?"

Sam nodded. "Yeah, it's in the other room. We haven't done anything with it yet; he was killed the night we brought it in, and we've been waiting for authorization from the insurance company or somebody representing his estate."

"Well," I said, "I'm not the guy on that one, but I've been asked by Comstock's attorney to check something out in the car. Would it be possible for me to take a quick look at it? I won't remove anything—just want to look at something."

Sam furrowed his brows. "Gee, I don't know…buddy…we aren't supposed to let anybody other than the owners near the cars."

"Well, this particular owner won't be around for quite a while," I said, reaching into my wallet for O'Banyon's card. "But maybe this will help."

I handed Sam the card, which he examined carefully and, apparently dutifully impressed, gave back to me. "Well, sure, I guess we could let you take a look," he said. He stepped out from behind the service desk and motioned for me to follow him.

The main shop was vast, and behind it was another only slightly smaller area, separated by a large, closed roll-down door. We entered through a smaller walk-through door beside it. It was in this area, apparently, that the more…uh…cosmetically disadvantaged cars were kept and major body work done. In one corner sat—or more appropriately, given the condition of its tires, squatted—a shiny, brand new canary-yellow convertible with a badly slashed top.

I walked directly to it and knelt down in front of the driver's side front wheel well. Feeling my way along the inside of the fender, I found what I was looking for…a small, magnetized metal box. Pulling it loose, I slid open the small lid. It was empty. I closed the lid and replaced the box under the fender. Standing up, I reached into my pocket for the newer of the two keys I'd found in the alley and moved to open the driver's door. Sliding into the driver's seat—which was a hell of a lot more comfortable than any recliner I've ever sat in—I put the key in the ignition. It turned easily, and the car murmured to life. I quickly turned the engine off and got out of the car.

"Thanks a lot, Sam," I said.

"Find what you needed?" he asked

"Yep. I owe you one," I said.

Sam grinned. "I might just hold you to that," he said.

We walked back into the main service area and, with another handshake, I left Sam at the Service Desk.

* * *

My next stop was 1101 Spruce, which was in a gay-gentrified area not too far from downtown. The area had been on a sharp decline for years until gays and lesbians began moving in and restoring the large old homes to their former elegance. What could be bought for a song ten years ago would now require a full-scale opera.

Comstock's house was a marvelous old gingerbread confection with scalloped fish-scale molding under the eves, and painted in crimson and cream. There was a small, iron-fenced and iron-gated front yard, and hoping no one would be home—I knew Comstock wouldn't be—I pushed open the gate and walked to the small front porch enclosed with delicate filagree railings. Hardly the kind of house I would have associated with Barry Comstock, but one never knows everything about someone.

To play it safe, I rang the bell, and when there was no response, I took the other key from my pocket and put it in the lock. It worked. Quickly re-locking it without opening the door, I went back across the porch, down the short sidewalk, through the iron gate, and into the street, closing the gate behind me.

* * *

Well, I thought, things were at least starting to fall into place. Comstock's killer had apparently been watching him—enough to know where he parked his car and how he got into Rage, at least. I wasn't sure how he'd found the magnetic key box, but again they were hardly rare at the time.

He'd removed all the keys since he didn't know for sure which one opened the side door. He probably just dropped the first one when it didn't work, and threw the second aside. Obviously there had been a third key...missing... which had opened the door. I assume it was just luck that no auditions were being held in the small room when he entered. Actually, it took a lot of balls to take all those risks. The guy must have been pretty determined.

As to why the cops hadn't found the keys themselves, it was pretty obvious they hadn't bothered much to look. They were going on the assumption that the killer had come from inside the building, not from outside. Even if they had considered that the killer had left through the side door, they probably wouldn't have felt a need to give it other than a cursory look—the murder weapon certainly didn't have to be looked for.

I stopped back at Rage to get the addresses and phone numbers of the members on the list Brad had given me, and to accompany him on another quick guided tour of the small room. I returned to my office to start calling the guys on the list. The few I was able to find at home were at first understandably reluctant to talk to anyone about that night—the cops had given them a hard enough time—but when I identified myself as being one of the family, they were more cooperative. I asked each one what time he'd arrived, and if he'd happened to come through or pass by the alley. A couple of them said they had passed the alley on their way to the entrance, but no one had paid attention to who might or might not be in the alley itself or hanging around it.

In short, I didn't learn anything at all that might be of help. And of course no one had seen anyone suspicious. I didn't think they would have. It occurred to me briefly that if the killer were either an average Joe or mildly unattractive, most of these guys wouldn't have noticed him if they'd tripped over him.

I also asked each one if he might have heard anything negative about Rage's membership policy, and if so, what was said and under what circumstances. Over half of the guys I talked to hadn't even been aware that Rage discriminated so blatantly. Probably not really that surprising, after all, since *they* had gotten in with no hassle. The rest had just heard general grumbling in the community, but nothing so specific as to warrant further investigation. And three had been approached by Comstock at one time or another to join his little porno enterprise—only one had taken him up on it.

I knew Jared didn't get off work until 4 or 4:30 and that he probably wouldn't be home much before 5, if he didn't stop off for a couple rolls in the hay along the way. But he had given me his home number, and I had an urge to call him, for a couple of reasons other than the obvious. I'd not talked to him since before Comstock's murder, and I had been thinking about Brad's version of how Jared had lost his Rage membership. I wanted to see if Jared's version might differ in any significant detail. Plus, I was curious to know if he might have heard anything in the course of his delivery routine and/or bar visits that might be useful. I took a chance that though he'd not be home yet, he might have an answering machine. He did.

"Jared; this is Dick Hardesty," I said. "Can you give me a call at home? I should be there by 5:30. Thanks. Bye."

The phone was ringing as I walked in the door. I caught it just before my answering machine did.

"Hi, Dick. It's Jared. What's up?"

"Jared, hi," I said. "I was wondering when we might be able to get together: I've got a couple of questions for you, and would like to see if you've heard anything of interest…"

"About Comstock's getting killed?" he asked, anticipating the rest of my sentence. "Couldn't have happened to a more deserving guy. Everybody's talking about it, of course."

"Well, would you like to get together to talk for a while?"

"Tonight?" he asked, then added "And you mean just talk?"

"Well, that last part is certainly open for negotiation, but yeah, if you could."

"Sure," he said. "What time and where?"

"How's 8:00—we could grab a bite to eat, if you'd like."

"Sure," Jared said. "I hate cooking. And maybe afterwards we could stop by Glitter for a few minutes. I've got a buddy who's subbing for the regular D.J. tonight, and I told him I'd come by if I could."

Glitter was the city's leading disco and it attracted much of the same type of guy who went to Rage—though Glitter had a far more relaxed policy regarding who could get in. I almost never went there because I tend to avoid "in" places—too crowded, too noisy, too much narcissism. But I was willing to give it a shot, especially with Jared.

"Sure," I said. "Why don't we meet at Rasputin's around 8?"

"Deal," Jared said. "See you there."

We exchanged our goodbyes and I got undressed to head for the shower.

* * *

Of course I got to Rasputin's 20 minutes early, and was sitting at the bar when I felt a hand on my shoulder.

"Started without me, huh?"

As I turned to see Jared, I noticed the clock behind the bar said 7:48.

"Well, I'm impressed," I said. "I thought I was the only guy who always shows up early."

Jared pulled the empty stool next to me closer, and sat down. "I hate being late," he said. "So I always set my watch 10 minutes fast."

The bartender came over to take Jared's order, and when he'd left, Jared swung around on his stool to face me, making the now-familiar knee-thigh connection. "So what's going on?" he asked.

I told him that I'd been hired by Comstock's partners to investigate his murder.

Jared smiled broadly. "Hey, that's great—two pieces of good

news: Comstock's dead and you've got a new case!"

The bartender brought Jared's drink and he raised it in a quick toast. "Good luck," he said. He was still facing me, and his knee was still pressed into my thigh. I was getting to like it. But business before pleasure.

"So you were the guy who punched Comstock?" I said, making it only a half-question.

Jared looked into his drink, then back up at me. "Ah, you heard," he said. "I'm kind of surprised I was the only one. And he was damned lucky I didn't mop the floor with him."

"Exactly what happened?" I asked, without telling him I'd heard Brad's side of the story.

Jared took another sip of his drink, then set it on the bar. "Well, you know that hot little blond at the registration desk?"

"Brad," I said.

He nodded. "Brad. I'd been going fairly regularly, and every time I saw this Brad, I kept getting stronger and stronger vibes from him. That last night, I hadn't even shown him my card when he said: 'How'd you like to fuck my brains out?'"

Jared grinned and his eyes had a devilish gleam. "Kind of hard to pass up a subtle offer like that, so I said 'Sure... when?' and he said 'It's my break time. Now's good.' And he picked up the phone under the counter and punched in a number and said 'Tom, come watch the desk.' He motioned me toward the door and buzzed it open, and just as I entered, a guy comes down the hall and goes into the office without a word. Brad comes out, and I follow him just a little way down the hall to a room on the left—right next to Comstock's office."

"Yeah," I said. "I've seen it."

Jared gave me a raised-eyebrow look and a grin, then picked up his drink and drained about a third of it in one gulp. "Did you know it's got a fucking two-way mirror in it? I should have known, but I had all my attention glued on Brad's hot little ass."

He sighed, then continued. "So we did it, and just when we're leaving the room, the door to Comstock's office opens up and he comes out into the hall. 'Come in to my office for a minute,' he says, and I haven't got a clue as to why he might want to talk to me. Brad just nods and goes back to the registration office, and me, dumber'n owl shit, I follow Comstock into his office. He closes the door and motions me to a seat.

"'You ever done any porn?' he asks. 'No,' I says, 'why do you want to know?'

"I'm sitting in this chair, and Comstock's standing practically right beside me, and I'm getting pretty uncomfortable.

"'I've got a video company,' he says, 'and I'm always looking for really hot studs to be in them. The pay isn't that good, but you get to fuck some of the hottest guys in town.'"

Jared paused for a moment, then continued. "Now, when I get uncomfortable, I also tend to get pissed, and Comstock was coming mighty close to pissing me off big time. 'I already fuck some of the hottest guys in town,' I said, 'and I don't have to do it in front of a camera.'

"'Don't knock it 'til you try it,' he says. 'And it's kind of hard to find a guy hung like you who's uncut these days.' Jeezus, but I'm dumb! That went right over my head: how the hell did he know how I'm hung, or that I'm uncut? Besides, I was getting too busy trying to keep the lava from coming out of my ears to let it register. But then he says…get this: 'There are other perks, too,' and he fucking unzips his fly and whips out his cock about a foot in front of my face! That did it! I jumped up out of the chair and slugged him so hard he stumbled back against the wall and knocked that big picture off center, and I saw there was a fucking two way mirror behind it! That son of a bitch had been watching Brad and me fucking!"

He looked at me, wide eyed, shaking his head. "I tell you, Dick, I almost lost it! I had to get out of that room before I killed the bastard—and, oh, I wanted to! So I left, and I never went back. I was afraid that if I ever saw Comstock again, I *would* kill him."

He noticed me looking at him, and he suddenly realized

what he'd said. He gave a quick, not totally convincing smile, and said: "I didn't, of course. Somebody else beat me to it. I owe him one."

I just sat there, listening. Jared drained his drink and motioned to my almost empty glass. I drained it as well, and he waved to the bartender, pointing to the glasses.

"Maybe we should get a table," he said. Which, when the drinks came, we did.

* * *

Glitter occupied the entire second floor of a huge old warehouse in the river front district. The dance floor took up at least half the space, with an assortment of bars scattered around the edges. In the back and separate from the dance area was a show lounge which attracted some well known but B-level entertainers. It had a separate outside entrance for those who didn't want to fight through the dance floor crowd to get there.

The whole huge space was painted all black, of course—exposed girders, pipes, factory-style windows which pushed out from the bottom to let air in when even the air conditioners couldn't handle the heat generated by the crowd.

The combination D.J.'s/lighting booth was suspended from the girders in the center of the room, and was reached by a catwalk extending to a side wall where a narrow metal- caged stairway led to a locked metal gate on the side of the dance floor.

The volume was set just below "stun". Nobody talked much at Glitter—not that most people there were in a talking mood anyway. A makeshift U-shaped loft/balcony ran across the main-entrance end of the room and enabled those so inclined to look down on the milling throngs below. It was a good place for the predators to spot their prey.

Jared and I paid our cover charge and pushed our way through the mob to the stairway leading to the loft/balcony.

Jared thought he'd have a better chance of being seen by his D.J. buddy from up there. There was yet another small bar at the top of the stairs, and we each ordered a beer—easier to keep control of in all the jostling. We managed to work our way to the railing where we could have an unobstructed view of the action.

Jared's buddy was doing a pretty good job of keeping both the volume and the excitement level high, and whoever was working the lights was doing an impressive job as well. The two of them worked well together, with the room going pitch black at exactly the right spot in the music, then bursting into a minute or two of full strobes, the jerky, freeze-frame effect never ceasing to fascinate me. Every time a sweeping spotlight would move across the balcony, Jared would wave toward the D.J. booth and finally the spot swept back and zeroed in on Jared for just a second, then blinked on and off before moving on.

"Mission accomplished," Jared yelled into my ear.

I was being slightly distracted by an incredible blond standing at the far end of one of the ends of the U, staring down at the crowd. A firm believer in ESP, I kept staring at him until he happened to look my way, and our eyes met, even over that long distance. He smiled and nodded, as did I. I know I was there with Jared, but as I said, it was my slut phase; while I wouldn't have gone home with the guy that night, a phone number's as good as a rain check.

But just then there was some sort of commotion on the dance floor, and a circle cleared around two figures in the center—a really hot kid with black, curly hair, and a neatly dressed guy around 60. The dark-haired kid was really in the older guy's face, literally, like a drill sergeant, screaming something we could not hear over the music, but clearly infuriated. The older man turned and moved toward the door, with the younger one right behind him, yelling, and the crowd melting back from them as they progressed. They passed under the balcony and were lost to our sight.

Jared leaned toward me and yelled: "Richie. What a fucking sonofabitch." I merely shrugged, wanting to know more, but deciding to wait until we got somewhere we could actually talk.

I left Jared at the railing while I pushed my way through to the bar for two more beers. When I got back, the dance floor had returned to its usual frenetic normalcy, and it was as if nothing at all had happened. Rather like dropping a stone into a shallow bowl of water. Ripples, then calm. Though calm was hardly a word you could ever apply to Glitter.

I looked around for the blond, but he was gone.

When we'd finished our second beer, Jared yelled "Are you about ready?"

I nodded and we fought our way to the stairway, down to the main dance floor, and then out into the blessedly quiet street—though you could still hear the muffled thump-thump-thump of the music's bass line.

"A little of that goes a *long* way," Jared said, and I nodded again in agreement.

* * *

We'd left Jared's car in Rasputin's lot and as we were driving over to get it, my curiosity got the better of me.

"What was that all about on the dance floor?" I asked. "And who's Richie?"

Jared leaned back in his seat and put his left arm on the back of mine. "Richie Smith. He's a card-carrying Arrogant Prick of the First Order," Jared said. "He's a fixture at Glitter…and at Rage: I understand he was one of Comstock's golden boys."

"You mean in the porns?" I asked.

Jared nodded. "Richie is a classic case of a guy who's been told he's hot so many times, he gets elephantiasis of the ego. He can have anybody he wants, any time he wants them, so he doesn't have to bother to even pretend he gives a shit about anybody but himself."

"Speaking from experience?" I asked.

Jared's hand dropped from the back of my seat to my shoulder. "Unfortunately, yeah. I made it with him when I first got into town. He's got a fantastic face and an incredible body and a dick you wouldn't believe. But he's what I call an 'Adore Me!' He just basically lies there, expecting you to fall all over him. I got the impression that all I—and I imagine every other guy he goes to bed with—was to him was a walking dildo."

"And what do you suppose tonight was all about?" I asked.

Jared shrugged. "Who knows? Maybe the guy had the audacity to hit on him. Richie's on a really slippery slope. Lots of booze, lots of dope inevitably lead to too much booze, too much dope. If he lives to see 30, it'll be a miracle."

* * *

As we drove into Rasputin's parking lot, Jared retracted his arm from my shoulder and moved his hand to my leg, then to my crotch. "Got time for a quick one at my place?" he asked.

"Take a wild guess," I said as we pulled up behind his car.

Jared grinned as he opened the door and started to get out of the car. "Good," he said. "You can follow me, okay?"

"Sure," I said. He was just about to close the door when I said: "But, hey, promise me something?"

He looked puzzled. "Yeah?" he said. "What?"

"You won't just lie there, will you?"

He grinned again and closed the door, saying "Trust me."

* * *

I did manage to make it to the office on time in the morning. Jared had to be at work at 8 and told me to sleep in if I wanted, but I wouldn't have felt comfortable being in his place alone—we didn't know each other quite well enough for that yet. Though it was nice of him to suggest it.

Before picking up the morning paper at the newsstand in the lobby of my office building, I stopped at the coffee shop on the ground floor to get a large black coffee to go.

The place had been there since Noah, and looked it. It had two waitresses who had been there just about as long: identical twins Evolla and Eudora, who had found a hairstyle they liked somewhere in the mid 1940s and had never found it necessary to change since. Every now and then I'd stop in at lunch time for a bowl of soup just to hear one or the other of them yell the order to the cook: "BAW-el!" I get a lot of fun out of the little things.

I'd just sat down at my desk and was prying the lid off the coffee when the phone rang. I waited for the second ring before picking it up: "Hardesty Investigations."

I recognized the voice immediately. "Dick! It's Jared." *I know*, I thought. "Have you read the morning paper—the late edition?"

"No," I said. "Why?"

"Remember Richie Smith from last night?"

"Yeah…" I said, something in the back of my head telling me I knew what was coming next.

"Check out page 3. I was right about his never seeing 30. He's dead."

CHAPTER 4

Jared gave me the sketchy details from the short article in the paper: Richie had been found dead in his closed garage with the car engine running. A neighbor had called the police at around midnight—a little over an hour after we saw him screaming at the guy in Glitter.

"Pretty odd coincidence, huh?" Jared said.

"Yeah," I agreed. But something told me it was a little more than coincidence.

"You suppose...?" Jared asked, apparently reading my mind.

"No idea," I said. "But do me a favor, will you? Keep your ears open today and see if you can find out anything at all about that incident at Glitter last night."

"Will do," Jared said. "Now that I think of it, I saw a couple guys I know down on the floor right near where we saw Ritchie go into his number. I'll see what I can come up with, and I'll give you a call later, okay? Right now, I've got to get back to work."

"Thanks for the call, Jared," I said.

As soon as we hung up, I checked the paper I'd just bought—it was the early edition, of course, so I went back downstairs to see what time the late edition arrived. Fortunately, Charlie, the guy who ran the newsstand, was just cutting the string on a newly arrived bundle. Making sure it was indeed the late edition, I bought one and returned to the office and my by-now-cold coffee. I immediately turned to page 3, and found a short, two paragraph article in the lower right part of the page under the headline: 'Man, 27, Found Dead.'

The article said basically what Jared had told me, of course: a Richard Eugene Smith, 27, had been found dead in the garage of his home at 1414 Greenbriar. He'd been found around midnight by police who had received a call from a neighbor walking his dog, who had heard a car motor running inside the closed garage and smelled exhaust fumes.

My gut told me that those two paragraphs only hinted at the real story, and that Richie's death, so closely following Barry Comstock's, went beyond coincidence. I wanted very much to find out more of the details, but wasn't sure where to find them.

My contract with O'Banyon did give me the leeway to look into "other possible connections" to my investigation of Comstock's death, and I somehow strongly felt this qualified. While I didn't want to start running to O'Banyon every time I came across a problem, and I knew neither he nor I wanted to get involved in any way with the police department, it occurred to me that he might possibly have some connections in the department which might allow me to make an end run and tap into more of the details of Richie's death. I called his office and left a message requesting that he call me when he had the opportunity. In the meantime, I decided to start my first official report to O'Banyon, even though it wasn't due for several days. I began by outlining in detail everything I'd done (except for Brad, of course) and discovered in the course of my investigation thus far.

I still had a number of Rage members who'd been in the bath when Comstock died. While I was almost positive they couldn't tell me anything, I couldn't dismiss the possibility, however remote. But I didn't want to tie up the phone until after talking to O'Banyon; and most of them probably wouldn't be home until evening, anyway.

* * *

My stomach was starting to growl around 11:30 when the phone rang. It was O'Banyon.

"Dick, this is Glen O'Banyon. I've just gotten in from court. What can I do for you?"

Not wanting to take up too much of his time, I told him I was working on my first report on Comstock's death, then quickly outlined the facts of Richie Smith's death, my suspicion that it might very well be somehow related to Comstock's murder, and asked if he might possibly have a police connection he'd feel comfortable with allowing me to contact.

O'Banyon was quiet a moment, and I was afraid I might have crossed some sort of line, but at last he spoke. "Well, there is one I can think of—he's straight, but an excellent policeman with an open mind and a lot of empathy for what the community's gone through over the years. But we're walking on eggshells here, you realize. We don't want to even hint at the possibility of a link between Barry's death and this Richie character. Let me think a moment." Another pause, then: "Okay, here's what we'll do. I'll call him—his name is Mark Richman. He just got a promotion to lieutenant and a transfer to Administration, but he keeps a pretty sharp eye on what's going on in the street. I'll tell him you've done some work for me in the past and I'd appreciate it if he could provide some non-classified information on the circumstances of Richie's Smith's death. I've not seen the paper, but I hope it didn't mention any suspicion of foul play, or anything about an investigation?"

"No," I said, "it was just a few paragraphs, and there was no implication that it might be anything other than an accidental death."

"Good," O'Banyon said. "That should make it easier. What will you tell him if he asks why you're looking into this particular death?"

"I'll just tell him Richie was a personal friend, and I wanted to be able to give his family all the information I could on how he had died."

"Hmmmm," O'Banyon said. "Okay. That should work. But I am relying strongly on your discretion to avoid even mentioning Barry or his death."

"You have my word," I said.

"All right. I'll get to him as soon as I can, and I'll have Donna call you to let you know if he agrees."

"I really appreciate it, Mr. O'Banyon," I said.

"Glen," he corrected. "And you're welcome."

* * *

I went downstairs to the coffee shop for a quick lunch—soup and a sandwich. I really didn't need the soup, but I couldn't resist hearing one of the waitress twins belt out "BAW-el!" Returning to the office, I'd just finished my detailed report on the progress of the case when the phone rang.

First ring. Second ring: "Hardesty Investigations."

"Dick: Jared. I've got the scoop on the dance floor incident. Can't go into detail right now—my truck's double parked. But my last route stop today is Ramón's—you want to meet me there around 4?"

"Sure," I said.

* * *

I managed to reach another two of the guys who had been in Rage the night of Comstock's murder. Neither of them had noticed anything at all out of the ordinary or had any other pertinent information. Oh, well.

That left only 8 guys who had been there who I had yet to talk to. I made a copy of their names and numbers and put it in my wallet to call after I got home. I also made a note to drop by Rage and pick up a list of employees who had been on duty that night. I could just have called Brad for it, of course, but it was my slut phase, remember? And I didn't want to miss a chance to see that little room up close again.

When the phone rang next, I was surprised to hear a woman's voice on the other end of the line.

"Mr. Hardesty, this is Donna Evans, Mr. O'Banyon's secretary. He asked me to call and tell you Lieutenant Richman will be expecting your call. You can reach him at the department, and his extension is 4821."

* * *

I had to look up the department's number, but when I asked for Richman's extension, the phone was answered on the first ring.

"Lieutenant Richman," the voice said, sounding very much like a police lieutenant.

"Lieutenant Richman, this is Dick Hardesty," I said. "I appreciate your being willing to talk with me, and I won't take up much of your time."

"How can I help you?" he asked.

"Well, sir," I said, lying through my teeth, "my friend Richie Smith was found dead last night in his garage, and I'd like very much to be able to tell his family exactly what happened. It might help them deal with it."

"I understand," Lieutenant Richman said. "I have the investigating officers' report here on my desk, and the coroner's preliminary report just came in. I'm not sure Mr. Smith's family will find much comfort in them."

I had a sinking feeling in my stomach. "Why is that?" I asked.

"Well, your friend Mr. Smith appears to have been a walking pharmacy. He had traces of no fewer than three different controlled substances in his system, not to mention a blood alcohol level considerably above the legal limits. It's a wonder he even made it home without killing himself or someone else."

I felt it wise to do some fancy back-stepping. I waited a moment before giving a large sigh. "I was afraid this would happen," I said. "To be honest with you, lieutenant…" *HA!* I thought, "…Richie and I have been growing apart recently. I saw that he was headed for disaster, and I tried to warn him, but…." Another significant pause, then: "So , what was the cause of death, if I may ask?" I asked.

Richman, too, was silent for a moment before saying: "From what we can determine, he made it home, into the garage, lowered the door with his remote, then probably passed out before he could turn off the engine. Apparently, he came to long enough to get out of the car and head for the door to his apartment, but he fell just short of it, and hit his head on the stoop—he had a bad gash on his forehead. But cause of death was carbon monoxide asphyxiation."

Yet another pause as I absorbed everything Richman had told me. Then: "Well, thank you for your cooperation, Lieutenant. You're right, it won't be of much comfort to the family. But thank you again for talking with me."

Well, so much for that, I thought. There was absolutely nothing to indicate that Richie Smith hadn't died exactly the way Richman had said. Maybe I was getting a little jaded, seeing sinister plots where there were none. There *are* such things as coincidences. But in the deep recesses of my brain and my gut, I still didn't believe it.

* * *

I walked into Ramón's at quarter to four—a tad early for the happy hour crowd. Hell, a tad early for me, too. But there were still three or four guys already there and I didn't allow myself to speculate why. Jimmy was behind the bar. He grinned and waved when he saw me, and I returned both.

"Bob's in the office, if you're looking for him," he said.

I suddenly remembered with no little embarrassment that I'd been carrying around a check I'd written to reimburse Bob for the bond he'd posted to get me out of jail and had completely forgotten about it.

"Thanks, Jimmy," I said. "If Jared comes in, will you tell him I'm in with Bob?"

"Sure," Jimmy said, then turned his attention to a patron waving his empty glass for attention.

I walked to the back of the bar and knocked on the office door. "Come on in," Bob's voice said.

The office was, like the offices in most bars, small and

crowded, but oddly comfortable. Everything in it was relatively
new, of course, since reconstruction following the fire that had
gutted the building some time before. And it was surprisingly
neat. On the wall above Bob's desk were several photos of him
and Ramón, taken in happier days.

Bob turned around in his chair, then got up to greet me.

"Dick!" he said, actually sounding happy to see me. "Come
on in."

We shook hands and I reached into my wallet for the check.
"Here," I said sheepishly…"I should have gotten this to you
sooner."

Bob nodded his head in mock seriousness as he took the
check and put it into his shirt pocket without looking at it.
"Yeah," he said. "It's been all of…what…three days?"

"Still too long," I said. "And, again, I don't know what I'd
have done without your being there for me."

"As if you'd never done anything for me," Bob said, sitting
back down and motioning me to a folding chair against the far
wall "So, what are you up to?"

"Well," I said, pulling the chair out and setting it across
from him, "this is just between you and me, but I'm looking
into Barry Comstock's murder."

"I assume you have a client, rather than just running
around trying to do it all yourself?" I nodded and started to
speak, but he quickly raised a hand to forestall me. "No, no,
I don't need to know who the client is. That's your business.
But have you learned anything yet? The police sure aren't
saying much, from what I hear."

"I'm onto a couple things," I said, "but nothing that'll nail
the guy who did it. I was wondering if you might have heard
anything about Comstock since his death that might help."

"I'm afraid not," Bob said. "Other than the fact that nobody
has been weeping much over him, nothing. Sorry."

I shrugged. "No problem," I said.

"So what are you doing here at this time of day?" Bob asked
"Not planning on getting sozzled again, I hope."

"No," I said with a grin. "I'm supposed to meet Jared Martinson here at around four."

"Jared? The 'how-in-the-hell-does-anybody-have-a-right-to-so-many-muscles' delivery guy?" Bob returned the grin and shook his head. "That boy does get around! And from what I hear, he's got a basket of goodies that would put Santa Claus to shame."

"All true," I said, smiling. Bob just gave me a raised-eyebrow look. "Speaking of which, I hear you've jumped back into the pool. No disrespect to Ramón, but it's about time; he wouldn't have wanted you to become a monk."

Bob gave a little smile, almost as if he were embarrassed. "Yeah, you're right," he said. "The guy's name's Mario, and I didn't mention it the other night because I'm still kind of ambivalent about it. As you know, I've been really hesitant about even dating again—and especially another Latino, but...." He sighed. "We'll just play it by ear and see what happens."

Time for a subject change, I thought. "I wanted to ask you if you happen to know a guy named Richie Smith?"

"I'm-too-fucking-hot-for-my-own-good Richie, you mean. Yeah, everybody knows Richie. Another arrogant prick—he and Comstock have a lot in common on that score. If he was only half as nice on the inside as he is on the outside, he'd be a lot better off."

"He's dead, you know," I said.

Bob looked only mildly surprised. "No shit? Too bad they couldn't have done a brain transplant and given his body to somebody who could really appreciate it. What happened? Drug overdose?"

"No," I said. "Carbon monoxide poisoning. Apparently passed out in his garage before he had a chance to turn the motor off."

I told Bob about my peripheral encounter with Richie at Glitter, and that I was meeting Jared to find out more about what actually happened on the dance floor.

"Interesting," Bob said. "But from what I know of Richie,

I don't imagine that incident was a first. He had a foul mouth and an even fouler temper. And while I'd never wish for anyone to be dead, with both Comstock and Richie gone, the community's better off by two."

There was a knock on the door and Jimmy popped his head in long enough to say "Jared's here, Dick."

"Thanks, Jimmy," I said, getting out of my chair and putting it back against the wall. "I'll let you get back to work now," I said to Bob. "Want to have dinner later this week?"

"Sure," Bob said. "How about Friday?"

"Great," I said, reaching forward to open the door. "And if you don't think it's too early to start introducing him to your friends, why don't you bring Mario? I'd like to meet him."

"I might do that," he said. "I'll call you."

As I left the office, I had to sidestep around a dolly stacked with empty beer cases. Jared was at the bar, getting Jimmy's signature on an order form. I moved up behind him and grabbed him by the ass with one hand.

Jared didn't even turn around. "You'd better be somebody I know, or have your checkbook handy," he said. He picked up the signed order form and turned around.

His handsome face split into a grin. "How goes it, Dick?"

"Fine as frog's hair," I said. "You about ready to get off work?"

Jared nodded. "Yeah, but tonight's class night, so I've got just enough time to get home, grab something to eat, and head out for school. But I did want to tell you what I'd found out about that incident at Glitter."

He moved around me to the dolly. "Walk with me out to the truck while I put these away, and I'll tell you while I'm working."

"Sure," I said and went ahead of him to push the back door open for him.

"Well," he said as we got outside and approached the truck, "Richie was apparently pretty high, and he was out on the dance floor with a drink in his hand—which is against the club's rules, but he was Richie Smith so rules didn't apply to him."

Jared slid open a panel on the side of the truck and began to put the empty cases in. "You know how crowded the floor gets," he continued. "So somehow this older guy bumps into him—totally by accident, of course, and sloshes Richie's drink all over him. The guy apologized, but Richie went off like a rocket, as always. Started screaming at the guy, calling him a decrepit, worthless old faggot who didn't belong there and that he should go back to the old folks home where he came from and do everybody a favor and die: stuff like that. The guy was really taken aback, of course, and tried to leave, but Richie just followed after him, screaming the whole way, trying to make the guy feel like dirt.

"I guess Richie must have left the club right after we did. I didn't hear what happened to the older guy, but I sure feel sorry for him."

Closing the side door, Jared moved around to the back of the truck to put the dolly on its rack, and I followed. Suddenly, Jared looked at me, and said: "You don't think that Richie's death was an accident, do you?" It was really more of a statement than a question.

I shrugged. "I honestly don't know, Jared," I said. And while most of me meant it....

* * *

I spent the remainder of the week trying to find information that might be of some assistance. I finally managed to contact all the guys who had been in Rage the night of Comstock's murder, including the three employees other than Brad. Nothing. I talked again with Glen O'Banyon to see if he could tell me anything further about Comstock and whether he might possibly have had enemies whose grudges might have been severe enough to lead to murder. As I suspected, Comstock had very few friends and enough people who ranged from mildly disliking him to sincerely hating his guts to fill several phone books. But again, nothing that rang bells. No word from Jared, which I assumed to mean he had heard nothing of specific interest in his rounds.

Bob called Thursday to set up a time for our dinner on Friday, and said that Mario would be joining us. He was a bartender at Venture, but had asked for Friday night off just, Bob said, so he could meet me. I was duly flattered, but I suspected the main reason was just to spend some more time with Bob.

We agreed to meet at Napoleon, a small, new restaurant in a former private home on the edge of The Central. The clientele was predominantly gay, and the food was reported to be excellent. Bob had made reservations for 8:30.

* * *

I arrived at Napoleon at 8:14 and was lucky enough to find a parking place within walking distance. I recognized the place immediately—it was a small bungalow modeled on the 7 Dwarfs' house in "Snow White," that had fascinated me for years. It had somehow been spared the fate of its neighbors which had been bulldozed and demolished as the area made the transition from residential to commercial.

The place was, indeed, small, and still maintained the comfortable atmosphere of a home. What had apparently been the living room was now a small, nicely appointed bar, with a low ceiling and a working fireplace. I sat at one of the six stools at the bar and ordered a manhattan which had just arrived when Bob and Mario came in.

Mario was taller than Ramón, several years older, and could be described as being more handsome than cute, as Ramón had been. But there were many physical similarities, and I wondered if Bob was consciously aware of it.

Mario's handshake was strong and warm, and his smile seemed sincere and natural. I was favorably impressed.

Bob ordered drinks for himself and Mario, then excused himself to let the maitre d' know we had arrived. The drinks arrived before Bob returned, so Mario paid for them and we moved to a group of chairs in front of the fireplace.

"This may be one of the oldest clichés in the book," Mario said as we set our drinks on the small table between each set of chairs, "but I have heard a lot about you from Bob. You're pretty special to him."

I smiled as we sat down. "The feeling's mutual, believe me," I said. "And I'm really happy that he met you. It was about time."

Mario smiled, a little sadly. "Yes. Bob doesn't talk much about...some things ...but I know what you mean."

Just then Bob walked up to the chairs. "Table's ready," he said. Mario handed him his drink and we followed Bob to where the maitre d' waited, menus in hand.

The main dining room was still relatively small...maybe eight tables in all. Nice, subdued lighting, lots of paneling, attractive individually lit pictures along the walls, crisp white tablecloths with red napkins and place settings. Our waiter stopped by to introduce himself and announce the specials, then said he'd come back when we were ready to order, leaving us to finish our drinks at leisure.

Bob and Mario had met, Bob explained as we relaxed with our drinks, when Bob paid a typical bar-owner courtesy call to Venture where Mario had been tending bar for nearly a year. The next night, Mario had come by Ramón's.

"Purely by chance, I'm sure," I said, and Mario gave me a wicked grin.

"Not exactly," he said.

The conversation got around to Comstock's murder and my whole involvement in the case (though I still didn't mention O'Banyon's role), and my mild frustration with not really being able to find out anything substantial.

"Did Jared tell you anything about Richie?" Bob asked, and the talk shifted to Richie's death and my inability to fully accept the coincidence scenario.

"That's kind of odd," Mario said. "Did you see yesterday's paper about the two guys who drove off the cliff coming down from the Hilltop?"

The Hilltop was a nice but slightly remote gay club located on the edge of the chain of bluffs running along the east side of the river. The shortest way up and down was via McAlester Road, which wound precariously from Riverside at the bottom of the bluff to Cortez, at the top, where the Hilltop was located. It was a general rule that if you were drinking, you didn't take McAlester down.

"Yeah," I said, "I saw that, but don't remember the article saying anything about the Hilltop. Though now that you mention it, it did happen on McAlester Road. Did you know those guys?"

"Yeah," Mario said. "They were regulars at Venture until I 86'd them the same night they got killed."

"Why were they 86'd?" Bob asked.

"Because I couldn't put up with their shit any more—they really crossed the line."

"How so?" I asked, curious. And somewhere in the back of my mind a little voice was saying *Oh, oh!*

"These were two old queens—and I use that term deliberately—who always hung out together. Not lovers; I don't think even they could have managed to put up with one another on a steady basis. But there's fun-bitchy and there's mean-bitchy: these two were mean, *mean*-bitchy. They'd sit there at the bar and get drunk and rip everybody to shreds—quietly, and to each other, so they wouldn't get punched out, I'm sure. I tried to ignore them as much as possible, but they really pissed me off. But I never said anything, because they were paying customers.

"But Wednesday night they were there, and Billy came in." He looked at both Bob and me. "You know Billy, don't you? Goes around to the bars selling flowers?"

Bob and I nodded. Billy was sort of a fixture in the bars

along Arnwood and in the Central. A sweet, innocent guy, pretty severely mentally disabled, but he managed to support himself and his mother by selling flowers in the bars and clubs. The clientele of a lot of the bars Billy had on his route weren't exactly flower-type guys, but everybody liked him. And since his pride would never allow him to take money from anyone unless they got a flower in return, a lot of guys who never bought flowers bought flowers from Billy.

"Well, it was pretty busy for a Wednesday," Mario continued, "and Billy came in and went around asking people if they wanted to buy a flower. I bought a couple, as always, and so did some of the other guys. But then he came up to the two queens at the bar, and they tore into him like a tiger after a lamb! They asked him if he was working his way through college, or if he'd written any good books lately, and then they'd look at one another and laugh at how clever they were. It wasn't clever, it was really cruel, vicious shit. Several of the other customers were getting really pissed. I told the queens to knock it off, but they kept it up. Poor Billy didn't fully understand what they were doing, thank God, but even he knew they were making fun of him, and he stood there, not knowing what he should do. All he wanted was to sell his flowers."

I could see Mario's anger building as he talked, and I found myself getting angry by proxy. He stopped talking for a moment, as if to calm himself down, then continued.

"Then one of those fucking fruits took a quarter from the bar and threw it on the floor at Billy's feet. 'Here's a tip for you, Einstein,' he said, and that did it," Mario said, his eyes narrowing. "I had to hold up my hand to keep a couple of the other customers from moving in on them, and I told those fucking faggots to get the hell out of my bar and to *never* dare show their faces there again, or I personally would come out from behind the bar and kick the shit out of both of them. They stormed out in a huff, and that was that. I told Billy not to pay any attention to people like them, and bought every flower he had out of my tip jar."

Bob and I were both impressed, and I think we both decided then and there that Mario was definitely a keeper.

"Apparently," Mario continued, not being privy to our thoughts, "they went on up to the Hilltop, got even more smashed than they already were, then were drunk enough or stupid enough to try to take McAlester, and lost control of the car on the way down. I guess what goes around does, really, come around."

Are you starting to see a pattern here? I asked myself, but before I could answer the waiter came by to see if we were ready to order. We were.

* * *

The niggling had started, and try though I might, I could not get the story of the two dead bitch-queens out of my head. I really hate it when I know something and won't tell me what it is. And something was telling me there was more to their deaths than met the eye. But what possible connection could there be between them and Comstock? With Richie, there was obviously a direct link, since he knew Comstock and had appeared in his videos. But two queens probably in their 40s or 50s if not older? What gave me any idea that their deaths might be related to Comstock's, or Richie's? My mind didn't know, but my gut did.

Early Saturday morning, I had the urge to get up early and take a drive to the Hilltop. I took the longer, less winding route to Cortez, drove past the Hilltop, then turned on McAlester and started down the bluff. There had been a sufficient number of accidents on this stretch of road over the years to prompt sporadic attempts to close it entirely. But it *was* the shortest way from Riverside to the top of the bluff, and the speed limit was set at 25 mph—which, unlike most speed limits, was pretty much heeded given the road's proximity to the edge of the bluff. It was a tricky road, but not really dangerous if you took it easy.

However, for anyone drunk and going too fast....

There wasn't much traffic that time of morning, so I drove even slower than the posted 25 mph, watching the road carefully. About halfway down I noticed a new section of guardrail at the start of a sharp turn. I pulled over onto the narrow shoulder on the uphill side of the road and got out of the car. Walking back to the new piece of guardrail, and looking uphill I noticed about 25 feet of skid marks leading directly to the guardrail. Looking over the edge, I saw a badly broken tree, and a smudged-clear area in the narrow strip between Riverside and the base of the bluff about 100 feet below.

Directly across Riverside from where the car had apparently landed was a gas station. I got back into my car and con~~jut~~tinued the drive down to Riverside, turning right to head for the station. I needed gas, anyway.

While I usually opt for Self-Serve, I pulled up to one of the Full Service pumps.

A teenager, who was well on his way to being a pretty attractive hunk when his acne finally cleared up, came out of the service bay, wiping his hands on a rag. I got out of the car on the pretext of stretching my legs.

"Fill it up," I said, and the kid nodded, opening the little door in the fender and removing the gas cap.

I motioned to the broken tree and smudged area across the street. "That where that car went over a couple days ago?"

The kid put the hose nozzle into the opening, and squeezed the trigger to start the gas flowing. "Yeah," he said. "I saw the whole thing."

"No shit?" I said.

"Yeah, I normally work nights—just on this morning for the extra money."

"So what happened?" I asked.

The kid topped off the tank, then removed the nozzle and replaced the hose onto the pump.

"I was filling up some guy's tank…It was just a little before closing, and I hear a couple 'Pop' sounds, then brakes squealing, then the crash of the car going through the guard rail. I looked up to see these two headlights just soaring out into open air, then arcing down to point at the ground. It plowed through that tree there, then landed on its roof. I ran in to call for help, but the guys inside were already dead when they pulled them out."

"What happened to the car?" I asked, taking a bill from my wallet to pay for the gas.

"Marv's Salvage came for it," the kid said, handing me my change. "Guess it's still at his yard."

"Thanks," I said, getting back into the car. I had a sudden thought from out of absolutely nowhere. "Oh, by the way...what kind of car was it?"

"It was a classic—a '53 Packard Caribbean. Looked like it had been in mint condition until it hit the ground. A real shame."

"Yeah," I said, starting the engine.

"Have a good day," the kid said, heading back to the service bay as I drove off.

* * *

'...a couple pops' the kid had said. What kind of 'pops? How many? What could they have been?' Don't ask me how, but something told me I knew.

I pulled up at the nearest phone booth and looked up the address for Marv's Salvage. Taking a chance they might be open on a Saturday morning, I drove over.

Luckily, there was an "Open" sign on the chain link fence beside the open gate leading to the auto graveyard inside.

I pulled up to the small shed which apparently served as an office, and went in. It smelled of rust and old oil. A short, heavyset man in grease-stained coveralls sat behind a battered desk piled high with bills and receipts, punching numbers into an equally battered adding machine. He looked up when I entered.

"Help you?" he asked.

"Yeah," I said, "I hope so. I'm planning on restoring a '53

Packard Caribbean and wonder if you might possibly know where I can find one for parts."

The guy got out of his chair, smiling.

"You're in luck!" he said. "I just got one in the other day. Pretty good shape, except for the flattened top. Let me show you where it is."

I followed him out into the yard and he pointed down the makeshift road between rows of junked vehicles of all ages, sizes, and descriptions. "Almost to the end of this row, then turn right. It's right there."

"Thanks," I said. "I'll go take a look."

He nodded and went back into the office while I got back in my car and started down the long row of cars.

There's something kind of sad about an auto junkyard—all those abandoned, once shiny-new cars, trucks, busses (and for some odd reason, a vintage WWII army tank with its tracks missing). All sitting there like they were hoping their owners would come back for them.

I kept looking off to the right and, near the end of the lane, another short path to the right showed a 1953 Packard Caribbean, top flattened almost to the level of the hood, doors pried open, looking much the worse for wear. I backed the car into the narrow lane so as not to block the main road, turned off the engine, and got out to look at the wreck. I walked first to the driver's side. A glance in through the pried open door revealed a mangled seat with dark stains I preferred not to think about. I noted that both tires on the driver's side were apparently still fully inflated. Well, the car had landed on its roof.

However, when I walked back to the passenger's side, I saw that while the rear tire looked perfectly normal, the front tire was shredded as though there had been a blowout. That could easily have contributed to if not caused the car to veer to the right and send it through the guardrail. I knelt to inspect it closer and found a large hole at the top of the tire, from which long, wide strips of shredded rubber dangled. The front of the car was resting on something on the ground underneath, so that the front tires were off the ground. Out of curiosity, I rotated the tire to bring the hole toward the bottom. As I moved it, with some effort, I heard a slight, sliding sound of something like a small stone inside the tire. Curious, I kept turning until the hole was at the bottom of the tire, then reached into it with two fingers. I felt something. Using my index and third fingers as a pair of pliers, I grasped it and removed it from the hole.

It was a spent bullet.

CHAPTER 5

I very carefully wiped the bullet with a Kleenex and then put it back into the hole and turned the tire back to the position in which I'd found it. Then I drove back to the shed/ office, where the owner was still at his desk, punching the keys on the adding machine.

"Find it okay?" he asked, not looking up.

"Yeah, thanks," I said. "I think I can definitely use some stuff off it, but let me check to see exactly what I need, okay?" He nodded. "It's going to be right there for a couple days, isn't it?" I asked.

"It ain't goin' nowhere. But if somebody else comes along wantin' parts from it... well, first come, first serve."

"Understood," I said, rationalizing that even if someone did want some pieces of the wreck, it wouldn't be likely to be a blown tire. "I'll get back to you as soon as I can."

* * *

I would have to wait until Monday to call O'Banyon's office, but I badly needed to talk with him. I was convinced that I was on to something that went considerably beyond Comstock's murder, but since I was working on O'Banyon's dime, I didn't want to do anything more until I'd gotten his okay. And there was the little matter of the bullet. While I couldn't prove Richie Smith hadn't died accidentally, there was no doubt in my mind that the car taking the two bitchy queens over the cliff was neither an accident nor a coincidence and the police should know about it. Obviously, they hadn't considered the accident anything *but* an accident. But they'd sure as hell be curious as to what I was doing sticking my fingers into a blown tire.

The pattern that I'd begun to see at dinner with Bob and

Mario was taking on a far more definite shape and I didn't like the picture I could sense emerging.

* * *

I called O'Banyon's office at exactly 8:30 Monday morning and told the receptionist that it was extremely important that I speak with him in person at his earliest convenience. She said she would see that Mr. O'Banyon got the message as soon as he came into the office.

Less than an hour later, O'Banyon's secretary called to say that he would be in court all day, but could see me at 4:30. I thanked her and told her I'd be there.

I spent the rest of the morning finishing, then rewriting, and rewriting again my first official weekly report for O'Banyon. It was hard putting everything in words, since a lot of my suspicions were largely that—just suspicions and gut-level reactions, neither of which really have extensive vocabularies. Hard facts, which are always easiest to work with, were in sadly short supply. The specific investigation into Comstock's death—which had been the reason I was hired in the first place—was going nowhere, and I was less than happy with myself.

And I suddenly found myself wondering whether Comstock's murder had merely been the first-identified link in a chain that could extend back in time for who knows how long, or whether his death had been the first act that set the killer off, and that now he had embarked on a personal crusade of some sort.

* * *

I stepped out of the elevator on O'Banyon's floor at exactly 4:28. The receptionist smiled and, before I had a chance to announce myself, said "Mr. O'Banyon has been slightly delayed, Mr. Hardesty, but he should be here shortly. May I get you some coffee while you wait?"

"No, thanks," I said, and moved to one of the expensive-looking upholstered chairs against the wall and picked up a copy of the latest *U.S. News & World Report* on the small table beside it.

At 4:45, the elevator door opened and O'Banyon stepped out, carrying a briefcase and looking every inch the successful attorney he was. He saw me, came over to shake my hand, and said: "Just give me a minute, would you, Dick?"

"Sure," I said, as he exchanged greetings with the receptionist and then passed through the glass doors and disappeared down the hall toward his office.

Another ten minutes passed while I paged through the Wall Street Journal looking for the comics section. Finally, Donna, O'Banyon's secretary, appeared at the door and invited me to follow her. The door to O'Banyon's office was already open and Donna just motioned me in.

O'Banyon hung up the phone and rose from his chair for another handshake.

"I apologize, Dick," he said, and sounded as though he meant it. "When I have to be in court all day, there just isn't enough time to get much else done." He gestured me to a seat, then sat himself.

"Now," he said, "what can I do for you?"

I leaned forward to hand him the large envelope with my report. "Basically," I said, "everything is in here. I'm not happy with the way things are going…or rather, not going… in regards to getting any real leads on Comstock's death. But what really bothers me is that I think Barry's death may have somehow started a chain reaction. As I say in the report, a lot of it is just gut reaction, but…."

I proceeded to tell O'Banyon the account of Richie Smith's death I'd gotten from Lieutenant Richman, my gut-level feeling that some key elements were missing, and about the two queens at Venture and their subsequent deaths.

"And here's what I consider the clincher," I said, and told

him about finding the bullet in the shredded tire. O'Banyon's eyebrows raised and he pulled back his head, and stared at me.

"A bullet!" he said. "You're sure it was a bullet?"

"A .22," I said. "I used to do a lot of target shooting."

O'Banyon sat back in his chair, still looking at me. "I'm sorry," he said; "I didn't mean to doubt you, but this does put a whole new light on things." He sat quiet for a full minute, apparently lost in thought. "The police will have to know about this," he said, finally.

"I know," I said. "The problem is how to do it without opening up the whole can of worms and telling them everything. If we do that, my involvement in the case will of course come to an abrupt end—which is fine if that's what you think should happen. But I have a deep feeling that something's been started here that isn't anywhere near over yet, and if the police take it out of our hands, there's not much we can do to stop it."

I paused to give O'Banyon a chance to speak, but he remained silent, so I continued. "I'd thought about making an anonymous call to the police, but they'd be sure to find out from the yard's owner that somebody had been nosing around the wreck."

We both sat another moment or two in silence, until I had an idea. "What about Lieutenant Richman?" I asked. "Could he be brought in somehow? Or do you think he's too hard-line when it comes to anybody interfering in police business?"

O'Banyon pursed his lips. "Hmmm," he said, nodding his head several times, almost imperceptibly. "Richman might be good. I think he could be convinced that we're not trying to circumvent the police investigation, but to supplement it. And I know he'd be interested in hearing about the McAlester incident. I don't know if we can avoid telling him everything, but we'll see. Let me give him a call, and see what develops."

It was my turn to nod. "Okay," I said. "And in the meantime?"

O'Banyon sighed. "In the meantime, keep on as you have

been. And keep your radar going. I'll do the same—I tend to hear a lot of different things, and I've tended to ignore a lot of them. But now we have something of a filter, and if anything gets caught in it, I'll be sure to let you know."

I knew full well, of course, that I'd been specifically hired to track down Comstock's killer, and that I should concentrate every bit of my effort to that end. But Richie Smith's death, and the death of the two bitch-queens were, my gut told me, not coincidental to Comstock's, and while everything I'd tried had led to a dead end with Comstock, these other deaths might offer leads that would lead to the one guy I believed was responsible for them all.

After leaving O'Banyon's office, I made a stop at the library to check out back issues of last Thursday's paper to see what it said about the accident in general and the two guys who had gone over the cliff in particular. I found a brief article on page 3, giving the essentials of the accident and listing the names of the two guys who were killed as Timothy Breck, 57, and Matthew Sharp, 59. I wrote their names down on a piece of paper and stuck it in my wallet.

If their last stop had, indeed, been at the Hilltop, perhaps there might be some sort of clue there. I hadn't been to the Hilltop in nearly a year—it was a nice place, but a little off the beaten path. I knew the owner casually, but had heard he'd been ill recently and was very seldom actually there—the rumor was that he'd come down with that 'gay cancer' people were whispering about. So the person I'd really want to check with would be the bartender on duty the night of the accident. Although I hadn't a clue who he might be, it occurred to me that Jared might well know, and as soon as I got back to my office I called his apartment and left a message on his machine asking him to give me a call.

What had been bothering me, in the back of my mind, is how the killer could possibly have known that the queens would be coming down McAlester—it was pretty clear that he'd have to have been somewhere in front of them in order to be able to shoot out the passenger's side tire. The 'couple of 'pop's' the kid had heard had undoubtedly been the shot and the tire blowing. I decided it might be a good idea to drive back up McAlester to the Hilltop, and then to follow Cortez along the top of the bluff paralleling McAlester to see where the killer might have been to take the shot.

This time, I drove up McAlester from Riverside. I pulled off the road onto the narrow shoulder just before the curve with the new guardrail, got out of the car, and looked up at the bluff behind me, trying to see if I could spot where the killer might have been standing. There were one or two places, and making a rough mental approximation of how far they were in relation to the Hilltop, I continued up the bluff to Cortez and turned right. There were no houses on the bluff side of Cortez, and when I got close to where I'd estimated the line-of-sight spots were, I parked and walked along the bluff as close to the edge as I could get. Sure enough, there was one little promontory which afforded a perfect straight shot forward and down to the curve below. And it also was in direct line of sight to the Hilltop.

The killer could have followed the queens to the Hilltop, taken a few minutes to scout out the promontory, and waited there for the queens to leave. If he'd followed them there, he'd have known what car they were driving and which one to watch for when it pulled away from the Hilltop. A classic '53 Packard Caribbean would be pretty hard to miss.

I spent a few minutes searching the ground for an empty .22 casing, but with no luck It was quite probable that if the shooter were standing close enough to the edge, the casing's being ejected from the rifle—and I assumed it was a rifle since it is hard to sight a pistol at that distance—had sent it over the edge of the bluff. But at least I was pretty confident in the scenario.

* * *

I got home a little after five, and was just fixing my evening manhattan when the phone rang. As always, I picked up on the second ring:

"Dick Hardesty."

"Hi, Dick;" Jared said "Got your message. What's going on?"

"Hard to say, " I said, honestly. "But I was wondering...you deliver to the Hilltop, don't you?"

"Yeah, why?"

"I was wondering if you might know the bartenders—especially who might have been on duty last Wednesday night."

Jared was silent a moment, then said: "Yeah, there's Mike and Tony and Irv, but he's only on weekends."

"Would you have any idea who might have been on last Wednesday night, then?"

"Tony," he said without hesitation.

"Boy, you *do* keep a close eye on everything, don't you?" I said, admiringly. "You know all the bartenders *and* their schedules?"

"Well, not quite," Jared said, "but in this case I know for sure—I was there. Tony and I had a...well, let's call it a sort of date...Wednesday night after he got off work."

"Aha!" I said, picturing a faceless Tony getting royally plowed by Jared. "What time did you get there, do you remember?"

Jared thought a minute, then said "Must have been around 11, I'd guess. I had class Wednesday night 'til nine, and I had Thursday off from work—otherwise I'd never have gone out."

I took a sip from my manhattan...not enough vermouth...before saying "Do you remember hearing about the two guys who went over the bluff on McAlester Wednesday night? It happened just around midnight, and they were probably coming down from the Hilltop."

"Shit, of course!" Jared said, and I could almost see him slapping his forehead. "I never put two and two together. How fucking stupid! It was those two creeps, I'll bet. They were an accident just waiting to happen."

"What do you remember about them?" I asked, stretching the phone cord to reach the vermouth.

"I was standing back by the door," Jared said, "watching some guys play pool, when these two came in. They looked pretty well sloshed already, and they went up to the bar and ordered drinks. While I was too far away to hear everything they said, I could tell they were being pretty loud and obnoxious. When they ordered another drink, Tony cut them off and told them to go home, and they really threw a fit." Jared paused. "Do you know Tony?" he asked.

"No, I don't think so," I said. "Why?"

"Well, Tony's a great guy, and pretty damned hot, but he was in a car accident a couple years ago, and got his face smashed up pretty bad. He's had a lot of surgeries on it, and they've done a great job, but he still has a really deep scar from his left eye down to his jaw, and he's pretty sensitive about it, though he pretends not to be. Anyway, when Tony cut them off, they got all indignant, and the whole place sort of quieted down. One of them said 'Well, who needs a dump like this anyway? We can do down to the Troc where they appreciate our business.'"

The Troc's a sleazy beer bar on Riverside, about six blocks from McAlester. "They got up and started for the door, and Tony called out to them 'Hey, guys, don't take McAlester down, okay?.' They were just about to the door, and the one turns around and says 'Yeah, thanks for the tip, Scarface.'"

"Jesus!" I said.

"Yeah, Jesus is right," Jared said. "If I hadn't had the pool table between me and them I'd have made them wish they were dead! But they did it for themselves, I guess."

"Well, I wouldn't bet that they might not have had a little help. I have strong reason to suspect their deaths were about as 'accidental' as Richie Smith's."

"No shit? You think somebody's out knocking off bastards? Good for them! Oh, and speaking of rotten bastards, did you see this week's issue of *Rainbow Flag*? Just came out today?"

"Not yet," I said, pouring a little more vermouth into my manhattan. "Why?" I asked, taking another sip. Better.

"You know Carlo D'Allesandro, the fashion photographer?"

"Ah, his Gay Royal Highness," I said. "Yes. Another charter member of the Bastards Club. What did he do now?"

"He fired his top model—John... Peterson, I think his name is. I made it with him one time at Rage."

"Is there anybody in this town you *haven't* made it with?" I asked, realizing that my envy made it only half kidding. "That guy is too beautiful to be real. But I hear he just got out of the hospital. What a lousy time to get fired, but it sounds like typical D'Allesandro to me." Carlo D'Allesandro was yet another of those arrogant pricks who assume fame freed him from any laws of common civility.

"Well, he outdid himself on this one. You've heard about this gay cancer people are talking about?"

"Yeah," I said, "but only rumors. I find it pretty hard to believe, to be honest with you. Is that why Peterson was in the hospital?"

"So I've heard," Jared said. "And I'm not too sure it's just a rumor. Pretty fucking scary, if you ask me. Anyway, D'Allesandro is doing this big fashion shoot—had several magazine fashion editors on the set—and John Peterson comes in to get dressed for the shoot, and D'Allesandro says 'Go away. You're fired.' He could have fired the guy in private, of course, but that's not his style. When a couple of the reporters asked him what was going on, D'Allesandro says...here, I've got the article; I'll read it to you... 'My models epitomize beauty, vitality, and health. I've recently been told that John has gay cancer and is going to die. I do not use dying models.' Can you believe that? Can you actually *believe* that?" Jared's voice echoed his incredulity.

No, I couldn't. I stood there, my drink suspended halfway to my mouth "It's a joke, right?" I said after a long pause.

"No joke," Jared said. "And again, if you're right about

these other guys..."

I had a very strange, but by now all too familiar, feeling in the pit of my stomach.

"Jared," I said, "I think I'd better make a phone call—now."

"Sure," Jared said. "And let me know if there's anything I can do to help."

"You've already been a real godsend," I said—and meant it. "Talk to you later."

* * *

The minute I hung up the phone I called Glen O'Banyon's office, hoping against hope someone might be there at that hour. I got a machine. *Damn!* And of course O'Banyon wasn't listed, and I didn't have his home number! *Damn again!*

I do not like being confused and frustrated, but I was totally both. I frantically reviewed my options: there weren't many. Having no way to contact O'Banyon, the only other thing that entered my mind was to call Lieutenant Richman and warn him that D'Allesandro might be in danger. The operative word there was "might." I had no solid proof that he actually was in danger—hell, I had no solid proof of anything except that four men were dead. What could I possibly say to him? There was nothing tangible that I could offer—just theories and hunches. Even the causes of death were different in each incident. Comstock stabbed, no doubt about murder there; Richie asphyxiated—with nothing but a hunch that it wasn't accidental. The two drunk queens? A freak accident; some kid shooting off a rifle somewhere. The whole thing would involve a whole lot more explaining than I cared to—or probably even could—do.

And everything else aside, I was *still* on O'Banyon's dime. Unless I could go to Richman with something other than hunches and conjecture, I really couldn't justify it without checking with O'Banyon first.

Shit, Hardesty! In addition to feeling helpless and

frustrated, I was thoroughly pissed at myself. So I decided just to wait until morning and catch O'Banyon whenever and however I could.

I made dinner then plunked myself down in front of the TV for another exciting evening at home. By 10, I was ready for bed and got out of my chair to turn the TV off just as the local news was coming on. The opening shot of the newscast was of the anchorman sitting somberly at his desk in front of a large full-background photo of someone I recognized immediately, even before the anchor opened his mouth to say:

"Tonight's top story concerns the shooting death earlier this evening of famed fashion photographer Carlo D'Allesandro...."

CHAPTER 6

The morning news, and the local morning papers, centered on the D'Allesandro shooting, of course. Apparently he had been shot on the front steps of his mansion at around eight o'clock as he was leaving for some social function. His male 'personal assistant'...*uh huh*...had gone to bring the car around and heard the single shot as he entered the garage. He'd run immediately to the front of the house to find D'Allesandro dead, but had seen no one, though attempted robbery was not ruled out as a motive.

Just as I was unlocking the door to my office, the phone began to ring. I ran across the room and picked it up on the third ring.

"Hardesty Investigations," I said.

"Dick, this is Glen O'Banyon. I wonder if you might be able to join me for a quick lunch today? I've got to be in court in a few minutes, but if you could meet me at Etheridge's around 12:15, we can talk."

From the background noises, he apparently was calling from a pay phone. Obviously, he didn't want to go into specifics over the phone, but I had little doubt as to the purpose for the call.

"Of course," I said.

"Fine," he said. "Just ask them for my usual table. And please excuse me if I'm a few minutes late."

"No problem, I'll see you there," I said and, hearing a click at the other end of the line, I hung up.

* * *

Etheridge's is sort of a local landmark. Located directly across the street from the City Building, it's a combination of a very upscale coffee shop (no counter) and a limited-hours restaurant, in that it serves a complete and elaborate lunch menu, but closes at 6 in the evening. It caters almost exclusively to workers from the City Building, including the lawyers, judges, and staffers from the various courts.

Naturally, I got there about fifteen minutes early and killed some time walking up one side of the block and down the other, sending out little mental sonar waves...and picking up some decided "Blip"s from interesting-looking business types coming and going from the City Building.

Entering Etheridge's at exactly noon, I asked for Mr. O'Banyon's table and was shown, without the slightest question being asked, to a booth at the far back of the restaurant. The high-backed booths guaranteed a maximum of privacy, and were obviously designed for just that purpose. I asked for coffee, which the waiter brought immediately, with two menus.

It was about ten minutes later when O'Banyon appeared, exuding efficiency, confidence, and control. I half rose to accept his handshake, and he slid into the thickly padded bench opposite me, carefully placing his briefcase on the seat, against the wall.

"I'm glad you could meet me," he said. "You know why I called."

"Carlo D'Allesandro," I said. "I assume you got the message I left with your office."

He looked puzzled. "No," he said; "I normally check in first thing, but I was running late this morning and came directly from home to court. I called you from a pay phone in the hall."

I nodded.

"I was out of town yesterday," he said, removing his napkin from the table and placing it on his lap, "and didn't get back until late. I heard the news about D'Allesandro in the car on the way from the airport just as I was thumbing through a copy of *Rainbow Flag* my driver had picked up. When I read the piece on D'Allesandro's having fired John Peterson, I put two and two together."

The waiter appeared, and O'Banyon smiled at him and said

"We'll need just a minute or two more, Alex, if you would."
The waiter smiled back, and disappeared as we picked up our menus.

"Well," I said, noting to my delight that they featured a Monte Christo sandwich, "it looks like we don't have any choice but to go to the police now—even though we still don't have a single actual piece of evidence unless, as I strongly suspect, the bullet in the tire matches the bullet that killed D'Allesandro."

There was a brief pause as O'Banyon glanced at the menu and then set it aside.

"You're right, of course," he said, "But I'm afraid I'm walking on pretty thin ice here. As you know, I prefer to keep my involvement in all this as low-key as possible: I obviously can't afford to alienate too many homophobes still in positions of authority in the police department by giving them any reason to be less cooperative in my future dealings with them than they already are. They'd love nothing better than to think I've been going behind their backs on Comstock's death."

I thought a moment. "Were you able to talk to Lieutenant Richman?" I asked.

O'Banyon shook his head. "I'm sorry, I fully intended to call him as I told you I would but I got tied up in some other business, and…"

"Maybe it's just as well you didn't, with D'Allesandro's death making a complicated case even more complicated," I said. "Perhaps I could just approach him on my own and lay out the basics of my suspicions. I won't even mention Comstock if I can avoid it. As far as he knows, I was a friend of Richie Smith, and I'll just tell him that in light of Richie's death, I'd followed a hunch with the two queens and found the bullet, and that he might want to follow up on it in light of D'Allesandro's shooting. Once they have the bullet from the tire, I can't imagine that it wouldn't be linked to D'Allesandro's death."

"And you're sure the two bullets will match?" O'Banyon

said.

"I'd bet on it," I said.

The waiter reappeared, refilled my coffee and poured some for O'Banyon, then took our order and left.

"All right, then," O'Banyon said. "If for some reason Richman won't hear you out, let me know. Otherwise, I'll let you handle it and stay as far out of it as I can. But do keep me posted."

* * *

Since the two dead queens had been at Venture before heading off on their fatal trip to the Hilltop, I thought maybe I should talk to Mario on the outside chance he may have noticed something or someone he hadn't mentioned when telling Bob and me about the night he 86'd them. I could, of course, have just called Bob to ask for Mario's phone number and called him at home, but thought I might as well combine a little business and pleasure and go directly to Venture. I called Bob to verify that Mario was working that night, and asked Bob if he'd like to join me. He had some work to do at Ramón's, but said he would try to meet me at Venture around 11 o'clock.

I arrived at Venture at around 10. It was fairly busy for a weeknight, and Mario pretty much had his hands full waiting on customers. He smiled and waved when he saw me walk in the door, and I took a stool at the far end of the bar and waited until he had the time to come take my order.

"Hi, Dick!" he said as he came up. "What can I get you? A manhattan?"

I was pleased that he'd remembered what I'd been drinking the night we'd had dinner. But then, that's what good bartenders do.

"I think I'll go for an old fashioned, whisky sweet."

Mario grinned: "Always keep 'em guessing," he said.

"Oh, and when you've got a second, could I ask you a couple quick questions about those two queens you were telling us about at dinner?"

"Sure," Mario said. "Let me get your drink first."

Between frequent interruptions to attend to thirsty customers, I was able to determine, as I expected, that other than his direct involvement in the incident between Billy and the two queens, and the fact that they had pretty well pissed off most of the other guys in the bar by their behavior, Mario couldn't think of any one customer who might have been displaying particular interest in or antagonism toward the queens.

"Sorry, Dick," he said. "It was a busy night, as I said."

"That's okay, Mario," I said. "It was worth a shot. I'll let you get back to work."

Picking up my drink, I walked to an empty spot along the wall opposite the pool table. There were maybe four or five guys against the wall, most of them leaning back against the small elbow-level shelf where you could set your drink. I took my time looking around, spotting a couple guys I knew and exchanging nods when our eyes met.

Standing closest to me, about five feet down to my left on the wall, was a very tall, very skinny kid who looked like he couldn't possibly be more than 15—though he must have been, because they check IDs pretty carefully in this town. He still had a serious case of acne, and he almost exuded a sense of awkwardness. It wasn't hard to figure out that he was brand new to the game.

I continued looking around, and the next time I glanced to my left, the kid had moved about two feet closer to me. I didn't look directly at him, but I could see out of the corner of my eye that he was looking at me every time he thought I wasn't aware of it. I wanted to smile, but didn't. He somehow reminded me of a puppy—or more honestly, of myself at that age.

Someone walking past smiled and said "Hi, Dick." I recognized him as a guy down the hall from my office, and said "Hi, Chad." And when I glanced to my left, the kid was practically at my elbow. I turned to him and said "Hi."

Dark as the bar was, I could see him blush. "Hi," he said, only meeting my eyes for a fleeting second, then looking down at his drink. I didn't say anything else, and pretended to be staring at something in front of me, but though he didn't move his head, I could feel his eyes darting back and forth from his drink to me.

I really felt sorry for the kid; he was excruciatingly uncomfortable, but the need was there. He just hadn't been playing the game long enough to know how to express it.

Finally, he turned to me and blurted out: "Wouldyougohomewithme?"

I turned to him and smiled. "My name's Dick," I said. "What's yours?"

The kid looked like he was going to fall over. "Devon," he said. "My name's Devon."

"Well, Devon," I said, "I'm really flattered that you would ask me, but I'm waiting for a friend."

Devon looked as though he'd been slapped. His eyes dropped again to his glass. "Oh." he said, his voice flat. "Okay. That's what everybody says."

I kept looking at him until his eyes came back up to meet mine. "Well," I said, smiling again, "I really mean it. But don't ever let it bother you if people turn you down—most of the time it has nothing to do with you. Maybe, like me, they *are* waiting for a friend. There'll be a lot of guys who will jump at the chance—you just wait; you've got all the time in the world."

Devon smiled. "Thanks," he said.

We talked for a few minutes, and I learned not to my surprise that he had just turned 21 and this was only his third time in a gay bar. He'd known he was gay since before puberty, but had never gotten up the courage to act on it. And because he had always been taller than the other kids his age, and skinny, he'd had a rough time of it. As a result, he was firmly convinced that he was ugly. The gay world was totally new to him, and totally frightening. Like a lot of kids coming out, he automatically assumed there were a set of rules to follow; rules that everyone knew but him. I did my best to assure him that there weren't, and that the best thing he could do was to simply be himself.

We were quiet for a minute, and then Devon said: "Well, I'd better go get another drink. Thanks again for talking with me. Maybe we'll see each other again sometime?"

I offered him my hand, and we shook. He had a nice, firm grasp. "I'll look forward to it," I said. "Good luck."

Devon smiled again, nodded, and headed off toward the bar.

"You did that very well," a voice said, startling me. I turned to my right to see an incredibly hot-looking blond I instantly recognized—though I had no idea from where. A wet dream, maybe? He wasn't an ex trick, that's for sure. I'd never have forgotten a face and body like that.

"Thanks," I managed to say. "He's a nice kid."

The blond kept staring at me, smiling. "And are you?"

I was puzzled. "Am I what? A nice kid?"

"Waiting for someone."

"Oh...yeah. I am, actually," I said. "A *friend*," I hastened to add, hoping he believed me. "He's dating the bartender."

"Ah," the blond said.

I extended my hand. "I'm Dick," I said, as he took it.

"I heard," he said. "I'm Toby."

"Nice to meet you, Toby," I said, and wondered if he had any idea how much I meant it. There was something about his voice. It wasn't nelly or effeminate... more...soft? gentle? His body was "Don't fuck with me, Buddy" butch, but his voice betrayed that image. It was... well, *gay*, if that makes any sense at all. Not effeminate: gay.

At that moment, Bob came in the door and walked directly to the bar as Mario smiled and waved a greeting.

"Speak of the devil," I said, as Bob looked around the room, spotted me, and waved.

Toby grinned. "Well, you'd better get over there, then,"

he said. "Besides, we wouldn't want Devon to think you'd turned down his pass and then accepted mine."

This is a pass? I thought. *There **is** a God!*

"Wow," I said.

"Wow indeed," Toby said. "But don't worry about it. Like you told Devon, there's all the time in the world. We'll see each other again soon, I'm sure."

"Okay,"I said; "How about here? Saturday night around 10?"

"I'll be here. Now you'd better go see your friend," Toby said, extending his hand again. "See you Saturday." Our handshake tightened briefly into a something more than a handshake, and I had to literally force myself to release it, pick up my drink from the ledge, and move through the crowd to Bob.

Bob watched my approach with a raised eyebrow. "Now you *sure* as hell didn't leave that U.S.D.A. Premium hunk just to come over here," he said, wonderingly.

"It's a long story," I said, "but yes."

"Well get your ass back over there!" he said. "You can see me any day. That's one fish you sure don't want to risk letting off the hook."

"Like I said, a long story," I repeated. "But we're going to meet up here Saturday, I hope." I emptied my glass and put it on the bar as Mario came up. "One more for the road, barkeep," I said. "Tomorrow's a workday."

"Hey, Babe," Bob said as Mario returned with my drink, "Do you know that stud Dick was talking to?"

Mario shook his head. "Sorry, Bob… I've been too busy to notice much of anything. Which stud was that?"

Bob gave a slight jerk of his head. "That blond over there against the wall. In the sprayed-on tee shirt."

Mario looked without appearing to look. "Oh, yeah," he said. "Toby, I think his name is. Really nice guy, from what I can tell. Kind of quiet but…"

"Is he a regular?" I asked.

"I wouldn't call him a regular," Mario said, busying himself dunking glasses into a sink of soapy water, then into another of clean water, then placing them on a towel on the drain counter directly behind the bar. "Once every couple weeks or so. Hard not to notice somebody who looks like that, though."

Bob grinned. "Who knows, Dick? You may have found Mr. Right at last."

"From your lips to God's ear," I said. When I glanced quickly over to where Toby was still standing, I saw that Devon had moved over from wherever he had been and was standing next to him. *Good luck, kid,* I thought, with a mental smile.

"So did you find out anything?" Bob asked.

"No, I'm afraid not," I replied. "Apparently those two had the magic ability to piss off anyone who came within a hundred yards of them."

"Talk about pissing people off," Bob said, "what did you think about D'Allesandro getting shot? Now there was a guy just begging to be offed. What an unmitigated asshole. I'm just surprised it took somebody this long to kill the jerk. Whoever did it deserves a Public Service award."

I hadn't told Bob everything I knew...or suspected...about D'Allesandro's death, or about my growing hunch that somebody had apparently set out to rid the world—or at least the gay world—of its human vermin. And with the deaths of Barry Comstock, Richie Smith, the two queens, and Carlo D'Allesandro, he was off to a good start.

I glanced at the doorway just in time to see Devon leaving...with Toby.

* * *

I'd only been home about ten minutes, and was just getting undressed for bed, when the phone rang. There was so much background noise it took me a minute to recognize the voice: it was Jared.

"Jared?" I asked. "You'll have to speak up...I can barely

hear you. What's going on?"

"Dick, I hate like hell to bother you, but do you have $150 handy?"

"$150?" I asked. "What for?"

"Bail," Jared said. "I'm in jail."

* * *

When I got to the Central Precinct station, several leather types were emerging, and there were several more in the lobby. I made my way to the desk and told the utterly bored-looking policewoman behind the counter that I wanted to pay the bail for Jared Martinson. Without a word she handed me a form and a pen, took my money, and turned her what-passed-for-attention to the guy behind me in line. When I completed the form I handed it back and she took it and dropped it onto a tray with several other forms. "Wait over there," she said, indicating three already-full chairs near the entrance.

The place looked like a leathermen's convention. More leather than a furniture store full of desk chairs. A good 10 people in the lobby at any given moment, with more coming and going as the door beside the desk kept opening to regurgitate still more.

"What happened?" I asked a paunchy older guy wearing a motorcycle cap, a pair of leather chaps and no shirt.

"A fight at the Male Call," he said. "Sort of got out of hand. The cops busted the whole place."

Another officer came into the lobby through the inner door and picked up the slips from the tray, disappearing back inside.

About ten minutes later, Jared came out. I'm not really all that much into leather, but in Jared's case... It was a side of him I'd never even suspected existed. Some guys in leather look like they're playing some sort of game. Jared was dressed like he was born in leather. He was wearing a black leather armband, black leather pants that I have no idea how he could have possibly gotten into, and black leather vest and boots.

Period. Oh, and he was also wearing a matching black eye.

He came immediately over to me. "Jeezus, Dick, I appreciate this. I didn't know who else to call, and I've got to be at work in the morning."

"No problem," I said as we left the station and headed for the car. "What happened?" I asked as we pulled away from the curb.

Jared looked just a little sheepish as he said: "Well, I was just in one of my leather moods. I don't get them very often, but every now and then...So I went to the Male Call."

"And the fight started, and you got caught up in it," I said.

Again, he looked like a little boy caught at something. "Well, not exactly," he said.

"Meaning?"

"Meaning I was sort of the one who started it."

"Well," I said, "that sounds like the beginning of an interesting story...care to elaborate?"

Jared shrugged and looked out the side window. "I hadn't been there very long," he began, "when three or four college kids came in like they were taking a tour of the local zoo. They were pretty well bombed, and one of them took a shine to a guy who practically lives there—Mitch, his name is. A real hard case, mean as they come: the kind of guy who gives leather a bad name. So this kid's buddies wander off to the back of the bar somewhere, and the kid's coming on to Mitch, real strong. Mitch starts playing with him like a cat with a mouse and the kid's too dumb or too drunk to know what's really going on. So Mitch starts telling the kid what he's going to do to him, and the kid thinks it's as exciting as all hell and that Mitch is just fooling around. Big mistake. Mitch asks the kid if he likes getting fisted and the kid laughs and says 'sure' and it's clear as hell he doesn't even know what fisting is. But Mitch knows."

Jared interrupted his narrative to say: "My car's on Arnwood, about a block down from the bar."

I nodded.

"Anyway," he continued, "I'd just been minding my own

business, but I started to see where this was headed, and I didn't like it. Mitch had the kid backed up against the wall, and it was beginning to dawn on the kid that maybe he was in a place he didn't want to be. Mitch has both arms on the wall, pinning the kid in, and all the time talking to him about what he was going to do to him. The kid started looking around, getting scared, and I walked over and told Mitch to let the kid go, now. Mitch told me to go fuck myself, and turned back to the kid. The kid tried to duck out from under Mitch's arm and Mitch grabbed him and slammed him into the wall so hard it knocked the breath out of him.

"I told him again to let the kid go, and Mitch grabbed him by the arm and said 'Oh, yeah, we're going all right,' and started to drag the kid to the door. That did it. My temper kicked into overdrive, and as they walked past me, I grabbed hold of Mitch's shoulder and spun him around. It must of surprised him, because he let the kid go, and the kid ran for the door. Mitch shook me loose and started after the kid. By this time, I was *really* pissed. I ran up and grabbed him again and turned him around and punched him in the midsection so hard he doubled up and fell on the floor and puked his guts out. One of Mitch's buddies came running over and took a swing at me, and that's all she wrote. Pretty soon it's one big brawl, and then the cops came, and everybody was hauled off to jail, and I called you."

"Well, just remind me never to piss you off," I said.

Jared shrugged again. "Yeah, I guess I do have a little bit of a temper," he said.

"As Mitch can testify," I observed.

"Hey," he said, "Mitch is Mitch. If he'd pulled that number on one of the regulars, I wouldn't have given it a second thought. Everybody who goes there regularly knows what to expect, and everybody knows Mitch. But for him to try that shit on some kid who didn't know what was going on...Mitch should have fuckin'-A known better. He could really have hurt the kid, and I wasn't about to let that happen."

We were turning on Arnwood toward the Male Call. I

looked over at Jared and saw him watching me. "I've got to admit," he said, "all this excitement has made me pretty hot."

Oddly, I realized I was getting a little warm myself, seeing a bare-chested, chisel-muscled, bulging biceped, unbelievably handsome walking poster for Every Gay Boy's Masculine Fantasy sitting next to me, fondling his crotch.

I spotted Jared's car and pulled up beside it. Jared made no move to get out.

"Ever fucked a leatherman?" he asked.

It was definitely warm in that car.

"Not lately," I said.

"'Ya wanna?"

Let me count the ways, I thought. "Oh, yeah," I said.

Jared grinned and opened the door. "Follow me," he said. I did.

When we got to Jared's apartment, it became immediately clear that Jared had been expecting to bring home some company that night. I'd noticed before, in his bedroom, that there were four large hooks in the ceiling to one side of his bed. Since there'd been nothing hanging from them, I hadn't given it much thought. But tonight I saw why they were there, and what they were there for. Suspended from the four hooks was a large, leather sling.

Okay, I've got to admit it...I've been around the gay world for quite a while, and I've had a little experience in a lot of different areas of gay life. But the leather scene was pretty much terra incognita for me. Normally, the sight of a leather sling hanging from a guy's ceiling would give me considerable pause, but with Jared...

I knew he realized I wasn't really familiar with the whole leather scene, and that he was just giving me a brief guided tour, as it were.

Without a word, Jared peeled off his leather pants, walked to his closet and pulled out a pair of leather chaps which, of course, exposed a hell of a lot more than the pants had. Putting them on, he walked to the sling, grabbed two of the straps and effortlessly hoisted himself into the sling. I noticed the two straps closest to me ended in stirrups. As I undressed, getting more turned on by the minute, I watched him lie back in the harness, raise his legs and easily insert them through the stirrups. The resulting position and view were impressive, indeed. Now fully undressed, and totally into the fantasy, I took stock of what an incredible hunk Jared Martinson really was—all solid-muscled 6'3"of him. From where I was standing, Jared's muscular thighs looked like tree trunks, with a truly impressive third column between them, and with a perfect bull's-eye below. Everything was at just the right level. He put his arms behind his head and grinned at me through his spread legs as I kicked my pants to one side and moved toward the sling.

"Welcome to the Master Bedroom," Jared said with a truly lecherous grin.

CHAPTER 7

I was a little late getting to the office the next morning, tired but happy. I took my time drinking the coffee I'd picked up at the coffee shop downstairs, and did the crossword puzzle (in pen) until I was fairly sure Lieutenant Richman would be in, then called the police department and Lieutenant Richman's extension.

It rang four times before being picked up. "Lieutenant Richman's office." I didn't recognize the voice.

"Is the lieutenant in?" I asked.

"He's in a meeting, but he should be out in about fifteen minutes. Would you like to leave a message?"

"Uh, no," I said. "I'll call back in about half an hour." The fewer people in the police department who had to hear the name "Dick Hardesty" the better, I figured.

"Fine," the voice said. "He should be here by then."

"Thanks," I said and hung up.

* * *

Some things take a little time to register with me, and it wasn't until I had been on my way to work that day that I suddenly flashed on something Jared had said when he called me about the interview D'Allesandro had given to the fashion magazine. John Peterson had been a member at Rage. So had Richie. Richie had appeared in some of Comstock's videos, Jared had punched Comstock out when he was approached to be in them. And, as beautiful as John Peterson was, it wasn't a stretch of the imagination to think that Comstock may have tried to recruit him, too. I'd sort of let the whole fact of Comstock's porn business slip past me, but now I realized that I should definitely look more deeply into it.

And since both Comstock and D'Allesandro used beautiful men in their work, it was very possible that they knew each other—and, by extending that thought, that they might possibly have some sort of working relationship.

* * *

I realized my coffee had grown cold and that my pen was still on the "r" in "hierarchy" on the crossword puzzle in front of me. A glance at my watch showed that 45 minutes had gone by. *Did it again, Hardesty,* I thought as I picked up the phone.

"Lieutenant Richman," the voice said after three rings.

"Lieutenant, this is Dick Hardesty calling. We spoke some time ago about the death of Richie Smith."

There was only the slightest of pauses, and then: "Yes, I remember. Glen O'Banyon referred you to me. What can I do for you?"

Good luck, Hardesty, I thought, and then plunged right in. "I have some information I think the police should know," I said, "but I'm in a very awkward position here, and the situation is sufficiently complicated as to be difficult to explain under any circumstances. I wonder if we could meet and talk privately."

"There are proper channels for these things," Richman said. "If you have information regarding, say...a suspicious death..." The lieutenant was no dummy, obviously, "you should contact the homicide division."

"Of course you're right," I said, "but as I say, this is extremely complicated and it would be much easier if I could pass it by you first, then I'll be glad to do whatever you suggest."

A longer pause, and then: "I suppose we might be able to do that. My wife and family are out of town this week, and I stop for breakfast at Sandler's on my way to work. Do you know the place?"

"Right across from Warman Park," I said. It was about two blocks from the City Building Annex where the police administrative offices were located.

"That's the one," he said. "I'm usually there at 7, so if you'd like to meet me tomorrow morning, we can talk about your problem then."

"Thank you, Lieutenant," I said, and sincerely meant it.

"See you then." And I hung up.

* * *

I called Rage in hopes of finding Brad on duty, but was told it was his day off. Taking a chance anyway, I identified myself and told whomever it was manning the phone that I needed him to give me the address and phone number of one of their members: John Peterson.

"Who did you say this was, again?" he asked. "We aren't allowed to give out information on our members."

"This is Dick Hardesty, of Hardesty Investigations," I said. "I believe you were told it was all right to talk to me."

A pause, then: "Oh, yeah. Yeah. Sorry. Hold a second."

I held a second. Then a minute. Then two. I was about to hang up when I heard the receiver being picked back up. "Sorry," he said, "he was in our 'inactive' file. He lives at 1818 Oak, and his number is 281-3487."

"Thanks," I said, and hung up, then immediately dialed Peterson's number.

The phone rang four times before a tired voice said: "Hello?"

"John Peterson?" I asked.

"Yes." Again, he sounded as though I'd gotten him out of bed.

"I'm sorry," I said, "...I hope I'm not disturbing you. My name is Dick Hardesty. I'm a private investigator, and I thought you might be able to answer a few questions I have."

There was a long silence from the other end, and then: "About what, specifically?" he asked.

"Well, actually the questions are really more general than

specific, but I'm working on a case with an awful lot of holes in it, and I'm mainly trying to fill some of them in," I said. "I know this is an imposition, but could I come by and talk with you in person for a few minutes? It's really quite important or I wouldn't be calling."

"Well, I'm not exactly in a having-guests-over frame of mind right now."

"I understand," I said, "but it would be just for a few minutes, I promise."

More hesitation, then "Well, okay. I don't get many visitors these days—the place is a disaster area."

"Not a problem," I said. "When would be convenient for you?"

"Anytime, I guess," he replied. "I don't go out much these days."

"An hour, then?" I asked.

"Sure, why not? You have my address?"

"Yes, thanks. I'll see you in a little while. 'Bye."

* * *

The door was opened by a devastatingly handsome but somehow drawn and very tired-looking John Peterson. He was wearing a bathrobe, and I noticed an odd purple blotch of skin above his left eye, and another on his neck, which looked almost like a hickey—but a sinking feeling in my stomach told me it wasn't.

I hadn't meant to stare, but he gave a small smile and said: "Those go away with makeup; but I was just too tired today to bother. Come on in."

I followed him into the large, expensively furnished living room, which looked …well…very much lived in. Newspapers and magazines lay scattered on the chairs and floor, the coffee table had several filled-to-overflowing ashtrays and an empty beer bottle. Several dirty coffee cups and glasses were on the end tables.

"I had a houseboy," he said, pointing me to a chair, "but he quit when I got sick. I should clean this mess up, but I just haven't been in much of a mood to do housecleaning lately."

"Don't worry about it," I said. "This is 'House Beautiful' compared to my place."

I picked up a magazine from the seat and put it on the lamp table beside the chair.

Peterson sat on the only clear section on the sofa. "So what can I do for you?" he asked.

"I understand you're a member at Rage," I said.

Peterson smiled, but there was no humor in it. "Was. No more."

I wasn't quite sure what to say, or how to ask what he meant.

"Did you get to know any of the other members?" I asked, then realized how stupid that must have sounded.

Peterson smiled quickly and naturally. "Does anybody go to a bath to get to know someone?," he asked. "I sure didn't. I went there so I wouldn't *have* to get to know anybody."

I gave him an embarrassed grin. "Sorry…let me rephrase that. Did you know a guy named Richie Smith?"

Peterson gave me a quick raised eyebrow. "Sure, I know Richie," he said, "though I'd just as soon not. I did see him in Rage a couple times, and we mutually ignored one another."

"So you knew him from outside," I said.

"He was one of D'Allesandro's hangers-on," Peterson said. "Richie thinks the fact that he's in porn makes him better than print models. He hit on me once, just before Ron, my lover, died, and I turned him down flat. He acted like that had never happened to him before—maybe it hadn't. But he was really insulted. And the first time I saw him after Ron died—Ron was 31 years older than I—he said: 'Too bad about your *old* man—but, hey, I bet my grandpa could use a hot fuck.' And he laughed."

He shook his head. "I've never spoken to him since," he said, "and I never will."

No, I thought, *you won't*. If I thought telling him that Richie was dead would bring him any comfort, I would have. But "dead" was a word I preferred to avoid using any more than necessary.

"I should fill you in on a few things," Peterson said, reaching into his bathrobe pocket for a pack of cigarettes and matches. He offered me one, but I shook my head and waited while he lit up and reached for one of the full ashtrays on the coffee table in front of him.

"Ron and I had been together since I was 19," he continued, leaning back on the sofa. "And I still haven't gotten over his death. It was Ron who urged me to become a model. I resisted at first, because I was having a hard enough time in the real world dealing with guys hitting on me all the time. And I was pretty sure being a model would just make it worse. Not that I'd ever give in to temptation …Ron and I were each other's whole world, and we never cheated. But then when he died, I decided I really should see if I'd been missing anything. Rage had just opened up, and I joined. I thought a bathhouse would be a good place to catch up, especially since I certainly didn't want to get into another relationship. About my second visit, Barry Comstock invited me to come into his office and asked if I'd like to be in his porn videos. I told him 'No way in hell'—I had a good, legitimate career going, and I wasn't about to risk it. But every time I'd go to Rage, he'd approach me. He really got to be a pain. I kept saying 'No' until finally I just stopped going to Rage at all. But by that time, too, I'd decided that fucking my brains out just wasn't what I really wanted. So I just sort of retreated into myself and my work.

"And then I got sick. My doctors still aren't sure what it is, but they told me they do think it's sexually related, and that it's probably highly contagious—they're seeing more and more gay guys with the same symptoms." He put out his cigarette, moving other butts aside to get to the bottom. "And more and more of them are dying," he added softly, almost to himself.

He looked up at me quickly, as though he had momentarily

forgotten I was there.

"Jesus, but I was scared," he continued. "I still am. I don't want to die. But I knew that if I did get it from having sex, the only place I'd *had* sex since Ron died was at Rage. I felt that something terrible was happening and that it was probably happening at Rage, and I felt obligated to go see Comstock, to warn him. That was my big mistake."

"How so?" I asked, but knowing Comstock as briefly as I did, I could pretty much guess the answer.

"Do you know what his reaction was? 'Prove it.' *Prove it.*' And then without missing a beat, he said he still wanted me to do his porn films. 'If you're sick, you can use the money,' he said. I told him that even if hell froze over and I was willing to go along with him, if this thing is sexually transmitted, I'd be putting everyone I came in contact with at risk. He just waved it off. 'They're all big boys now,' he said. 'They can take care of themselves.'

"I told him I'd rather die than do porn, and he laughed out loud and said 'Like you had a choice.' I have never hated another human being so much in my life as I hated that man at that moment. But I didn't say another word; I just turned and walked out.

"Two days later I heard he'd been murdered, and my only reaction was: 'thank you, God!' That same night I developed a chill and by the next day I was back in the hospital with pneumonia. They told me I almost didn't make it. But I was out within a week, and I pulled myself together enough to go the shoot that had been scheduled several weeks before. And when I walked on the set, D'Allesandro fired me. In front of all those people."

He looked at me, his face reflecting true disbelief and an almost tangible sadness. "How could any one human being do that to another?" he asked. "What had I ever done to him? In less than ten seconds, he totally destroyed my career. Why? Even if I beat this thing, no one will ever hire me as a model again."

I suddenly had the overpowering urge to find Comstock's and D'Allesandro's killer—and I had absolutely no doubt it was just one guy—just so I could shake his hand.

"And you think Comstock told D'Allesandro about the nature of your illness?" I asked.

Peterson sighed. "How else could he have known? He'd certainly never bothered to come see me or even call while I was in the hospital."

"Do you know if he and Comstock might have had some sort of...well, working arrangement?" I asked.

He thought a moment before answering. "I don't know for an absolute fact, but I do know that D'Allesandro was very particular about who he hired as models; he wanted a specific body type, or a specific look, or a specific attitude, and he turned down a lot of really good looking guys—but he'd always tell them to go see Comstock. In return, Comstock would keep D'Allesandro supplied with hustlers."

"And what did you think when D'Allesandro got shot?" *Stupid question, Hardesty,* I thought immediately.

Peterson gave a sad, weak smile that somehow reminded me of a painting of an early Christian martyr. "As they say, there is a God."

* * *

After talking with John Peterson, my first reaction was to put him right at the top of the suspects list. If anyone had a better motive to kill both Comstock and D'Allesandro— or a stronger case for justifiable homicide, I couldn't imagine who it might be. The motive was a little weaker with Richie. Peterson had a damned good reason to dislike the guy—break both his legs, maybe, or cut off his balls, but murder was stretching it a bit. But even so, that would wrap up who killed those three, but what about the two queens? There was no indication—though I cursed myself for not having at least pursued it when I was there with Peterson—that he even knew them, and it was pretty hard to think of a scenario where those two—bastards that they may have been—could have done anything to him. They lived in a totally different world from the others. Still, I made a mental note to check them out a little more closely to see if there might be some remote tie-in.

And while I was on the subject of suspects, far-fetched though it may be, I had to admit reluctantly that Jared just might be one. He had a temper, he had good reason to have a grudge against Comstock...but that's about it without stretching things. Granted, he'd known and disliked Richie, and he'd been at the Hilltop just before the queens went over the bluff...but even on the most illogical scenario that they had really pissed him off—as they pissed off just about everyone who went anywhere near them—getting mad enough to kill them...? Even giving the benefit of the doubt there, that left D'Allesandro. I had no indication that Jared ever met or even seen the guy, and while he was obviously furious with what D'Allesandro had done to John Peterson, it was via a newspaper article. Plus the fact that tempers burn hot, but fast. And having a flash of temper isn't necessarily the same thing as carefully, calculatedly plotting a murder.

And why was I zeroing in on people I'd already met, anyway? I'm sure every one of those guys had enemies I'd never even thought of yet. Yeah, but what one guy had it in for all of them? Puzzle time.

And for some reason, what Peterson had said about his illness and Rage really bothered me. A bath would be an ideal place for spreading any infectious disease ...especially one that might be transmitted by sex. I had, as I'd told Jared, been really skeptical of the rumors I'd been hearing in the community about a "gay cancer," but after seeing and talking with Peterson, I had tended to agree with Jared that they may not have been unfounded. I'd have to remember to bring it up to O'Banyon the next time we talked.

It was getting fairly late in the day, but I decided to stop by the office and jot down a few notes, and maybe do a rough draft of my next report to O'Banyon. I was a little surprised to find, when I checked with my service, that I'd had another call from O'Banyon. I returned the call immediately, hoping he might still be in, and wondering what was up. When I identified myself to the receptionist, I was put through to O'Banyon's secretary.

"Mr. O'Banyon's office." I recognized her voice immediately.

"Donna, this is Dick Hardesty. Is Mr. O'Banyon in?"

"No, I'm afraid he's left for the day. He should be home by now, and he did want me to put you through to him as soon as you called. Could you hold a moment, please?"

"Sure," I said. There was a slight click and a moment later another, and I heard O'Banyon's voice. "Thank you, Donna," he said, and there was yet another click as she disconnected. "Dick, I'm glad you called. Something has come up and we should talk."

"Fine," I said, wondering but not asking why. "Name the time and place."

There was a brief pause, then "Um...do you know a bar called Hughie's?"

Hughie's? Now *that* caught me totally by surprise. Hughie's was a hustler bar about two blocks from my office. Not the kind of place I'd have associated O'Banyon with in a million years.

"Yes, I know it," I said, now *really* curious.

"Could you meet me there in about an hour?"

"Of course," I said

"Good. I'll see you there." And he hung up. I held the phone about a foot from my face and looked at it as though it had a life of its own and had just told me something that puzzled the shit out of me. Then I realized how stupid I must look, so I put it back in its cradle, mildly embarrassed.

* * *

My curiosity kept me from doing anything much constructive, so after a couple abortive tries, I just gave up. I changed into a tee shirt I kept in the bottom drawer of a file cabinet along with a couple changes of clothes (you never know when you'll need one), and headed out the door to walk down to Hughie's. I figured if I had a choice of looking like a hustler or a john, I'd go for the hustler.

Walking into Hughie's at any time of day is like walking into a movie theater from broad daylight...it always takes a couple minutes for your eyes to adjust. As usual, the place smelled of stale beer and damp air conditioning. While I wasn't exactly a regular at Hughie's, I'd been there several times, mainly because it was so close to work, and because it served dark beer on draft...in frosted mugs, no less.

Bud, the bartender, gave me a heads-up nod when he saw me, and automatically reached into the cooler for a mug. Drawing a dark, he brought it over to me, putting it on a fresh napkin which immediately became waterlogged from the condensation of the ice running down the sides of the mug.

"How's it going, Dick?" he asked.

"Great, Bud," I said. "You?"

He shrugged. "Same as the past 15 years behind this same fucking bar."

Before he could elaborate, someone at the far end of the bar yelled: "Hey, Bud, how about some fucking service here?"

"That answer your question?" he asked, and moved off down the bar.

I'd only taken a couple droughts when I felt hand on my shoulder.

"Thanks for meeting me," O'Banyon's voice said. But when I turned around, the guy beside me sure as hell wasn't the Glen O'Banyon I knew! He was wearing a battered football jersey and Levi's with a hole in one knee.

Obviously my surprise was written all over my face.

"I know," he said with a smile. "But I can't spend all of my life in court."

"Well," I said, "this is about the last place I'd ever expect to see you!"

"Which is exactly why I come here...seldom, admittedly, but it's good just to get away for a couple hours every now and then. Actually, this place is a lot closer to my roots than that penthouse office of mine—though that fact's just between you and me, of course."

I nodded my agreement, then said "I gathered from your call that there *is* a problem. What is it?" Somehow, knowing that Hughie's was not exactly terra incognita made him seem a lot more...well, like me, I suppose.

Bud came up and said "What'll it be?"

"Miller's."

Bud nodded and turned to the cooler to extract a bottle and seemingly in one motion pop the top off on the opener just out of sight on his side of the counter. He put a napkin on the bar in front of O'Banyon and set the bottle on it, taking the bill O'Banyon handed him. He didn't ask if he might like a glass. Hughie's wasn't exactly a glass type of place.

When Bud turned away to take care of another customer, O'Banyon took a long swallow and set the bottle on the napkin.

"We seem to be getting deeper and deeper into the woods, here," he said cryptically.

"Meaning?" I urged.

"Meaning that I got a call today from Bob Kimmes at Kimmes Associates—the accountants for Rage. It appears there's a problem with the books. A lot of money seems to be missing."

"Embezzlement?" I asked.

"Well, Kimmes is calling them 'irregularities' at the moment. But if it is embezzlement, it could throw a whole new light on possible motives for Barry Comstock's murder."

I drained my beer and put it at the inner edge of the bar to attract Bud's attention.

"How did all this come to light?" I asked.

"Standard procedure, really. When Comstock died, it was natural to do an audit for purposes of the surviving partners' interest."

"Kimmes is one of the best firms in the city," I said. "How could they not have had some idea that something was wrong?"

O'Banyon leaned forward, resting both elbows on the bar and staring at himself in the mirror on the wall opposite him. "That was my first question, and it appears we'll never know. The C.P.A. who handled the Rage account was killed in a car crash recently, I understand, and when a new accountant started going through things for the audit, the discrepancies started to show up."

There were those damned sirens in the back of my head again!

"Do you happen to know the accountant's name?" I asked, feeling a tightening in my stomach. My mind and stomach always seem to know things before I do.

O'Banyon took one elbow of the bar so that he could turn toward me. "I'm sorry, no. I met him with Kimmes when we first went with them, but I don't recall his name. As I've said, Rage was primarily Comstock's baby. We get quarterly financial reports, but there's never been any indication of anything amiss. Our other partner took a lot more interest in it than I did, but he didn't mention anything either. Why did you ask about the name of the accountant?" he asked.

"A hunch," I said, and let it go at that.

"Well, you can call Kimmes' office if it's important."

My mind and stomach told me it was. "I think I'll do that," I said.

Bud came over to bring me another mug, and when I laid a bill on the bar, O'Banyon waved it away and handed one of his own to Bud.

"Thanks," I said. We were quiet a moment, and then I said: "So there's no way of telling at this point whether the...irregularities ... come from Kimmes' end, or Rage's?"

O'Banyon shrugged. "Not at this point, no."

There was something else that had been on my mind since I first took the case, and thought it might be the time to bring it up.

"You know," I said, "up to now it hasn't been any of my business and while I've never asked before, I think it might help for me to know the name of your other partner in Rage."

O'Banyon stared at me for a full ten seconds, face impassive. I met his eyes and held them, not blinking or looking away. Finally it was he who broke the stare.

"Bart Giacomino," he said.

Well, well, another surprise! I thought. Bart Giacomino was also one of the original owners of Glitter, though I'd heard he'd recently sold his interest in it. He fancied himself a real wheeler-dealer, as Comstock did, but Bart's money reportedly came from what was euphemistically called "family connections." His relatives were rumored to be big in casinos and other gambling, but had distanced themselves from Bart when they found out he was gay.

It might have been the beer, or the fact of O'Banyon's being more in my territory than his at the moment, but I decided to press my luck a little. "Ah," I said. "If you don't mind my asking...how did you ever hook up with Bart Giacomino? Or Comstock, for that matter."

O'Banyon sighed, motioned to Bud for another beer and waited until it had been delivered before answering.

"Bart and I were roommates in college," he said. "and I spent several weekends at his family's place in my senior year. Then, when I first opened my practice they threw some business my way, which really helped get me started. This was before they found out he was gay."

I got the strong impression that Glen O'Banyon was not in the habit of revealing much about his personal life, and I could certainly understand why—the higher you climb on the ladder, the more people there are waiting to pull you down. I probably should have been grateful that he apparently trusted me enough to tell me as much as he was. But I knew there was more, so I just continued to look at him until he met my eyes again and continued.

"I owe Bart a lot," he said, taking a long pull from his beer. "And when Barry was doing porn, Bart and he had something going for awhile. Barry pretty much used Bart, I think, but Bart never seemed to mind. So when the idea for Rage came along and they asked me to come in with them, I did. As I told you, Barry was very good about making money."

"And Bart?" I asked.

O'Banyon gave a slight shrug. "He does okay, I guess, but he's always lived pretty close to the edge. Bart's attitude has always been that money's there to be spent, and he does that very well. Luckily, he's had partners who were able to keep the reigns on him."

I was busily jotting down mental notes to go through later, but wanted to take full advantage of the opportunity to learn as much as I could while I had the chance.

"Would he talk to me?" I asked.

O'Banyon stared at me again for a few moments, and I could tell he was debating just how far out on a limb he was placing himself by letting me in on things that he'd undoubtedly prefer I didn't know.

"I think I see where you're going with this, Dick," he said, "and I'm not sure I'm too happy about it."

"I'm sorry, Glen" I said, aware that I was calling him by his first name for the first time. *Well, he asked you to,* I reminded myself. "But I can't do the job you hired me for if there are places I can't go."

O'Banyon shrugged again and took another drink from his beer. "You're right," he said at last. "But let me talk to him first."

"Sure," I said. And we were both quiet for awhile. Not uncomfortable, exactly, but just the quiet of having reached a natural place for a pause.

O'Banyon looked at his watch. "I really should get going," he said. "I've got to be in court tomorrow, and there are things I have to do yet to get ready."

"No problem," I said. "I should go, too—I'm meeting

Lieutenant Richman early tomorrow morning. But there is one last thing, if you've got another minute."

"Fire away," O'Banyon said.

"I went to see John Peterson today, and he told me some really disturbing things."

O'Banyon cocked his head and gave me a raised eyebrow questioning look. "About Barry?"

"Yeah, but more importantly, about Rage."

O'Banyon had his nearly-empty bottle raised halfway to his mouth, but he quickly set it down again. "What about Rage?" he asked.

"Peterson is ill—really ill—and he's convinced he got whatever he has from his visits to Rage." I filled him in on everything Peterson had told me about his sexual history and the doctors suspecting the mysterious ailment being sexually transmitted. "If that's true," I said, "Rage could be a breeding ground for it, and a lot of guys are in real, serious danger."

O'Banyon looked troubled, and shook his head back and forth slowly as if in disbelief. "Damn!" he said at last. "The minute I started hearing about this gay cancer thing, I was sure it had to be related to sex. Maybe it's a new form of clap or syphilis, and we know those are sex-related. But this new thing...? I convinced Barry to make condoms readily available in every room, but you know guys: most of them don't want to be bothered."

He continued to shake his head, slowly. "But we can't go overboard and just shut the place down," he said. "There's way too much money involved here, and until we know more about this thing, all we can do is warn the members to be careful. Bart is interviewing for a new manager this week, as a matter of fact, and I'll be sure that he puts up signs. It may hurt business, but it's worth it if it keeps even one guy from getting this...whatever. Then, when we know more...."

"That's all I can ask," I said.

We finished our beers, shook hands, and left the bar to go our separate ways.

CHAPTER 8

Five thirty is much too early to expect any civilized human being to get out of bed, but if I was to meet Lieutenant Richman at seven, I had little choice. I staggered into the kitchen, fumbled for the coffee filter, coffee, and water, turned the coffee maker on, then stood leaning against the sink with my forehead resting on the cabinet above, trying to convince myself I was still sleeping. When I figured there was enough coffee in the pot, I sloshed it into a cup, momentarily grateful I took it black and was therefore spared the complexities of adding cream and sugar, and somehow found my way to the bathroom to begin getting ready.

It was going to be a long, long day.

* * *

Since it was still early, I was able to find a parking place with relative ease, and as I walked the half block to Sandler's Café, it suddenly occurred to me that I'd never actually seen Lieutenant Richman and had no idea what he looked like. But for once, I wasn't early, and I was fairly sure there wouldn't be that many uniformed police there having breakfast.

I was right. When I entered, I immediately saw a really kind of hot guy seated in a booth against the far wall, wearing a police lieutenant's uniform. I went immediately to him and extended my hand.

"Lieutenant Richman, I'm Dick Hardesty."

He turned slightly to be able to take my hand, then motioned me to the seat opposite him. As I slid into it, my Scorpio nature kicked in, and I determined that Lieutenant Richman's being straight was definitely the gay world's loss. Mid forties, short-cut brown hair greying at the temples, very handsome; obviously but discreetly butch.

The waitress had followed me to the table, stopping on the way to pick up a carafe of coffee and a cup and saucer, which she placed in front of me as soon as I sat down.

"I'll get you a menu," she said, but I shook my head.

"Just coffee, thanks," I said. It was still a bit early to even consider eating anything.

She turned to Lieutenant Richman, who ordered a typical man-sized breakfast: pancakes, two eggs over easy, ham, toast, and juice, and a side dish of oatmeal.

"I often don't have time to get lunch," he explained as the waitress headed off toward the kitchen.

He looked at me for a moment the way heterosexual men tend to look at one another when they are not too uncomfortable to do so. "So what is it you wanted to tell me, Mr. Hardesty?"

"Dick, please," I said, mentally taking a deep breath before continuing. "I think it might be to your advantage to check out the car in which those two men were killed a week or so ago, coming down McAlester. The car landed on its top, but the front passenger's side tire is blown, and there's a hole at the top of the tire. If you'll rotate it so you can reach inside, you'll find a bullet—a .22."

Lieutenant Richman gave me a raised-eyebrow look and leaned slightly forward. "And how did you come across this information?" he asked.

I deliberately took a sip of my coffee before plunging ahead. "Well, you remember my asking you about the circumstances surrounding Richie Smith's death..." I began.

I told him about the incident at Glitter and of my subsequent suspicions when Richie was found dead the next day, and about the two queens' having been kicked out of Venture and their comments at the Hilltop, and about talking with the gas station attendant who'd heard the 'pops'.

The waitress brought the lieutenant's breakfast, but he made no move to eat it.

"Very flimsy stuff, I know," I continued, "but I've found that going with my hunches pays off more times than not. So I decided to check the car out on the hunch that a blown tire had sent them through the guardrail, and the blowout might not have been an accident. That's when I found the bullet. And then when Carlo D'Allesandro was murdered, I was pretty sure it was related to these other deaths."

Lieutenant Richman slowly put his napkin on his lap and picked up his fork. "And the motive for these apparently unrelated deaths would be...?"

I waited until he had taken a forkful of his eggs, trying to hold down the sudden feeling that Richman must think I'm a loon, before saying: "Before I get into that, just let me ask you one question, if you can tell me without it interfering with your investigation: was D'Allesandro shot with a .22?"

He reached for the small pitcher of syrup the waitress had brought and poured it carefully over his pancakes before looking up at me.

"Where did you say this car was?" he asked.

* * *

The first thing I did when going in to the office was to call Kimmes Associates. I had been battling with myself ever since my encounter with O'Banyon at Hughie's to *not* open the Fibber McGee's closet of speculations that presented themselves the minute the possibility of embezzlement from Rage was mentioned. I had first to find out the name of the Kimmes accountant killed in the "car accident." I wasn't sure I wanted my gut instinct to be right, but I was pretty sure it was. I fished out the piece of paper I'd kept in my wallet since my trip to the library, unfolded it, smoothed it out, and laid it on the desk in front of me.

I identified myself to whomever it was who answered the phone, told her I was an associate of Mr. O'Banyon, and asked the name of the accountant who had been handling the Rage account before his death.

"That would be Mr. Sharp."

"Matthew Sharp?" I asked.

"Yes, sir. Is there someone else who could help you?"

"No, thank you," I said. "I've found out what I needed to know." And I hung up.

Matthew Sharp had been one of the two queens who went over the bluff on McAlester.

* * *

And the doors of speculation burst open and sent me tumbling ass over teakettle into complete confusion.

Sharp had been handling Rage's account. Therefore, there *was* a trail of breadcrumbs—hell, make them croutons! —between one of the two queens and Comstock, and of course there was one from Comstock to D'Allesandro, and one between both Comstock and D'Allesandro and Ritchie.

All of which sort of blew out of the water my moral vigilante theory. They were still all bastards, but maybe that wasn't what got them killed.

And now we had Bart Giacomino thrown into the mix. If money was missing from Rage, was Comstock responsible? Or maybe Giacomino, who O'Banyon indicated had problems with money? If it was Comstock, did Giacomino—who was in Europe when Comstock died—find out about it and use one of his family connections to have Comstock killed? Or if it was Giacomino, did Comstock die because he found out about it? Or was Sharp, the accountant, just doing a little creative bookkeeping on his own? Or...

Oh, shit, Hardesty, give it a rest!

I was suddenly reminded of when I was in Junior High, and one of our science classes had to do with a map of the stars. I came to the amazing realization that I could draw a straight line from any one of those stars to any other star. I was sure I'd made a scientific discovery of major proportions until the

teacher gently pointed out that you can *always* draw a straight
line between any two given objects if you want to. Was that
what I was doing here? Hell, who knows?

I finished up my official weekly report to O'Banyon and
kept trying, mostly unsuccessfully, to keep from getting back
on the speculation merry-go-round.

Luckily, the phone rang around 11:00. It was O'Banyon,
asking how my meeting with Lieutenant Richman had gone,
and telling me that Bart Giacomino would be at Rage to
interview a couple of manager prospects at 1:30. He'd agreed
to see me when he finished, around 2 or 2:30. I assured him
I'd be there.

A quick lunch at the coffee shop downstairs—a ham salad
on rye, a "BAW-el" of chicken & dumplings soup, and a
chocolate shake: gourmet dining at its finest, then a stop at the
dry cleaners for a drop-off and pick-up, and it was time to head
off to Rage.

I found a parking space just up the street from Rage, and
as I walked past the alley I noticed a gleaming black Jaguar
parked across from Rage's side door.

Brad was on duty, and I stood on the lobby side of the
registration window and shot the shit with him for awhile. With
Giacomino using the office for interviews, neither Brad nor
I mentioned taking advantage of the little room, though when
I asked Brad if they'd taken out the two-way mirror, he said
'no.' Maybe they were just waiting for the new manager to take
over. Or maybe the new guy would decide that a fine old
tradition like voyeurism deserved to be maintained. And I did
mention to him—without naming John Peterson specifically—that there might be a health problem he should be aware
of, and guard against

A few members came and went, and finally the inner door
opened and a nice-looking guy with pecs the size of Butterball
turkeys and biceps only slightly smaller around than his waist
came out. I recognized him as the manager of one of the local
gyms...Jim Hicks, I think his name was and, since he wasn't

carrying a gym bag, I assumed he had been Giacomino's interview.

A minute later, the inner door opened about halfway, being held by a large, oddly ...well, odd-looking...man. He reminded me instantly of a painting of a very handsome man done by a third-rate artist: either something was there that shouldn't have been, or something wasn't there that should have been. Hard to explain, but... And I first thought he was a mulatto until I realized he just had one of the darkest tans I have ever seen. His hair was so black it would make tar look like a pastel. He wore a suit the cost of which I could only imagine. A white silk shirt open at the collar revealed about six gold chains over a mat of curly, solid black glistening chest hair, and on the hand holding the door, one of the largest and most garishly ugly gold-and-diamond pinkie rings I've ever seen.

"Dick Hardesty?" he asked, and I smiled and walked to meet him.

He smiled broadly, revealing a mouthful of perfectly capped teeth, and held the door open with his elbow while he shook my hand, then said "Come on in to my office."

That one didn't get past me, you can be sure. *Your office, huh?*

When we entered the office, he closed the door, motioned me to a chair, and walked behind the desk to sit in Comstock's chair.

"Glen tells me you wanted to talk with me," he said, casually.

"Yes, I did," I said, hoping I sounded equally casual. "I appreciate your taking the time to see me...I know you've been busy."

He gave a casual flip of his pinkie-ringed hand, and said: "Busy isn't the word. I just got back from my villa in Cannes last week, and next week I have to be at my beach side place in Molokai for a dinner for the governor. But business before pleasure."

Uh huh.

"I understand you were in Europe when Barry Comstock was killed," I said.

Giacomino leaned back in his chair and sighed. "Yeah. I was skiing with the crown prince at Luftsenhagen when I got the word. I was devastated, of course. Barry was one of my best American friends."

Okay, Charlie, I get the picture. You can knock it off, now!

"Exactly what is your involvement with Rage?" I asked, as though crown princes and Luftsenhagen cropped up a lot in normal conversation. "...Other than being a financial backer."

He pursed...no, make that puckered...his lips, which made him look very much like a chimpanzee, and furrowed his brows—a very disconcerting combination, I have to admit. "Mostly financial," he said, resting his elbows on the arms of the chair and placing his hands under his chin, spread wide with fingertips touching, as though he were holding an imaginary basketball. "I'm so seldom in the country, of course. At first I'd intended to be a lot more involved, but Barry wanted to run the whole show, more or less, until Glen talked him into turning the books over to...ah..."

"Kimmes Associates," I finished.

"Yeah, them. I could have done it, of course, if I had the time. I'm very good with bookkeeping. But I simply don't have the time."

"What do you make of the apparent...irregularities... Kimmes found?"

Giacomino shook his head. "No idea at all. I'm sure it's just a minor error somewhere. To even think that Barry might have been...no, it's impossible. Of course, he did live pretty high on the hog for a former porn star. But, no...he would never have..."

I had to give the guy credit—he could bob-and-weave with the best of them.

"Did Barry have any..." I started to say 'enemies,' but I knew the answer to that one before I even asked it, so I

switched track in mid-sentence, especially since it was obvious
Giacomino wouldn't be adverse to putting the finger on
Comstock "...recent financial problems or setbacks you were
aware of?"

That puckered-lips, furrowed brow thing again. Creepy.

"No, not at all. Barry was always very good with money.
Of course, that house of his was something of a bottomless
money pit, and I'm sure he rued the day he bought it. As a
matter of fact, he'd tried to sue the realtor who sold it to him,
as I recall. Oh, and then there was that lawsuit..." He suddenly
raised his eyebrows in patently obvious fake surprise. "Oh, but
you didn't know about that, did you? No one did, and I was
sworn to secrecy." He shook his head as if mentally scolding
himself, but I wasn't fooled for a minute. I did notice that his
eyes never left me. When he didn't see whatever reaction he
apparently expected, he continued. " But I'm sure that since
you're working for us, it would be considered privileged
information. Glen handled it, and it was settled out of court.
It was a scam, of course, but Barry did not like being scammed."

I sat back in my chair and crossed my legs. "Could you
sketch in the details, now that it's been mentioned?"

I had the distinct impression that Bart Giacomino had his
own agenda in all this, though of course I had no idea what it
might be. Whatever it was, he was probably trying to cover his
own ass by the old "Oh, look over there!" routine.

"It was about two years ago," he said. "A cameraman who'd
done some work on Barry's videos brought him two incredibly
hot identical twins, blonds—farm boys just in from Nebraska.
The cameraman and the kids swore up and down they were
eighteen—they even had fake ID's, and they could easily have
passed for it. Barry always had this special thing for blonds,
so of course he had to 'audition' them personally. And the next
day the kids' irate father showed up screaming that Barry had
raped his two innocent sixteen-year-old babies, and threatening
to sue him for every penny he had. It was, as I say, all a set-up
to extort money from him, but Barry was uncharacteristically

stupid enough to fall for it, and he settled, just about the time Rage opened. Even I don't know how much was involved, but I know it was a big chunk of change. And I do know that Barry was not happy about it."

From what I knew about Barry Comstock and his reluctance to part with money, I could imagine just how not happy he must have been. Might he have decided to use a little of Rage's money to restock his coffers?

"As partners, I assume all three of you have access to Rage's books?"

There was what I found to be a rather significant pause before he responded: "Well, yes, of course. But the accountants are doing all that now. They're responsible for looking after the money. We get quarterly reports."

In the back of my mind, I could swear I heard the quiet sound of tap-dancing. I saw him subtly push one sleeve of his jacket up with an index finger to reveal his Rolex. He looked at it rather pointedly.

"I think I've taken up about enough of your time," I said, getting the hint, but hastening to add "…for now. But I do have one more question."

His expression did not change, but I was sure there was an almost imperceptible narrowing of his eyes as he said: "Of course."

"I understand you were one of the founders of Glitter," I said.

He nodded. "One of my many successful business ventures," he said.

I gave an "I see" return nod. "And I'd heard that you recently sold your interest in it."

He again…this time with no subtlety whatsoever…pushed up his sleeve to look at his watch. "I'm sorry, Dick, but I have another interview waiting. Maybe we can talk again when I get back from Molokai. Bob Redford called yesterday to ask me to set up a charity function with him and Liz Taylor in New York on the 19th , so I know I'll be back before then."

Uh huh, I thought, but only said: "I'd appreciate that," and followed his getting-up-from-the-chair motion to lean forward across the desk and take his extended hand.

He walked with me to the outer lobby, where a clone of the gym manager I'd seen when I came in was standing at the registration window talking with Brad. From the bulge in his pants, I gathered it had been an interesting conversation.

Giacomino and I shook hands again, and he turned immediately to the hunk at the window, who was suddenly and obviously awkwardly aware of his condition—which was not lost on Giacomino, either, I could tell.

"Chuck Roth?" Giacomino said, holding the door open with his elbow, "Come on in to my office."

Roth managed an embarrassed smile as we passed one another, and I winked at Brad, who stood behind the window with a huge, shit-eating grin.

"I like this job," Brad mouthed slowly without speaking.

"Gee," I said, "who'd'a thunk?" I was tempted to go over and talk with him more, but the outside door opened and a member walked in, so I just gave Brad a wave and left.

* * *

It's one thing to be able to draw a nice, clean straight line between any two points and something quite different when you start connecting every point to every other point: the whole thing starts to look like a big blur.

Obviously Giacomino was hiding something when it came to Rage's books. Why, I wondered, had he sold his interest in Glitter? It was, from everything I could tell, a cash cow, and the obvious conclusion to be drawn from his having given up his place at the udder was that he needed money. And if even half of his Bob-and-Liz-and-the-crown-prince-and-villas-and-beachfronts routine was true, that must involve one hell of a large and continuous outlay of cash.

I made a mental note to call O'Banyon Monday morning

to see if he knew more about Giacomino's financial condition than he was telling.

* * *

Since I knew full well that once I started a case I felt compelled to work nonstop until it was solved, I'd determined some time ago that I had to make a conscious effort to make my weekends my own. It wasn't easy, especially in a convoluted case like this, but I really had to try to shut my mind off and step away from it. I hadn't had much actual practice at it, but was determined to try.

I tried to force myself to sleep in, which of course didn't work, so got up and, after dragging out my coffee/breakfast routine for as long as I could stand it, and telling myself yet again that I should have the paper home-delivered every day instead of just on Sunday so I'd have a Saturday crossword puzzle to work on, I studiously applied myself to doing really fun things, like dishes and laundry and cleaning the oven.

The day went relatively fast, and before I knew it, it was time to think about getting ready to go to Venture to meet Toby—assuming he would be there. *Well, his loss if he's not*, I told myself—I just wish another little voice in there didn't snicker.

* * *

I arrived at Venture around 9:30, and noted they had two bartenders on duty—well, it was a Saturday night. I was glad to see that Mario was one of them. I made my way to the end of the bar closest to Mario who smiled and, both hands occupied with making a drink, gave me a head-nod 'hi'. No sign of Toby yet, but we weren't supposed to meet until 10 so I wasn't concerned.

As soon as he was able, Mario came over to take my order. "How's it going, Dick?" he asked, as he put a napkin in front of me.

"Pretty good," I said. "Don't you ever get a night off?"

Mario grinned. "I've got two days starting tomorrow," he said. "Bob and I are going to drive out to Tilton to a gay bed and breakfast there."

"Ah," I said, "a romantic getaway."

Mario just grinned.

"I'm glad for you." I said. "You both need a little time to relax."

"If I'm lucky, I don't think there'll be too much relaxing," he said. "What can I get you?"

"Whiskey old fashioned..."

"...sweet," Mario finished.

"You *are* good," I said, grinning.

"So I've been told," he said and reached for a glass.

* * *

I took my drink and went to my usual spot along the wall. At about five til ten, I glanced at the door to see Toby coming in. He went directly to the bar without looking around, said a few words to Mario and, still without any indication that he was looking for me, walked directly over to where I was standing. I noticed he was carrying two drinks—one of them a Whiskey old fashioned.

"Hi, stranger," he said, looking directly at me for the first time and putting the old fashioned on the ledge by my side.

"Hi yourself," I said. "Glad you made it."

He gave me a little smile. "Like you thought I wouldn't?" he asked. "I always do what I say I will."

"Nice to know," I said. "And if the old fashioned is for me, thanks."

He nodded a "you're welcome."

Not recognizing what was in his glass, I said: "What are you drinking?" I obviously hadn't been paying attention the night we met.

"Cranberry juice," he said. "I don't drink."

Interesting, I thought.

We idle-chatted with the usual mild clumsiness of a first conversation, dropping in little bits of personal information as we went. Toby, I discovered, was relatively new to town. He'd first worked as an orderly at a local hospital, which may have had something to do with his being a health fanatic. No alcohol, no caffeine. Strict vegetarian (so much for the fantasy of quiet dinners-for-two at home of burnt pork chops, mashed potatoes and gravy); three hours a day, every day, at the gym, which I might have expected—nobody has a body like that without a lot of effort. He'd left the orderly job to go to work for a construction company, which in effect boosted his per-day exercise regimen to 11 hours.

It showed. He was wearing a white Polo-type short sleeved shirt which set off both his tan and his muscles to full advantage, but I didn't get the impression of wildly overt narcissism too often present in guys who live at the gym. Nor did I envision him standing for hours in front of a mirror looking for the perfect combination of clothes for the evening. His tan was dark, but natural—not like Giacomino's. And where Giacomino wore about a dozen gold chains around his neck, Toby had the same single, simple thin silver chain I'd noticed the first night I met him.

And all the time I was looking at that beautiful face and body and counting the minutes until I could get him into bed, there was...something else. For some reason, I got the impression again of there being two people in there. The hard-muscled hunk on the outside and something...I couldn't find the word...inside. For some reason it brought out the...well, the big brother instinct in me.

Oh, great, I thought. *So now you're into incest?*

But my primary impression of Toby was also the same as the night I'd first seen him—that he was a genuinely nice, warm guy. I of course did not bring up his having left the bar with Devon—I sensed that he hadn't taken Devon home because he felt sorry for him, but because he wanted to help the kid feel better about himself—and that was a pretty damned nice thing for him to do. Of course, he just might like tall, skinny young kids—but then he'd hardly be standing here talking with me.

As I was returning from the bar with another old fashioned and glass of cranberry juice, I noticed Jared come in with somebody who had obviously been yanked out of the pages of Wet Dream Weekly. *How in hell does he do that?* I wondered. Jared saw me, smiled and waved, and I, hands full, merely smiled and nodded.

When I got back to Toby, I noticed a guy I knew from my days with Chris standing about two spots down the wall from us. George...Atkins, I think. Another really nice guy who had finally found a lover after looking unsuccessfully for several years. Unfortunately, the guy he took up with was a real cunt—possessive, bitchy, demanding. Most of George's friends at the time...including Chris and me...had drifted away from them; or more accurately, been driven away by the new lover. I'd one time asked George why he put up with all the abuse the guy was giving him, and he just shrugged and said something to the effect of "Better the devil you know," which I read to mean "Better to be miserable with someone than to be alone."

I was relieved to see him alone, though, and assumed he'd finally gotten wise and kicked the guy out. I gave him a big smile and said "Hi, George...great to see you" as I passed him. I didn't want him to think I was ignoring him, but I was, after all, with Toby and this was really our first time together.

About ten minutes later, my conversation with Toby was interrupted by a loud "There you are, you fucking sonofabitch! I knew I'd find you here! How dare you walk out on me when I'm talking to you!"

Startled, Toby and I both turned to see a prissy skinny queen I recognized immediately as George's lover. So he hadn't dumped him. Jeezus!

George, obviously embarrassed, made a "Shhhhhh" sound and said quietly: "Don't make a scene, Lynn."

Wrong thing to say. Lynn upped the volume about five notches. "Don't you tell me not to make a scene, you limp-pricked bastard!" And he suddenly slapped George across the face...hard. The sound was like a guillotine, cutting off every bit of conversation in the bar, leaving only the sound of the jukebox to fill the large room. I instinctively made a move toward the fucker, but Toby reached out calmly and held me back. All this was in the space of five seconds, and it didn't slow Lynn down for as much as one of them.

"I'll make a goddamned scene any goddamned time I fucking well feel like it and there's not a goddamned motherfucking thing you can do about it!" he yelled. "Now put that drink down and get out of here!"

By this time, every pair of eyes in the place was glued on poor George, who was obviously so embarrassed and angry he didn't know what to do. I saw Mario pushing his way through the now silent crowd.

"Okay, guys," he said, "that's enough. Take it outside."

"Take it outside is fucking right!" Lynn yelled. "You bet your ass we'll take it outside." He reached out and grabbed George by the sleeve, yanking it so hard it tore the material.

"Lynn, for Christ's sake!" George said, and Mario reached out to remove Lynn's hand.

"I said that's enough," Mario said calmly to Lynn. "Now get out of here before I throw you out."

George gave me a fleeting, embarrassed glance and followed Lynn through the crowd, which parted as if by magic. Mario just gave me a poker-faced look and shook his head. As soon as the door closed behind them, the place slowly resumed its normal noise level, until it was as though nothing at all had happened.

I turned my attention back to Toby. "Sorry about that," I said.

Toby shook his head. "Hey, you didn't have anything to do with it." Then he was quiet a moment before saying: "I can never understand how people can treat each other the way they do. I can't stand violence."

"Well," I said, "some people just let others walk all over them."

"Yeah, but they shouldn't," Toby said. There was a pause, and then: "And you know those two?"

"I know George," I said. "George Atkins. The other one's name is Lynn but I can't remember his last name and would just as soon not. What a sorry excuse for a human being!"

We were quiet again for a minute until Toby said: "Are you ready to go?"

Our eyes met and little ESP. messages went darting back and forth between us.

"I think so," I said.

We finished our drinks, carried the glasses to the bar, and I waved goodbye to Mario and Jared, who was deep in conversation with the Wet Dreams hunk, and we left.

"Do you mind if we went to your place?" Toby asked.

No, Toby, I don't mind at all, I thought.

"Sure," I said.

CHAPTER 9

Think about all the times you've had sex in your life. Now think about how many of those times—or people—you can really *remember*. Sex is always fun and sometimes it can be really intense. But most of the time you're having sex and the guy you're having sex with is having sex, but you're not really having it *together*. That's one of the major dividers that separate tricks from lovers But every now and then, if you're really lucky, there's a Toby.

Toby was incredible; he seemed to sense exactly what to do and when to do it. And always, every minute, I was absolutely sure he really, sincerely *meant* it. And while I really hated to admit it, there was that weird incest element—Toby made me feel...well, the word that pops to mind is "butch", but that didn't really do it. I can be butch with a lot of guys. It wasn't so much a matter of "Me Tarzan, You Jane" as it was "Me Tarzan, You Boy" if that makes any sense This was more a matter of being the leader, the protector...I don't know. Like I say, weird.

Sex with Jared was always fantastic—but that was just it: Jared was a walking sex fantasy—it was largely sex for the mind. If you could imagine it, Jared would be willing to do it with you. With Toby, you were aware that sex could sometimes be more than just a great meshing of body parts.

But as we all learn at a pretty early age, the gods keep perfection for themselves: we mortals can come close...but only *so* close. So, while I was absolutely sure that Toby was somebody's—hell, a *lot* of guys'—Mr. Right, I knew he wasn't mine. I could see Toby as a kid brother, but I could take the incest analogy only so far:.... But then, as we were lying in bed afterwards Toby leaned over and kissed me and said: "I'm sorry, Dick, but I've got to be getting home."

That brought me back in a hurry, you can bet. "Can't you spend the night?" I asked. "It's almost three already." Hearing myself say that rather surprised me—usually I didn't care if they stayed or not.

Toby smiled, his face only inches from my own. "I wish I could, Dick, but I've got to get some sleep, and I couldn't sleep here."He noticed my look of puzzlement and smiled again. "It's got nothing to do with you—it's kind of hard to explain."

He looked just slightly embarrassed as he said: "I always keep the foot of my bed two feet higher than the head—it helps blood circulation. And all my supplements are at home. And I want to be at the gym when it opens—sex is great, but it takes a lot out of me, and exercise is the only thing that will put it back."

He kissed me again, then rolled over and sat up on the edge of the bed, reaching down to pick up his shorts. "Can I use your phone?" he asked. "I'll take a cab home...my car's in the shop until Monday."

I threw off the sheet and sat on my edge of the bed. "No way! I'll drive you back."

"You're sure?" he asked. "Calling a cab won't be any trouble, and that way you can get some sleep."

We both stood up on our respective sides of the bed, adjusting our shorts, and in unison leaned back down for our pants. "I can sleep when I get back," I said. I really didn't want to let him go. Why?

Innocence! That was it! I somehow sensed inside that hunk's body, there was an almost child-like innocence—and an indefinable aura that he'd been hurt because of it. That must have been what triggered my Hardesty-the-Protector reactions.

But altruism aside, Toby was also damned good sex. God, what ingrates humans are. We hope and pray for just one night with someone as good as Toby, and then when we get it, we're not satisfied because we want more.

We got dressed, spent two or three minutes at the door locked in a bear hug, and then went downstairs to the car.

"Would you like to have brunch after the gym?" I asked, then immediately thought: *You're pushing it, Hardesty!*

Toby turned slightly to look at me with a soft smile. "Thanks, but I can't. I almost never eat in restaurants. I have a pretty strict food regimen, I'm afraid. But can I call you next week some time?"

"Sure," I said,. "There's a piece of paper and a pen in the glove compartment—I'll give you my number."

"Great," he said.

* * *

On the way back home, I had a one of my little Hardesty-to-Hardesty talks.

Think you'll ever grow up, Hardesty? I asked myself. I was thinking of how, as a kid, I'd made myself self-appointed guardian of the smaller kids, protecting them from the local bullies. The fact that Toby was a big boy and gave no outward indications of needing to be protected didn't matter.

God, I hope not! I replied.

* * *

I managed to sleep 'til almost noon on Sunday, got up, put my bathrobe on, put on a pot of coffee, then stepped out into the hall to get the Sunday paper which the delivery guy invariably left outside the custodian's closet next door. Maybe if I had it delivered every day he'd remember which door was mine.

Curious as I was about Jared and his hot friend, and what he'd thought of the confrontation at Venture, I managed to keep myself away from the phone. He was probably still asleep, anyway.

Read the paper, drank coffee, fought down the urge for a morning cigarette, did the crossword puzzle, and was just thinking about making breakfast when the phone rang.

"Dick Hardesty," I said.

"Hi, Dick," Jared's cheerful voice replied. "Wondered if you'd like to go out for brunch?"

"Saved by the bell!" I said. "You just caught me in time. When and where?"

"How about Calypso's? I think they serve until 2:30. What time is good for you?"

I glanced at my wrist and realized I hadn't put my watch on yet, so looked at the clock beside the refrigerator. "Ah...I can be there by about quarter 'til. Will you be alone, or..."

Jared laughed. "I was just going to ask you the same thing!" he said. "I'll be alone."

"Me too," I said

"Pity," he said. Then: "See you at 1:45 then. Bye."

I hung up, took the last swig of coffee left in the cup...cold, of course...and headed for the shower.

* * *

Calypso's has two things going for it...a nice private patio and a great Sunday brunch. But the clientele tended toward those with one foot in the closet and one hand on the doorknob. None of the usual brunch-bar boisterousness, since openly using the "g" word was frowned upon. I hate games like that, so despite the good food, I seldom went.

Jared was just walking up to the entrance as I got out of my car. He saw me, waved, and waited for me to join him. The place was pretty well filled, as always, but the main wave of brunchers was ebbing.

"In or out?" I asked Jared as we stood by the maitre d's podium.

"How about a little in *and* out?" he said with a wicked grin.

"'Get off the table, Mable, the quarter's for the beer,'" I said, laughing. "We can talk about ins and outs later. Let's see if we can get something on the patio first, okay?"

"Fine by me," he said as the maitre d' came up, giving Jared an appreciative once-over.

Luckily, a table had just been vacated on the patio, so after a very brief wait while it was cleaned and set up, we were shown to it, seated, and had our drink order taken.

"So," Jared said, leaning back in his chair, "how was last night?"

I grinned. "You first," I said.

"Our new district manager," Jared said, anticipating my question while leaning forward to pick up his napkin from the table. "The guy has a great future."

"So I noticed," I said. "How in the hell do you manage to *find* these guys?"

Jared shrugged. "They find me, mostly," he said with not a hint of ego. "Stan... the district manager...is a new-hire, and he's going around to the various branches in the area, learning the ropes. He rode with me on my shift Friday, and asked if I'd show him around town after work. Well, we didn't actually see much Friday, so we tried again on Saturday."

I strongly suspected Jared showed him a lot more than the town. "And where is he now?" I asked.

"On his way back to the wife and kids in Pecksburg."

"Ah," I said. "I trust you gave him a tour of the Master Bedroom?"

"Oh, yes," he said with one of those lecherous grins. "You'd think the guy was born in a sling!" He paused and then said: "And what about that number you were with?"

The waiter came with our drinks and we decided in the interest of the hour, to order. When he'd left and we'd had a sip of our drinks, I said: "Toby. A really nice kid."

"He sure looks like more than a kid to me."

I grinned. "Long story."

"Going to see him again?" he asked with no trace of jealousy.

"I sure hope so, " I said, and Jared gave me a cocked-eyebrow look.

"Well, if you'd ever care for a three-way..." he said.

"Be still, my beating heart," I said, and we both laughed.

The waiter brought two small fruit compotes, which we ate largely in silence.

"What did you think of that little brouhaha?" he asked, finally.

"You mean at Venture?"

"Yeah, you were pretty close to the action."

"Yeah," I said, finishing my compote and nudging the bowl toward the center of the table to make it easier to reach my drink. "I know the two guys. George Atkins and Lynn something. George is a really nice guy, but that cunt he's with defies description."

"Why in the hell do they stay together?" Jared asked.

I sighed. "Because George is too nice a guy to kick the sonofabitch out, and Lynn knows it."

Jared nodded, solemnly. "Well, he wouldn't last ten minutes around me," he said, "and he should be damned grateful I wasn't close enough to get to him when he pulled that little number. It looked like you were going to make a move, but Prince Charming held you back."

Before I could reply, the waiter arrived with our food.

* * *

The only thing nicer than a great Sunday brunch with Jared is spending most of the rest of the afternoon in bed with Jared. I didn't for one minute even think of comparisons between Jared's brand of sex and Toby's. Apples are apples and oranges are oranges—and both are delicious.

Jared left around five to go home and work on some paper for school, and I thought of calling Bob Allen to ask if he'd like to go out for pizza, until I remembered that he and Mario were gone for a couple days. I was glad I didn't have Toby's number or I knew I'd have been tempted to call. I wondered if he ate pizza—even cheese pizza.

Okay, Hardesty, give it a rest.

Instead of pizza, I opted for a short trip to my favorite deli for a fresh-baked bagel with lox, cream cheese, and a thick slab of Vidalia onion, washed down with a vanilla egg creme and followed with a piece of chocolate whipped-cream cake. Heaven.

* * *

When I got to the office Monday morning my answering service told me I'd had a call from a Lieutenant Richman at police headquarters, asking me to call. I'd planned to call O'Banyon first thing, but decided to see what Richman had to say first—though I pretty well could guess. I dialed the number, asked for Richman's extension, and was put right through.

"Lieutenant Richman," the now familiar voice said. I identified myself, and Richman said "I'm just going in to a meeting, but was wondering if you could meet me tomorrow morning at Sandler's around the same time. There are some things we have to talk about."

"Sure," I said. "I'll see you there."

Well, though he hadn't come out and said it, it was fairly obvious that I'd been right—the bullet that had blown the queens' tire had come from the same gun that killed D'Allesandro. What I wasn't at all sure of was what was going to happen next as far as the police department and my involvement in the case was concerned.

I next called O'Banyon's office and was put through to Donna, his secretary. Mr. O'Banyon, it seemed, was in court but would be calling in shortly for some information she was getting him for the case in trial. I asked her to see if we might possibly set up a very brief meeting at his earliest convenience, and she said she'd pass the word on and get back to me.

Next, Kimmes Associates. I'd toyed with the idea of checking with O'Banyon first, then decided I couldn't run to him for everything, and I was sure he'd okay it anyway. I called the firm, identified myself as working with Mr. O'Banyon on the Rage matter, and asked if I might speak with Mr. Kimmes himself. A minute or two on hold was followed by a male voice saying: "Bob Kimmes here. How can I help you, Mr.... Hardesty?"

"Mr. Kimmes," I said, "I'm checking on a few facts relating to the irregularities in the Rage account, and wonder if you could give me a little information."

There was the muffled sound of throat-clearing on the other end and then: "I'm afraid I can't discuss the details with you, Mr. Hardesty. We're still going over everything in great detail."

"I'm sure you are," I said, "but what I'd like to know has nothing to do with the figures involved. I was curious as to how often the individual partners in Rage may have been in contact with you...or with Mr. Sharp."

"In person, you mean?"

"Yes, if you might know."

"Well, while we work closely with all our clients, we do not encourage their person-to-person contacts with the C.P.A. handling their accounts. We do have, as a matter of policy, a...well a sort of 'Introductory' meeting when we first take on a new account, during which time we outline our services, agree upon the clients' specific needs, go over any financial laws and regulations which may apply to their particular account...that sort of thing. I normally conduct such meetings, as I did with the partners in Rage. However, at that time Mr....one of the partners...was out of the country."

"Mr. Giacomino," I said, lest Kimmes think I might not have been privy to all the partners' names.

"Yes, Mr. Giacomino. And so I never personally met with him. When he returned, I was vacationing in Jamaica, so Mr. Sharp met with him in my stead."

"Had Mr. Sharp been with you long?" I asked.

"He had been with the firm 18 years," he said. "His unfortunate death was a great loss. And for it to come just at this time..."

"I understand," I said. "Would you know if Mr. Sharp was in frequent phone contact with Mr. Giacomino?"

There was another long pause, and then, with the slightest note of suspicion in his voice: "I can't imagine that he would have been. Rage was primarily Mr. Comstock's concern."

"Would you happen to have telephone records?" I asked.

"Yes, of course. Our accountants keep scrupulous records of their time."

"Would it be possible for me to get a log of the partners' calls to or from Mr. Sharp?"

His response was just what I expected it to be, of course: "We keep our dealings with our clients in strictest confidence, Mr. Hardesty and, if you'll excuse me for saying so, you are not our client at the present time."

Nor would I ever be unless the bank made a *big* error in my favor.

"I can certainly appreciate your position," I said. "Would it help if Mr. O'Banyon made the request? While he is as you know extremely busy, I'm sure I could ask him to contact you."

There was a significant pause. "You are working for *both* Mr. O'Banyon and Mr. Giacomino, is that correct?" he asked.

Good question. Actually, it was O'Banyon who had hired me, but he had consulted with Giacomino first, so I felt technically justified in replying confidently: "I am representing Rage's surviving partners, yes." I didn't go into such details as the fact that neither one of them knew I was even talking with Kimmes at this point.

Yet another pause and a barely-distinguishable "Hmmm." Then: "Very well. I can have the receptionist prepare a log of calls for you. Would tomorrow afternoon be soon enough?"

"That will be fine, Mr. Kimmes," I said. "And I very much appreciate your cooperation, as I'm sure do Mr. O'Banyon and Mr. Giacomino."

We exchanged goodbyes and hung up.

I'd barely set the phone back in the cradle when it rang again—Donna, O'Banyon's secretary, saying he could meet me at Etheridge's at noon.

Busy day.

---

* * *

I spent what was left of the morning making out an itemized billing for my time on the case thus far, and working on my next official report for O'Banyon. I realized the report was more than a little redundant, since I'd once again be telling him everything that was in it when we met. Still, I guess it was good to have some sort of written history. And it looked quite different there on paper—a lot neater somehow, not all cluttered up with hunches and suspicions and gut reactions.

I wrapped it up around 11:15 and headed for Etheridge's, knowing full well I was going to be early again.

The clouds had rolled in and it was starting to drizzle by the time I reached the restaurant, which precluded my taking a stroll up and down in front of the City Building to watch the passing talent. Instead, I went into the bookstore next to Etheridge's and browsed around, rather hoping the cute sales clerk would come ask if there was something he could do to help me. Just as he started to walk my way, a blue-haired matron lassoed him for help in finding the latest best seller on the care and feeding of geraniums. He gave me a quick, raised eyebrow "Sorry" look, and led the lady to the gardening section. Ah, well....

When I again walked into Etheridge's at exactly noon and asked for Mr. O'Banyon's table, I was led directly to it without question. I wondered vaguely if they ever let anyone else sit there. Again I sat at the bench facing forward and ordered coffee.

At ten after, O'Banyon appeared, all business-crisp and in-control-efficiency. After leaning forward to set his briefcase down at the far end of the bench, next to the wall, we shook hands and he slid himself into the bench.

"What's up, Dick?" he asked, then added: "...and what makes me think I don't want to hear it?"

"It's a little too early to tell," I said, "but I do have a suspicion you're not going to like it."

After the waiter came to take our order, I told O'Banyon of my Friday afternoon meeting with Giacomino and my subsequent call to Kimmes. "I'll have a little better idea after I look at the phone logs," I said, "but I wouldn't be surprised if something shady was going on between either Barry or Bart and Sharp, the dead accountant."

I then told him of Lt. Richman's call, and my scheduled meeting with him the next day. I sighed. "All of which adds up to more and more roads going off in more and more directions. But I did want to alert you that some of these roads may lead uncomfortably close to home."

O'Banyon held off replying until the waiter, who had arrived with our food, had headed off to attend to another table.

"We're both right," he said, reaching for the salt: "I'm not at all happy about this. But that's precisely why you were hired, and I'll do my best to see that nothing stands in your way in getting to the bottom of this mess—no matter how 'close to home,' as you put it, it may lead."

"I appreciate that," I said, and I meant it.

* * *

I'm not quite sure where the rest of the day went but, like most days, it went, and on my way home I passed by Barnes Park, a rather notorious cruising area on the edge of the Central. I noticed a number of police cars and a lot of activity around the public restroom, and assumed there was another raid going on. Though there had been some noticeable relaxing in official harassment of gays since former Chief Rourke's glory days, old habits die hard, and periodic tearoom and park busts were still routine.

Stopped at the store for some groceries, and made it home just in time for the local news. I didn't expect there'd be any mention of the raid, since they were still far too common to rate any attention by the media. I was a little surprised, though, when following a fascinating in-depth report on the pros and cons of a new school referendum, the ever-chipper anchorman announced that a man had been found beaten to death in Barnes Park, and that the police were investigating. Name of the victim was being withheld pending the notification of relatives. End of story.

Well, if it was Barnes Park, that pretty much meant the poor guy was gay, and gay bashing was a not completely unheard of pastime among the lunatic fringe. And since too many members of the police department still considered gay bashing a public service, the chances of an arrest being made any time soon were somewhat less then remote.

Since I had to be up very early to meet with Lt. Richman, I determined to try to get to bed relatively early. Fortunately, there was nothing much of interest on TV so I started to get ready for bed around 10. Then, on a whim, I rummaged through my porn videos and found my copy of "Comstock's Load" and popped it into the VCR. And there was a much younger Barry Comstock, long pre-Rage, alive and hot as all hell, doing what he did best. I decided yet again that the one thing I dislike most about time is that it passes, and that what was doesn't last forever.

* * *

Morning came much too soon, as mornings have a tendency to do, and I forced myself out of bed and into the shower. Nicked myself about a dozen times while shaving and cursed myself for having forgotten, yet again, to buy new razor blades.

I'd optimistically made a whole pot of coffee but only had time to drink one full cup and a couple swigs from a second before it was time to head out the door.

Once again, Lt. Richman was already there when I arrived at Sandler's. We shook hands, exchanged greetings, and I sat down opposite him. This time when the waiter came, I ordered a ham and cheese omelet along with my coffee.

Richman waited until I'd had a few swallows of coffee

before saying: "We have a problem...and you're part of it."

I'd expected that first part, but the second came as something of a surprise.

"How's that?" I asked

Richman sighed and added more sugar to his coffee before answering.

"The police department," he began, "prides itself on doing its job, and doing it well. However, when it comes to dealing with the problems of the city's minorities, we're too often hampered by long established, conservative, white-heterosexual-males-only tradition. Things are starting to change, but we still have a very long way to go, as you are very well aware."

He sat back while the waiter brought our food, then motioned me to start eating while the waiter went back for the side of pancakes he'd forgotten.

"When we started recruiting black officers," he said, "—which was a lot longer in coming than it should have been, due in large part to Chief Rourke's dragging his feet every inch of the way—we were finally able to become far more effective in dealing with the specific problems of the black community. White officers going into black neighborhoods could never achieve the same results or obtain the same information as black officers can."

I didn't need a road map to see where he was going with this.

The waiter brought the pancakes and a large pitcher of syrup, and Richman proceeded to pour a river of maple syrup over the hub-cap sized pancakes before continuing.

"We don't have any gay officers," he said, then anticipated my reaction by giving me a quick smile before adding "...*openly* gay officers, that is. It's one of the sad facts of life that in this city at this time you can be openly gay or you can be a police officer: you cannot be both. I wouldn't even hazard a guess as to how long it will be until that will be possible."

He paused long enough to take a couple forkfuls of pancake, and I knew I should say something to at least give the poor guy a chance to eat, but he was on a roll and obviously going somewhere with his part of the conversation, and I didn't want to sidetrack him in any way.

He cut a sausage in two with his fork, speared it, tapped it lightly in the syrup, and conveyed it to his mouth. After chewing and swallowing, he made a very slight gesture toward me with his fork.

"The problem is," he said, "that the department is also extremely protective of its own interests, and it won't tolerate anyone trying to do what it considers its business. That's where you come in, unfortunately."

I shrugged and nodded, waiting for the other shoe to drop. We both concentrated on our breakfasts for a moment, though I suddenly wasn't as hungry as I'd thought. I noticed as we ate, though, that Richman kept glancing at me. At last he said:

"You were right about the bullet, and the tire. We missed it completely, which was obviously our own fault. I looked at the report on the 'accident' again, and that's all it apparently was—two drunks going over the bluff. But from what you've said, I gather there's a whole lot more going on here."

I nodded again. I could have played coy, but decided to trust him and be honest. "There is," I said.

Richman sighed. "So now comes the dilemma," he said. "Now that we know that there is some link between D'Allesandro's murder and the death of the two men in the car, we'll be doing our own investigation and it's pretty likely that your involvement in all this will come out at some point. Some of the hotter heads in the department are not going to be too happy about what they will perceive as your 'interference' in 'their' business, and I'll do my best to protect you from harassment if it comes to that—I'll say you are my informant..." He looked at me and gave me another small smile. "Sorry about that, it sounds a little disreputable, I know, but..."

I had a quick mental picture of myself, a two-week beard, dirty clothes, rummaging through a dumpster with one hand while the other clutched a bottle of Ripple in a brown paper bag.

"Well," I said, "I hope it doesn't come to that, either. A private investigator with a reputation as police informant wouldn't exactly be a magnet for new clients."

Richman nodded, finishing the last of his eggs and pushing his plate off to one side. "The other alternative, of course, is for you to just back down, now. Drop the whole thing and let the department handle it from here."

It was my turn to sigh. I shook my head. "All well and good if it were just a cut-and-dried case of three murders. But I'm firmly convinced there's a *lot* more going on here...too many pieces and too many links between them, and all of them rooted in a community the police have little knowledge of or, let's face it, interest in. And even if the department did have openly gay officers who knew their way around the community and what to look for and what questions to ask and who to ask, there are so many different directions this case is leading I don't know how they could follow up on them all. Hell, I don't know how *I'm* going to be able to do it."

I drained the last drop of coffee from my cup and put it back on the saucer.

"The other hand of it for me," I said, "is that the police have a lot easier access to certain information than I might have." I was thinking primarily of Giacomino's past history and business dealings. "So is there any area of compromise here?" I asked.

Richman sat back and just looked at me for a moment. "I'm putting my neck out here," he said, "but I think we can probably find some way to work parallel, if not together. I'll have to insist that you keep me informed on anything concrete you come up with, and in exchange I'll, as I said, do my best to protect your identity and what you're doing. Agreed?"

"Agreed," I said, just as the waiter arrived with the check. I reached for it, but Richman got it before I could.

"I'll get it," he said. "I'll take it out of our 'informant's fund,'" and he grinned.

"Oh, by the way," I said, "I understand there was another murder in Barnes Park yesterday A gay bashing, I assume."

Richman nodded. "So it appears, unfortunately. Luckily, it's unrelated to these other cases—if he'd been shot, they'd have checked the bullet for a match with the other three deaths. This one died from a single blow to the back of the head. He was found in some bushes right behind the public restroom; apparently he'd been killed the night before."

"Have they released his identity yet?" I asked.

Richman nodded as he hoisted his rear off the chair to reach his wallet in his back pocket. "Barnseth, I think it is. Lynn Barnseth."

I felt the coffee rising up in my stomach. *Barnseth! That's it! Lynn Barnseth: George Atkins' lover!*

CHAPTER 10

I didn't say a word to Richman—I didn't want to make a complicated situation any more complicated at the moment—and we said our goodbyes outside Sandler's and went our separate ways. But my mind was working overtime. I was thinking of the scene Lynn... *Barnseth*...had caused at Venture and the fact that he'd always been an incredibly nasty piece of work. And with that thought, yet another piece of the puzzle fell firmly into place. I'd allowed myself be sidetracked by the pieces that had seemed to connect everything to Comstock and Rage. I now was positive that Comstock, Giacomino, and Sharp, the accountant's being linked in the embezzlement scheme were just three coincidentally connected pieces—but they weren't the picture. But I felt now without a doubt that illogical as it may have been, being a thoroughly rotten sonofabitch was *the* link between all these deaths. My original theory of a gay vigilante determined to take out the human trash was right.

I suddenly realized that I was just standing there on the sidewalk, staring off into space, and I'm sure some of the people walking by wondered what the hell this guy was doing—but if they did I wasn't aware of it...or them. But I did finally force myself to let my motor functions resume walking me toward my car.

* * *

Though I knew the timing was really bad, the minute I walked into the office I went to the phone book to see if I could find George Atkins' number. There were two "G. Atkins" listed, but I recognized one of the addresses and wrote it down on a piece of scratch paper on my desk. I did have the decency to wait until around nine thirty to call, though.

When I dialed, the phone was answered on the second ring.

"George?" I asked, not really recognizing the voice.

"No, this is John. Can I help you?"

"John," I said, having no idea who he was, "this is Dick Hardesty, an old friend of George's. I just heard about Lynn's death, and wonder if I might talk to him for a minute, if he's up to it."

There was a brief pause, then: "Hold a second, I'll see if he can talk with you."

A muffled hand-over-mouthpiece comment, pause, another comment then the sound of the receiver exchanging hands and George's voice. "Hi, Dick. It was nice of you to call." He sounded a bit tired, but not bereft. Considering all he'd put up with with Lynn, I hardly expected him to be.

"I just heard about Lynn," I said, "and wanted to extend my condolences."

"I appreciate that, Dick," George said, "but I think you know the situation between Lynn and me; condolences aren't really needed, to be honest."

I was somehow relieved to hear him say that. "I'm glad you're looking at it realistically," I said. "You've always been such a damned kind soul, I was afraid you might have been devastated in spite of what you've had to go through."

"Well, he was part of my life for a long time," George said, "so naturally there's some sense of...well...loss, if you will, but..."

I decided to push my luck. "I know this isn't a good time, George," I began, "but I'm working on a case and I think that somehow Lynn's death might be connected with it in some way. Would it be at all possible for us to get together for a few minutes and talk about it?"

There was almost no hesitation before: "Sure. It would be good to see you. We didn't have a chance to talk the...the other night. When would you like to meet?"

"The sooner the better, really," I said. "Whenever it's convenient for you, that is."

"Today's fine," he said. "I've got some arrangements to make on behalf of Lynn's parents later this afternoon, but if you wanted to come by this morning, yet, that'd be all right."

"Great!" I said. "How about in an hour?"

"Good," George said. "We'll see you then."

I hung up, not unaware of the "we'll" and wondering just who John might be.

* * *

John, I discovered, was a co-worker at the insurance company where George worked. And it was fairly clear that now with Lynn out of the way, George and John might be free to become something more. John seemed like a really nice guy, and I was glad to think that George might at long last have a chance to be happy.

"We'd been to an office retirement party Sunday night," George explained as the three of us sat in his living room drinking coffee. "And when the party broke up quite a bit earlier than expected, John suggested we stop by the Mardi Gras for a quick drink before heading home. I was a little hesitant after what had happened at Venture, but Lynn knew I was going to be late, so I agreed. They were having some sort of anniversary party, and the place was jammed for a Sunday. So we walked in and..."

George paused and stared into his coffee cup. John, who was sitting beside him on the sofa, picked up the story in mid-sentence, casually, as though they were already used to finishing each others' sentences.

"...and there was Lynn, at the bar, all over some guy. But when he saw us, he went ballistic. I'd never even met Lynn, of course, but he came storming over to us and started screaming and yelling really terrible things at George at the top of his lungs. I won't even begin to tell you what he said, but I'm sure you know the gist of it. The whole place just stopped dead. Finally, the bouncer who'd been checking ID's at the door came over and told Lynn he'd have to leave."

George picked up the story in a way that reminded me of two jugglers effortlessly tossing tenpins between them. "'Oh, I'll leave, all right,' Lynn yelled as the bouncer started to pull him toward the door. 'I'm gonna go out and get myself fucked by a *real* man, you fucking eunuch.' And that was the last time I ever saw him."

"We went out the back door just in case Lynn might be waiting out in front," John said, "and I insisted George come spend the night at my place."

"That finally did it for me," George said. "I knew I couldn't live one more minute like that, or with Lynn. John said I could stay at his place for awhile until I could get Lynn out of here or find another place. Almost everything here is mine, but I figured Lynn could have it all just to get rid of him."

"I loaned George a change of clothes so we could go to work Monday," John said, "and then Monday night we came over here to pick up some of his things. We were dreading having to have another encounter with Lynn, but of course we didn't have to; there was a message from the police on the answering machine."

"Did the police question you at all?" I asked.

George shrugged. "Not really. I guess they took John's word that we'd been together—we'd gone to a coffee house and talked for about an hour after we left the bar, and we had witnesses there. And the doorman at John's building saw us go in. To be honest, the police didn't really seem all that interested."

Why am I not surprised? I wondered. "Did you by any chance notice anybody who left the bar right after Lynn did?" I asked.

George gave me a weak smile. "A *lot* of people left," he said. "They went out the front, and we went out the back." We sat in silence for a moment, until George spoke again, quietly and almost to himself. "Lynn had no reason to be the way he was. I never cheated on him...never! And while I don't know how I could have gotten through the past few days without John,

I really don't know why he is being so kind to me—we've known each other for two years, but we'd never so much as touched one another, except for a handshake."

Well, maybe George didn't know, but John obviously did, and I certainly could make a good guess.

* * *

While there were several complicated and interwoven links between most of the six (and, I feared, six-and-counting) dead men, there was one other indisputable link other than their cruelty: the bars. While Comstock and D'Allesandro were more-or-less public figures who amply and regularly displayed their total lack of humanity in their workplaces, they, like every single one of the others, had been observed mistreating someone in a bar.

N'Uh-uh! my mind taunted like a little kid. *Not D'Allesandro.* Damn! That's true. I realized I didn't know if D'Allesandro even deigned to go to bars, though I was sure that if he did, being D'Allesandro he could hardly have avoided doing something to call attention to himself by hurting or embarrassing someone. I made a mental note to check that out much more carefully. So, if it *did* check out that the bars were the sole link, that would lead to one conclusion: Somebody was watching.

Well, that's a cheerful little bit of paranoia, I thought. But my gut told me it was true. And, of course, just when I'd started working up a nice lather over potential suspects among the guys I'd run into so far, the fact that the killer could be practically anybody neatly blew my little rubber duckies out of the water.

Well, I consoled myself, *it isn't quite that bad. We can narrow it down to: he's male and he's gay.* Sigh.

The route between George's apartment and Kimmes' office took me past one of my favorite little diners, so I took advantage of that fact to stop and have one of their gourmet delights: an olive cheeseburger. A half-pound hamburger patty piled with about half an inch of chopped green olives held in place by a slab of melted cheese—oh, and with a side of fries greasy enough to turn any paper napkin transparent in 20 seconds. Good eatin'!

As for Kimmes and the Rage probable-embezzlement problem, I thought as I ate, until I knew for absolute certainty that the bars were the key, I couldn't let myself get sidetracked again from the path...*Paths, Hardesty...lots and lots of paths...*I was already following.

A small part of me hoped it wouldn't be the bars: it would be hard enough if I were limited to just the vague suspects I already had, but to try to find out which one of any given 120 guys in any one of 20-odd bars might be looking for the next rotten s.o.b. to send to his reward....

Life ain't easy, kid.

* * *

For being one of the leading accounting firms in the city, Kimmes' offices kept a pretty low profile. The atmosphere was efficient to the point of being Spartan...the kind of place where you automatically knew when you walked in the door that levity was not a frequent or welcome visitor—where smiles never revealed teeth. Everything was neat. Very neat. You sensed that you could go through every single desk in the building and not find an unsharpened pencil, and that paperclips were kept in separate little compartments according to size. No polished oak or bronze raised lettering or Italian marble. Lots of chrome and extruded aluminum and good, sturdy stain-resistant upholstery.

The receptionist, whose neat metal nameplate identified as "Miss Zablonski"—God forbid she should be so informal as to have a first name—gave me a pleasant no-teeth smile and, when I announced myself, efficiently reached into a lower drawer of her desk and produced a relatively thick letter-size

envelope with my name neatly typed. I thanked her, asked her
to convey my thanks to Mr. Kimmes, and left.

* * *

When I got back to the office, I had a message from Jared,
asking if I'd like to meet him for a quick happy hour drink at
Ramón's. *Ah, ESP lives,* I thought. I had been planning to call
him when I got home. And meeting at Ramón's would enable
me to hopefully talk to both him and Bob Allen about what they
might know about D'Allesandro's bar habits—if there were
any.

Turning my attention to the envelope from Kimmes. I
opened it to find several pages of what appeared to be Xeroxed
copies of a detailed "Telephone Time Spent" form apparently
required of each accountant, showing Sharp's outgoing and
incoming calls: the person called/calling, the time and date the
call was made/received, and the exact duration of the call. I
would not be surprised to learn that each employee had to also
keep a record of their bathroom visits.

There were a total of 35 calls made between Rage's partners
and Sharp over the six months since Kimmes took the Rage
account. There were no calls to or from Glen O'Banyon, twenty
calls (nine out, eleven in) to/from Barry Comstock—averaging
six minutes each, and fifteen calls (three out, twelve in) to/from
Bart Giacomino averaging two minutes each. Thirteen of the
Giacomino calls were made in the month preceding Sharp's
death. Most interesting.

I decided I'd definitely like to talk to Giacomino again, but
that I'd better go through O'Banyon first to see if he might want
to talk to Giacomino himself—it was, really, a matter between
the two of them. And since I was technically working for both
of them it would be awkward to say the least to let one of them
think he was a suspect in the case he'd hired me to solve.

* * *

I got to Ramón's at around five fifteen and was rather surprised to see Bob behind the bar. No sign of Jared yet, and the place was pretty quiet since the Happy Hour crowd usually didn't start coming in until between 5:30 and 6:00.

"Jimmy's day off?" I asked Bob as I pulled a barstool out far enough so I could swing my leg over it and sit down.

"He'll be in a little later," Bob said, putting a napkin in front of me. "What can I get you?" he asked.

I ordered, and when he returned with my manhattan he handed me a small stack of quarters. "Do me a favor and feed the jukebox?" he asked. "It's kind of quiet in here."

I pulled out a bill to pay for my drink and picked up the quarters. "Anything special you'd like?" I asked.

Bob shrugged: "Surprise me," he said.

I left my drink on the bar and walked over to the jukebox. It was one of those old "flip the pages" affairs, with about a hundred or more selections. I ignored the few country and western, flipped quickly past Elvis, and started looking for the old standards.

When I got to Judy Garland's "Swanee" I got a very strange sensation in the pit of my stomach. Much as I loved her music, I just couldn't bring myself to listen to her anymore. Too many memories I'd just as soon keep shut away.

Luckily, Bob liked standards as much as I did, and I found some really great old classics: Glen Miller's "String of Pearls," the Andrews' Sisters "Don't Sit Under the Apple Tree," some Johnny Mathis. When I'd used up the quarters and headed back toward the bar, the door opened and Jared walked in. Actually, with the contrast between the bright sunlight behind him and the dimness of the bar, all I saw was a very impressive silhouette, but even in silhouette, Jared isn't the kind of guy you could easily confuse with anyone else. He waved, and we vectored in on my barstool near the end of the bar. I sat down and Jared pulled out the stool next to mine.

"How's it going, Dick?" he asked, his knee automatically finding my thigh.

"You got a couple hours?" I replied.

Bob came over to take Jared's order, and before he could turn to reach for a glass, I stopped him. "When you've got a second, Bob," I said, "there's something I'd like to talk over with both you and Jared."

"Sure," Bob said. "Be right back."

While we waited for Bob to return, Jared and I back-and-forthed on general topics: how school was going for him, the upcoming Olympics—zeroing in on the American and Russian male gymnastic teams and men's swimming, mostly.

Bob finished his conversation with one of the regulars at the far end of the bar, and came back to us.

"So what's up?" he asked.

"I'd like to know if either of you know anything at all about Carlo D'Allesandro; especially if he frequented any of the bars," I said.

Jared shook his head. "I couldn't tell you," he said. "I never heard anything that I can remember."

I looked at Bob, who had his brows-knit-in-thought look. Then his face relaxed and he too shook his head. "Nope. Afraid not. Sorry, Dick," he said.

"That's okay," I said. "Just thought I give it a shot."

Bob suddenly got his knit-brow look again and said: "Wait a second...there is something. Let me think."

We were all silent, except for Johnny Mathis singing "Chances Are" in the background. "Ah, that's right," Bob said finally. "Mario mentioned D'Allesandro once. He worked at Faces before he went over to Venture, and he was telling me something about D'Allesandro being a regular there."

"Bingo!" I said, both to myself and out loud.

"I-69?" Jared asked, grinning, and I grinned back.

"No," I said, feeling as though I'd just found that corner piece of the puzzle that joins two of the sides. "I knew there had to be a bar connection in there somewhere! I've got to talk to Mario."

The door opened to admit two new customers. Bob raised

his hand to me and said "Hold that thought"as he moved off to wait on them.

Faces was a very nice, expensive gay restaurant whose semi-exclusive clientele was comprised of two major groups: very wealthy, usually older, often married businessmen and very expensive male hustlers. I'd been there a couple of times for dinner, but I was most interested to hear what Mario had to say about the place in general, and Carlo D'Allesandro in particular.

"So," Jared said, bringing me back to reality with something of a start, "anything new on the case?"

I filled him in on Lynn Barnseth and his eyes grew wide. "No shit?" he said. "Jeezus, I heard that on the news the night they found him and read it in the paper yesterday, but I never put two and two together—of course, I wouldn't have recognized his name anyway, but... How many now? Six?"

I nodded "Jared," I said, "How about doing me a real favor?" I immediately caught the look on his face and added "Other than that."

"Sure," he said.

"I'd like you to ask all the bartenders on your route to tell you any time there's an incident in their bar like the one we saw with Richie at Glitter, or with that Lynn character at Venture. Neither you nor I can be in more than one place at a time, but every bartender in the city knows exactly what's going on in his own bar. If we can have some way of knowing when something is going on, we just might be able to keep some other rotten son-of-a-bitch from getting himself killed."

Jared started to say something just as Bob returned. "Mario's coming in in a few minutes and we're going to go grab something to eat," he said. "You guys want to join us?"

"Sure," I said, then looked at Jared, nudging his knee with my thigh,. "You got the time?"

He grinned. "Yeah, if we can make it a fairly early evening. I'm about halfway through my thesis and I've really got to spend some time on it tonight."

"Not a problem," Bob said, then looked at his watch. "Mario should be here any minute, and then as soon as Jimmy comes in, we can go."

About ten minutes later, Jimmy came in the back door just as Mario came in the front. We all exchanged greetings, and while Bob went over some business with Jimmy, Jared and I finished our drinks—Mario said he'd wait until we got to the restaurant. When Bob had done whatever he had to do to transfer the shift to Jimmy, we left.

* * *

Dinner, at a quiet little mostly-gay restaurant within walking distance of Ramón's, was very pleasant, actually. The food was good if not exceptional, the drinks were served in larger-than-normal glasses and were themselves larger than normal, the conversation was easy and relaxed. Jared, though he'd known both Bob and Mario only casually from his work, fit right in. It's always fun to watch friends interact, and it's especially nice when newer members of a group feel comfortable in it. Of course Jared was the kind of guy who could fit in anywhere—as, come to think of it, could Bob and Mario. Me, I'd have my doubts about, but...

Finally, after the waiter had cleared the table and we sat drinking our coffee, Bob looked at me and said: "You wanted to ask Mario...?"

I grinned. "Yeah, I'd been having such a good time I nearly forgot," I said—and I had. I slipped my hand under the table and laid it on Jared's thigh, then addressed myself to Mario.

"I'm trying to find out whatever I can about Carlo D'Allesandro," I said, "and Bob says you used to see him when you worked at Faces."

Mario's handsome face took on a look of total disgust. "Yeah," he said, "he was a regular. From what I gather he didn't deign to go to just bars—that's where the 'commoners' go, and he considered himself far above everybody else. Actually, the guy would have to climb up the evolutionary ladder about six rungs to be pond scum."

"I gather you didn't care for him?" I said, and Mario looked at me and then grinned.

"You might say that," he said. "What pissed me most about him, though, was the really dirty little games he really enjoyed playing with nice kids."

He had me and the rest of the table hooked. "Meaning?" I said.

"Meaning big-fucking-deal Carlo D'Allesandro loved cruising the bus stations. He'd watch for some fresh-faced kid obviously new to town to get off a bus, and he'd move in. Pick the kid up, be real friendly and helpful, promise him the world, take him home, impress the hell out of him with all the money and his fancy cars and big house, then he'd fuck the kid and throw him out."

Jared just stared at Mario, moving his head back and forth very slowly as if he couldn't believe it. Mario just looked at him and shrugged, then continued. "That was most of the time," he said. "Sometimes if he was in a particularly playful mood, he'd keep the kid around for a few days—really do a number on him; tell him he was going to make him one of his top models, that sort of shit. And then he'd bring the kid to Faces for dinner to show him off, and have one of his 'friends' join them. It was almost always the same guy. Now, there are older guys who can be overweight, or bald, or both and still be really nice guys. But D'Allesandro's buddy was old, fat, bald, and totally repulsive. He'd be all over the kid at dinner, and the kid would be miserable but not have a clue as to what he could do except look to his friend D'Allesandro to protect him. *Big* fucking mistake! And then at the end of dinner, D'Allesandro would get up and say to the kid: 'I'm giving you to him now' and walk out."

"I'd have killed him," Jared said calmly.

"Someone did," Bob noted.

"Yeah, and why didn't *I* do something about it after I'd seen it a half-dozen times?" Mario asked—I had the impression he was addressing the question more to himself than to us. He took a drink of his coffee before answering himself. "Because Faces is a nice place and it makes lots of money by catering to people who have lots of money. I could clear $500 a night on tips. But the rules of the house were you mind your own business or you're out." He sighed. "$500 a night is damned good money, but it's not good enough to have to watch that sort of thing going on. So I quit, and went to work at Venture. I don't make a tenth the money, but I can look myself in the mirror when I shave."

* * *

On the drive home, after a record-setting ten minute stopover at Jared's to take care of a mutual itch that needed scratching, I thought about what an unbelievable shit Carlo D'Allesandro had been—how could anyone have been so astonishingly, deliberately cruel? Of course, he had some pretty stiff competition in the other five dead guys...I found it hard to think of them as victims, though technically that's what they were.

I'd asked Mario, as we were leaving the restaurant, for the name of Faces' manager and any of the staff he knew who still might work there. I planned to stop by as soon as I could to see if perhaps D'Allesandro had had dinner there within a day or so before he was killed.

I got home, checked through my mail and was reading a letter from Chris, my ex, and his new lover Max, when the phone rang. I recognized Toby's voice immediately.

"Dick, hi, it's Toby. I know it's short notice and you probably have plans, but a guy at the gym gave me two tickets to 'Boy Meets Boy' at the Regis for tomorrow night. I know you said you liked musicals, and..."

"That's great, Toby," I said. "I'd love to go. Thanks for asking me. What time should we meet, and where?"

"How about meeting me at the theater about 7:30. The show starts at 8:00 and I'll be at the gym until 7:00, but I should make it in time."

"That sounds fine," I said. "I'll see you there. And thanks again."

"Good," Toby said. "Well, I hate to make this short, but I've got to get downstairs to the laundry room to get my stuff before somebody walks off with it."

"No problem. I'll see you tomorrow night. 'Bye."

* * *

One of my first tasks on getting to the office Wednesday morning was to read the paper carefully, looking for any stories on deaths—by any means other than illness or old age—of single men. Relieved not to find any, I did the crossword puzzle, drank the coffee I'd picked up from the café downstairs, and waited for O'Banyon's offices to open. I didn't expect to find him in, but the receptionist shunted me immediately to Donna, his secretary, who said: "One minute, Mr. Hardesty." And a moment later, O'Banyon was on the line.

"Good morning, Dick," he said. "Good news or bad news?"

He must have been expecting my call. "Let's say probably the negative side of neutral," I said. "I picked up the phone logs from Kimmes' office and...do you want to go into this on the phone, or...?"

There was only a slight pause before he said: "I'll be going over briefs this morning until around 11, then have to get ready for court this afternoon. If you wanted to come by right away, we could have a few minutes to talk—though not more than that, I'm afraid."

"I'm on my way," I said. I hung up, picked up the log information, put it back in the Kimmes envelope, and headed for the door.

* * *.

I was right: O'Banyon considered the news I had for him on the phone logs as considerably to the negative side of neutral. It was pretty hard to imagine a logical explanation for 15 calls between Giacomino and Sharp—especially since Rage was primarily Comstock's concern. I felt sorry for O'Banyon—smart and business savvy as he was to find himself hooked up with a potential embezzler he'd considered a friend. But I did offer the opinion—the hunch, really—that it was unlikely that Giacomino was behind Comstock's and Sharp's deaths. It still wasn't totally out of the question, of course, and had Comstock and Sharp been the only deaths involved in this case, he'd definitely have been the prime suspect. But I was becoming more and more sure that a lot of the little lines connecting the guys in this case were coincidences rather than clues. Someone had once said that you could link the entire population of the world just by following any given seven people—who they knew, who those they knew, knew, etc. I was beginning to believe it.

O'Banyon said he would have a talk with Giacomino, and I definitely agreed that was the best way to handle it at this stage. But, I told O'Banyon, I was not ready quite yet to erase Giacomino's name from my possibilities list. He agreed.

We left it at that.

* * *

Parking near the Regis was a bitch, and as I approached the theater, I saw that Toby was already there. And at the relative distance between us, I suddenly realized where I'd seen Toby before: I was positive he had been the guy I'd cruised that night at Glitter—the one who had disappeared while I was distracted by Richie doing his little number on the dance floor. Talk about small worlds!

I mentioned that to him as we took our seats in the small, comfortable little theater.

Toby smiled. "I know," he said. "That's why I came up to

you at Venture. I was wondering if you'd remember."

I was oddly embarrassed and stumbled all over an apology, but Toby just smiled. "Not to worry. We're here now; that's what matters."

And he was right.

"Boy Meets Boy" was an absolute delight: sweet, charming, funny and casually, openly gay—and it was a musical! Wonderful!

"Now that's the way the world should be," Toby commented as we left the theater.

"All singing, all dancing, all gay?" I asked.

He gave me another of those quiet smiles of his. "Maybe," he said.

Though it was a weeknight and I knew Toby had to be at work the next day—as did I—I asked him if he'd like to join me for a quick nightcap. I realized Faces was only two blocks away, and it would give me not only a chance to spend a little more time with Toby, but to see if I could find out anything about D'Allesandro. Business *and* pleasure.

"Sure," Toby said. "I don't usually go to bars *with* anyone. It'll be nice."

I don't know why, but that struck me as a little...well, sad, somehow. I mean, here's a guy almost any other gay guy would kill to spend time with—I'd have thought he would be beating them off with a stick. But then from the little I already knew of him I realized that he marched to a slightly different drummer.

"You've been to Faces before?" I asked as we walked, only because Faces didn't strike me as a place Toby would normally go.

He grinned. "Yeah," he said. "I've been just about everywhere. Interesting place."

Dinner hour was pretty much over when we arrived, but there were still a couple tables filled—mostly by older gentlemen with younger, very attractive companions. The bar was more active, with various older-younger pairings and some not-yet-connected singles. Toby was right: Faces was an interesting place.

We took a seat at the relatively empty far end of the bar and waited until the bartender, who had been filling an order for one of the waiters, noticed us and came over.

"What can I get for you gentlemen?" he asked.

I looked at Toby for unspoken confirmation, then said "A cranberry juice and a bourbon and seven." The bartender looked at Toby, smiled, and headed for the refrigerator at the middle of the bar.

"So how is your case going?" Toby asked.

I had to think a minute to remember what I may have told him about what I was working on. I don't like to go into too much detail with people I don't know all that well and Toby, sweet guy that he was, and despite our having been to bed together, still fell into that category.

"More twists than a truck full of pretzels," I said.

"Sounds like fun," Toby said.

"I wish," I replied, reaching for my billfold as the bartender came up with our drinks. I saw he was wearing a name tag that said "Kent."

"Kent," I said, fishing around for a bill larger than I needed to cover the drinks, "I understand Carlo D'Allesandro used to be a regular here."

"I wouldn't call him a regular," Kent said. "Maybe once or twice a month. A friend of yours?"

"Never met the guy," I said. "But I was wondering if you could tell me if he was in here within a few days before he got killed."

Kent didn't bat an eye. "Couldn't tell you," he said. "I was on vacation when it happened. You might ask Tod, though," he said, nodding toward a waiter refilling coffee for two of the last diners. "Tod was D'Allesandro's favorite waiter."

"Thanks," I said. "I'll do that. Keep the change."

Kent nodded his thanks and turned back to the other end of the bar.

Toby was looking at me, curiously. "Carlo D'Allesandro?" he asked. "Is that the case you're working on?"

"Only peripherally," I said as I put my billfold back in my pocket. "Did you know him?"

Toby shook his head firmly. "I wouldn't want to," he said. "I saw him a couple times. He...wasn't a very nice man."

"The understatement of the year," I said.

We made a silent, glass-click toast and sipped our drinks in silence for a moment.

"You know, I was just thinking," I said: "I don't think you ever mentioned exactly where you're from. I get just the slightest hint of an accent, but I can't put my finger on it."

Toby grinned. "Darn, and I've worked so hard to get rid of it." He took another sip of his cranberry juice and set the glass down on the bar. "No, as I think I told you, I've only been in town less than a year. We didn't have places like these where I come from. I guess that's why I go out so much—catching up for lost time."

"Ah," I said. "A small-town boy. They sure grow 'em nice in your part of the country."

He grinned again. "Thanks," he said.

Before I could say anything else, the waiter the bartender had pointed out came over to the waiter's station a couple stools away from us with a drink order.

"Excuse me...Tod," I said. "But could I see you for a second when you have a chance?"

He smiled and nodded, then gave his order to the bartender. While Kent was making the drinks, Tod came over.

"What can I do for you?" he asked.

"Just a quick question," I said. "I understand you used to wait on Carlo D'Allesandro regularly, and I was wondering if you might know if he was in within a couple days of his death."

"The night before," he said. "He pulled another of his numbers, and I think the manager had about had it with him. I know I had. He was a good tipper, but I can do without that kind of money."

Kent brought Tod's order to the waiter's station and gave a heads-up nod. Tod returned it, said "'Scuse me," and left.

I turned back to Toby. "I'm sorry, Toby—I didn't drag you in here so I could do business. I just thought as long as I was here..."

Toby gave me one of those little smiles which made me feel like shit for some reason. "Don't worry about it," he said.

"Well, I do," I said.

"I know," he said. "But tell me, why do you care who killed that man?"

Actually, that was a pretty good question, and I wasn't sure I had a very good answer. I shrugged. "Because it's my job, mainly" I said, and then hastened to add: "And as I said, D'Allesandro is only one part of what I'm working on."

Toby nodded. "It must be hard," he said, "always working with negative things and negative people." He looked at me and smiled. "I mean, people don't hire you for positive things, do they? Like finding homes for a box full of kittens."

I had to grin. "You're right," I said, "though to be honest with you, I'd never actually thought of it like that before. I guess I just concentrate on solving the puzzle, and don't let myself think too much about the negative. And if I'm lucky, the end result is usually positive."

Toby took another drink of his cranberry juice. "I guess," he said.

"So tell me, Toby, what do you do for fun?" I asked.

He gave me a wicked little-boy grin. "You mean other than...that?"

"Yeah."

"I work out. I guess that's fun, in a way. And tonight was fun. I never had a chance to go to plays much. And I'm just kind of discovering classical music—something else we don't have much of back home."

"Any particular favorites?" I asked.

Toby thought a minute. "Swan Lake," he said. "I found the

classical station on the radio on my way to work one day, and they were playing that. I listen to that station all the time now. I'm just beginning to learn what the songs are and who wrote them." Then he looked at me and blushed. "Boy, I do sound like a real hayseed, don't I?"

No, I thought, *you sound like a really nice kid.* "Not at all," I said. "And I'm really glad you like Tchaikovsky. I've got recordings of just about everything he ever wrote."

"Wow," Toby said. "I'm impressed. I'd like to hear them sometime."

"How about Saturday night?" I asked. *Jumping right in there, aren't you, Hardesty?* I thought as soon as the words left my mouth.

"Sure," he said.

"Would you like to try for dinner?" I asked. "I could fix something vegetarian."

Toby shook his head. "No, that's okay. I don't want to put you out. Why don't I just come over after dinner sometime?"

I wasn't about to push it. "Great," I said. "Whatever time you want—I'll be home."

We finished our drinks and got up to leave. I took out a couple bills from my billfold, left one on the bar for Kent and, as we walked past Tod, I handed him the other. "Thanks for the info, Tod," I said.

He took the bill without looking at it, put it in his apron pocket in one practiced movement, and smiled. "Any time," he said, and went about his business.

Toby and I walked back toward the Regis and said our goodnights at the corner; Toby's car was about a block down in one direction and mine a couple blocks down another.

"Thanks again, Toby," I said as we shook hands. "I really enjoyed it."

"Me too," he said. "I'll see you Saturday night."

"Great," I said, and meant it.

* * *

I'd made it a habit to check the paper carefully every morning, looking for anything that might be connected to the case. On Friday morning, on page 13, there was a brief article about a 26 year old single man, Ronald Baker, found hanged in the bathroom of his home. His father, it noted, was pastor of the 2nd Pentecostal Church, and Ronald had been active in the church's youth programs.

I wrote the name down and made a mental note to call Jared's house as soon as I'd gone all the way through the paper, leaving a message for him to call me. I'd have him check out Ronald Baker's name with the bartenders on his rounds. If Ronald had been gay, I wanted to know more about him. If he was one of those characters who periodically stood outside gay bars carrying homophobic banners and harassing patrons, he just might be another one of the guys I was beginning to think of as "the bar watcher's" targets.

The Giacomino side of the case was more or less on hold until I heard from O'Banyon as to what more, if anything, he wanted me to do about it. I wondered if they'd had a chance to talk, or if Giacomino had already left town for his latest jaunt. And in any event, I was pretty well convinced that the chance of Giacomino being the killer was almost negligible.

I also pondered the idea of getting out to the bars even more frequently than I already did, and hitting several every night, in hopes I might be there when an incident occurred—and more importantly, if I were, to make a careful note of who else was in the bar at the same time. It was all a process of elimination But I realized that was rather like running out into the back yard every night in hopes of seeing a falling star. You might, but chances are you wouldn't.

It was when I reached the Obituary section that my day really went down the toilet. About halfway down the long list of Mary Smiths, age 87 and Clarence Jones', age 103, there was a very small announcement which said:

Robert John Peterson, 28

Robert John Peterson, 28, died Wednesday in St. Anthony's hospital of complications of pneumonia. A former leading fashion model...

CHAPTER 11

I called Jared as soon as I got home, and caught him just as he was getting ready to leave for class. When I told him of John Peterson's death, he didn't reply for a moment, then said: "I'm afraid he won't be the last." Then he sighed and added: "Well, one thing's for sure...where he is now, he won't be running into Carlo D'Allesandro."

When I asked him if he could check around to see if any of the bartenders he dealt with might know anything about a Ronald Baker, Jared promised he would. Then there was another pause and he said: "Ronald Baker? The guy who hanged himself?"

"That's him," I said. "What do you know about him?"

"Marv, the bartender at the In Touch, was telling me today that one of his regulars, a guy named Ronnie, had hanged himself. He'd seen it in the paper."

"I'm kind of surprised that didn't ring a bell with you," I said.

"Oh, it did," Jared said. "But from what I understand from Marv, this guy was a real nice, quiet sort; really shy, never any problem. He did tell Marv once that he wasn't out to his family and it sounded to Marv like he was apparently terrified that they might find out. It looks like maybe they did." He paused again, then said: "What a fucking shame! What kind of parents make their children so ashamed of who they are that they'd kill themselves?"

Well, in the case of Ronald Baker, I think I could make a wild guess.

"Well," I said, "regardless of what Dr. Pangloss says, this is *not* the best of all possible worlds."

Jared sighed. "Maybe someday..."

"Yeah," I agreed. I glanced at my watch. "Well, I'd better

let you go get to class."

"Yeah, it's about that time," Jared said. "Oh, before I forget, I'm getting into one of my leather moods and was thinking of maybe going to the Male Call Saturday night. Want to come along? You might see what you've been missing all these years."

"Uh...thanks, but I think I'll pass this time. You just be sure you steer clear of Mitch."

Jared laughed. "Oh, I think he'll be the one doing the steering clear," he said. "You're sure you don't want to change your mind?"

"Actually, I'm going to be tied up...uh, let me rephrase that," I amended quickly. "I've got plans for Saturday. Toby's coming over."

"Emphasis on the 'coming,' I hope," he said with a laugh.

"I'll do my best," I said.

"I have no doubt," he said. "Well, I'd better head out. I'll be talking with you soon...oh, and I am putting the word out; I've talked to about 10 of my regular bartenders, and they've all agreed to keep me posted."

"Great! And thanks, Jared. Again, I owe you," I said.

"Don't worry," he said. "I'm running a tab. Later...."

"See ya," I said as we both hung up.

* * *

Just as I was finishing dinner, the phone rang again.

"Dick Hardesty."

"Dick, this is Mark Richman," the by-now-familiar voice said. "Sorry to bother you at home, but I've got a quick question."

"Sure," I said.

"Did you read about that single guy who hanged himself?"

"Ronald Baker," I said. "Yes, I read it in today's paper."

"Is it something we should be concerned about?" he asked.

I was once again struck by the fact that Lieutenant Richman was a pretty sharp cookie. Obviously, he'd been doing the same thing I had in looking out for suspicious deaths of single men.

"From what I know, Lieutenant, it pretty likely was a suicide—the guy doesn't come near fitting the profile of the others. And you know who his father is, so I don't think I have to draw you a picture. Though if anybody at all were to be a potential target, I'd put my money on the good reverend."

"I see what you mean," he said. "The Reverend Baker was one of Chief Rourke's buddies, by the way. It was always hard to tell which one was the bigger homophobe."

He was quiet a moment, then said "His own kid, huh? I guess they're right: what goes around comes around. Too bad it's always the kids who have to pay."

"I couldn't agree more," I said.

There was another pause, then: "Well, thanks for the input. I had a suspicion that's what the story was, but wanted to check with you. Do you have anything new on any of the other deaths?"

"I only wish I did," I said, "but right now it's still just ideas and intuition. Did you have any luck at all with the bullet?" I was pretty sure there wouldn't be—our killer wasn't your average criminal.

"No. Other than that they came from the same gun—and there are a lot of guns out there."

"Looks like we're both at something of a standstill," I said. "But I don't intend to give up—it's just a matter of time until it all comes together. And I'll keep you posted as soon as something solid comes along."

"Good," Richman said. "Let's hope it's soon. Good night."

"'Night," I said, and heard the click of his hanging up.

* * *

Friday night I set out on what I realized, even before I left, would be a futile random bar-hop on the outside chance of being present when something happened. I made it as far as the third bar before I made eye contact with a really hot guy I'd seen several times before but never talked to. Well, eye contact led to talk which led to my crotch running away with my head again, which led to going over to his place and that neatly took care of Friday night. My head was really pissed at me the next morning, but my crotch was very happy.

* * *

Saturday, while doing grocery shopping for the week, I made a point to stock up on cranberry juice. I gave the apartment a cursory cleaning—what it really needed would require a steam shovel and fire hose—, changed the bed, did laundry, wrote Chris and Max a letter, talked to Bob Allen and a couple friends on the phone...you know the routine.

Had an early dinner and went through my collection of Tchaikovsky's music, picking out some I thought Toby would particularly like—Swan Lake, of course, and some of the other better-known stuff like Romeo & Juliet, the First Piano Concerto and 1812 Overture, plus some he might not have heard too often, like the Pathetique and Francesca de Rimini. That was about 12 hours of solid music right there, but I'm nothing if not an optimist.

At about 8:30 the doorbell rang. I quickly put the Pathetique on, adjusted the volume, and rang the buzzer to let Toby in.

When I opened the door a moment later, Toby was standing there with one hand behind his back.

"Hi there, Toby," I said, genuinely glad to see him. "Come on in."

He came in, grinning, and brought his hand out from behind his back. "I got this for you," he said, reminding me very much of a small boy with a gift for his teacher. "I thought you'd like it."

I could see from the shape of the neatly wrapped package that it was a record. I was both delighted and a little embarrassed—I'm not used to getting presents.

"Thank you, Toby," I said, sincerely touched.

"Open it," he said, still grinning.

I tore off the wrapping as carefully as I could and saw it was an original cast recording of Boy Meets Boy. Being careful not to drop it, I moved forward and gave him a big hug, which he returned. "Thanks," I said again.

"You're welcome," Toby said. Then he said "You think we should close the door now?"

"Good idea," I said, releasing him from the hug and moving past him to push the door closed. "Come on in," I said, and led him to one of the chairs by the fireplace.

"Why don't we sit here?" he said, indicating the couch.

We sat down side by side, and Toby made a raised-head nod toward the stereo. "What's playing?" he asked. "I like it."

* * *

It was one of the most pleasant, relaxing evenings I'd had in a long, long time. We did very little talking, actually. Toby was absolutely enthralled by the music, and it's hard to describe what a delight it was to watch his reactions to it, and to know that this was for him something of a voyage of discovery. He knew the more popular themes, of course, but the rest was all new to him. When the principle theme of Swan Lake came welling into the room, he reached over and took my hand and held it throughout the rest of the score.

Ok, I know a lot of guys who'd have been running for the insulin about that time, and a lot more would think it was schmaltzy, and gooey, and maybe even B-movie corny. But it was also sweet and touching and...yeah, even at the risk of being thrown out of the Butch Gay Men's union, ...romantic. And most oddly of all, I kept thinking of how much I would have liked to have had a kid brother like Toby.

At about eleven o'clock, as Francesca di Rimini was ending, Toby turned to me and said: "Would you like to go to bed now?"

Being occasionally slow on the up-take, and still probably

a little lost in my kid brother fantasies, I must have looked a bit startled when I said: 'No...No, I'm not tired at all."

A slow smile spread across his face. "I meant *together*," he said.

I got up from the couch and extended my hand, which he took. I started to turn the stereo off, but he said: "No, leave the music on. Please."

So I did.

* * *

Everyone has heard the old jokes about having sex to Ravel's Bolero, and probably done it a few times, but if you've ever tried it and liked it, let me recommend Tchaikovsky's 1812 Overture. Time things just right, and it's got Bolero beat by a mile!

We lay there for quite a while after the music stopped, still not saying much. Toby had a wonderful air of calm and quiet about him, so the silences weren't awkward, just...quiet.

My hand, which had been resting palm-down on his stomach, which somehow reminded me of velvet-covered granite, slid idly up his chest to his neck, and I casually fingered the chain he always wore. "Nice chain," I said.

"Thanks," he said.

"A story behind it?" I asked.

Toby turned his head to look up at the ceiling. "It was my mom's," he said. "Actually, my grandmother's originally. It had a little locket on it, but I took it off. It's all I have left to remind me of them," he said quietly.

I knew well enough not to go any further on that subject right now. I could tell it was a very private thing for him, and I figured if he ever wanted to tell me about it, he'd do it on his own.

After another moment of silence, then: "I always wanted to be a musician," he said. "Not a rock star or anything like that. More like the stuff Tchaikovsky did...classical."

"Do you play any instruments?" I asked.

He turned on his side to put his head on my shoulder. "No," he said. "My folks could never have afforded any instrument—or even lessons. And the school I went to was way too small to have a band."

"Well," I said, "it's never too late."

Toby looked up at me without moving his head. "No, it isn't, is it? Maybe I will...."

I was really curious to know more about Toby—where he came from, if he had any brothers and sisters; that sort of thing. But I could sense that Toby had places inside himself where he wouldn't—or couldn't—let anyone go. There was a suggestion of it when he mentioned his mother—and we didn't know one another well enough yet for me to have a more sure sense about where those boundaries were.

I was pretty sure Toby didn't have much in the way of formal education, but what he lacked in "sophistication" he more than made up for in gentleness, sweetness, and a kind of inner serenity.

We lay side by side for another fifteen minutes or so, until Toby said: "Well, I'd better be getting home," kissed me, and got out of bed to begin putting his clothes on. I watched him dress in the half-light that filtered down the hall and through the open bedroom door. God, but he was a beautiful specimen! Again I couldn't help but..."compare" isn't the exact word, but I suppose it comes closest to what I was looking for...Toby and Jared. I'd thought before that if Jared were a horse, he'd be a Clydesdale; all mass and power; Toby was a thoroughbred; sleek and strong and fluid.

I got out of bed, put on my robe, and walked him to the door.

"Thanks again for the record," I said. "That was really nice of you."

Toby smiled, little-boy pleased. "I'm really glad you like it," he said. "And thank you for the introductions to Mr. Tchaikovsky. He's awesome."

You're kind of awesome yourself, Toby, I thought, but only smiled.

We hugged our good nights and I opened the door for him. "Give me a call," I said.

"I will," he replied. I stood in the doorway, watching him walk down the hall. When he reached the stairwell, he turned, smiled and waved, then disappeared down the stairs.

I closed the door and returned to bed.

I realized suddenly—again—that I didn't have Toby's phone number. Not only that, I didn't even know his last name! *And what do you do for a living, Mr. Hardesty?* my mind asked, sarcastically.

Well, I thought in my own defense, *the last-name issue has never come up, and actually, neither has the phone number. You should have just asked him for it. There isn't a mystery lurking behind every tree in the forest, you know.*

Glancing at the clock, I was surprised at how late it was. I had to get some sleep.

All right, already, I told myself. *I'll ask him for his last name. I'll ask him for his phone number. I'll ask to see his birth certificate, if it will make you feel any better. Now let's drop it, okay?*

And, turning over on my stomach and bunching the pillow up under my head, I went to sleep.

* * *

Bob Allen called shortly after I got up Sunday morning to ask me to join him and Mario for brunch, which I did. Other than that, it was a fairly quiet Sunday. I stopped in to the office for a few minutes after brunch to finish typing up my weekly report to O'Banyon, and was embarrassed by how little I had to say. I felt like I wasn't earning what I was being paid, and considered telling O'Banyon so. But then I realized that 1) I was doing whatever I could, and 2) this case was not over yet. The bar watcher was still out there, somewhere, and I knew

I would find him, eventually. The only question was how many others would die before I tracked him down?

* * *

Yet another week went by. I noticed in Tuesday's paper that the Chicago Symphony was coming to town and made a note to see if Toby would like to go. I cursed myself again for not having his telephone number so I could just call and ask him. *What a fucking poor excuse you are for a P.I., Hardesty,* I chastised myself for the ten thousandth time. I could go by his place and leave him a note, but thought that wouldn't be exactly right, either.

I talked to Jared a couple times. Three or four of his bartender contacts had reported incidents—fights, heated arguments, some drunk loudmouths making trouble. But none of them sounded like the kind of thing that would draw the bar watcher's attention—either that, or he just hadn't been there to see it happen. And despite the trepidation which always preceded examining the paper every morning for possible new victims, there was nothing that said: "Oh-oh, here he is!"

What did set my mental alarms off, however, was the increasing number of single men appearing in the obituaries as dying of "pneumonia" or "complications of pneumonia" or "after a long illness" or simply "in St. Anthony's (or City General or Atherton Memorial or…) Hospital." I had a chilling premonition that what had killed John Peterson was like the cow that kicked over Mrs. O'Leary's lantern, and that somebody had better start yelling "Fire!" pretty soon.

On what I sensed was far more than a whim, I went back over the entire week's papers, making a list of the names: there were twelve. I wrote them down, put them in my shirt pocket, and headed out the door for Rage.

* * *

The disappointment I felt when I saw that Brad was not on duty rather surprised me—I didn't know I cared. The guy behind the window was someone I'd not seen before— a very exotic-looking guy with skin the color of coffee-with-cream and shockingly blue eyes. Oh, yes, and—surprise!—a body to kill for. I identified myself and asked to see the manager. The guy nodded, picked up the phone under the counter, said something into it which I couldn't hear, and then replaced the receiver back out of sight. He gave me a smile that any toothpaste-ad executive would give his arm for, and said: "Jim will be right with you."

"You're new, I gather," I said, while waiting.

He smiled again. "I hope it doesn't show."

He has a slight accent I couldn't quite place. Not like Toby's, which was regional American. This one was...well, not American. "You could have fooled me," I said. "Is Brad still around?"

The guy nodded. "His day off," he said.

At that point the door opened and the guy I'd seen coming out of the interview with Giacomino...what was his name... Jim Hicks...came out to greet me.

"Dick," he said as though we'd known each other for years—which on having another good look at the guy, I wished we had, "good to see you again. We...well, I guess we didn't formally meet, but we saw each other the day I came to interview for the job." We shook hands and he motioned with his head toward the door. "Come on in to the office, where we can talk."

He smiled at the guy behind the window, who leaned forward to press the buzzer to open the door, and I followed him into the office. I noticed immediately that the carpet had been replaced and the wall where the two-way mirror had been had been repaneled. Hicks was apparently making a concerted effort to erase all traces of his predecessor—which in this case was a pretty good idea. Comstock's painting was gone, as were the framed photos of him and various celebrities which had hung behind his desk. In their place was a very nice seascape with a small light above it. And on the desk was a framed color photograph of Hicks and the guy behind the reception counter.

He's married, damn it! I thought. *Curses...foiled again!*

Motioning me to a seat, he went around to sit behind the desk. He looked a lot better there than Comstock had. He noticed my look at the picture.

"Christophe," he said with a smile. "We met in Sao Paolo six years ago, and haven't been out of one another's sight since then—and we don't plan to be. His being able to work here was one of the conditions of my taking the job—and I guess the partners liked the idea after how Comstock had made this his own little brothel."

He paused, leaned back in his chair, and said: "So what brings you here today... not that you're not always welcome."

I reached into my shirt pocket and got out the list of names. "Could you run these through your membership list? I'm curious how many are on it."

"Sure," he said, leaning forward to take the list. He looked at it and then frowned. "Jake Hancock...." He shook his head. "Jake's dead, you know. Just this past week."

"I know," I said. "They're all dead."

He looked at me in silence, and I could see his face grow momentarily pale. "And you think...?"

I nodded.

He picked up the phone and pressed a button. "Christophe, can you come in here? Now?"

He sat back, face serious, shaking his head slowly. "I *knew* it!" he said, more to himself to me.

The office door opened and Christophe came in, looking a bit puzzled.

Hicks half-rose from his chair to lean forward to hand Christophe the paper. "See how many of these are on our members list, would you, Babe?"

"Sure," he said, taking the list. He looked at it and said: "Jake Hancock...Jake's dead. Just this past week. We went to his funeral."

See what six years together does? I thought. *I'll bet they finish each others' sentences.* And I thought of how Chris, my ex, and I used to do the same thing. And part of me was kind of sad, and very, very envious of them. *Wimp!* my mind taunted. *Screw you!* I replied.

"I'll be right back," Christophe said, and left the room, closing the door behind him.

I turned my attention back to Hicks. "What did you mean when you said 'I knew it'?" I asked.

Hicks sighed and sank back against his chair. "I started to notice something when I was managing Silver's Gym. Rumors, mostly. Then some of the regulars who'd been there since I started didn't come in anymore. Any gym has a pretty big member turnover, of course, but there's always a hardcore group of regulars. Then maybe four or five of those dropped out in my last six months there. I heard a couple of them had died; I don't know what happened to the others—maybe they just left for other reasons. I hope so, but I get the feeling it was more than that."

"I'm beginning to think you're right," I said. "And I'm pretty sure whatever it is is being spread by sex, like clap and syphilis. And that means that wherever there's a lot of sex going on..."

"Like Rage," he said.

"Like Rage," I repeated. "That list you gave Christophe is of the guys who died just this week."

Hicks was silent for a minute, then said: "But if we're right that whatever is killing all these guys is sex related, and Rage is part of it...."

As if on cue, the office door opened and Christophe came back in, looking more than a little unhappy. "Five of twelve," he said, "including Jake Hancock."

Jeezus! I thought.

"Jeezus!" Hicks said.

Christophe handed the paper back to me, with a red "X"

in front of five of the twelve names.

"Do you happen to know if Bart Giacomino is still in town?" I asked, taking the paper and putting it back in my shirt pocket. I thought it was time I had a talk with both Rage's surviving partners.

Christophe had moved to the open door, where he could look through to the reception area in case anyone came in.

"No;" Hicks said, " he left for Hawaii two days after I started. Nothing like jumping in with both feet. I've been spending most of my time since then trying to figure things out and get things in order. Comstock knew every detail of how this place works, but he didn't bother to write anything down."

"Have you met the other partner?" I asked.

"Glen O'Banyon? Yeah. But just once, after my first interview with Brent. Nice guy."

"That he is," I agreed. "I'm kind of curious as to why you took this job, though. I'd imagine it would be more of..." I realized I was painting myself into a corner, since I didn't know exactly what type of arrangement he and Christophe might have, and it was none of my business. But I couldn't stop in mid-sentence, so I went ahead: "...a single guy's job."

He and Christophe exchanged grins. "No problem. At Silver's, I was just one of three managers; here I'm it. And Glen O'Banyon, in particular, seemed to like the idea that Christophe and I are a couple—monogamous, in case you're wondering. And as I said, after Comstock's reputation for dipping his pen in company ink...."

Someone entered the reception area, and Christophe left to sign him in, closing the door as he went.

Hicks looked at me. "About this...whatever it is," he said: "Do you think there's anything we can do?"

"Well," I said, "I think I should talk to O'Banyon first. We'll see what he thinks, and maybe we can figure out a way to stop this thing before it goes any further." I realized the minute the words left my mouth how utterly naive I was probably being. Any deaths that could be directly linked to Rage were probably just the tip of the iceberg. Rage wasn't the only place gay guys had sex.

* * *

Whoa, Hardesty, I thought on my way back to the office. *You're getting in <u>way</u> over your head here. You're being paid to find Barry Comstock's killer, not to get up to your armpits in something totally unrelated to the case.*

Well, I countered, *this may not be directly related to Comstock's killing, but I'm afraid it's a lot bigger than any murder investigation. And since O'Banyon's and Giacomino's interests are seriously involved in both situations, nothing's written in stone.*

By the time I'd returned to the office and picked up the phone to call Glen O'Banyon, I'd pretty much convinced myself that I was justified in doing both.

I was put through to Donna, who said O'Banyon had just gotten out of court and was going directly home, but that he would be checking in with her. I asked her to have him call me as soon as he could.

About half an hour later, the phone rang. It was O'Banyon.

"Hi, Dick," he said, sounding pretty chipper for a guy who'd spent his day in court. I gathered it had gone well for him. "What's going on?"

Not wanting to spoil his apparent good mood but also not wanting to beat around the bush, I said: "I think we'd better talk, and probably the sooner the better."

There was only a slight pause, then: "Well, sure. Would you want to meet me at Hughie's again, say in an hour?"

"I'll be there," I said.

As soon as I hung up, I felt the old sense of frustration building up again. I was getting nowhere with the Comstock case, but at least I was absolutely certain there was a single human being behind it; and that sooner or later, I'd be able to find out exactly who. But with this whatever-it-was that was killing gay men, I felt totally helpless and—though I hated to admit it—hopeless. Why in the hell was it up to *me* to try to do anything about it, anyway? I knew damned well I wasn't the only one who was aware something very scary was happening. Where was the health department? Where were the doctors? Where was the gay *media*, for chrissakes?

And where were the leaders of the gay community? This was our people who were dying. Why wasn't someone out there beating the fire bells and sounding the alarms? Well, O'Banyon was a leader of the gay community: *he* could do something... *something*.

* * *

I'd forgotten that Friday afternoon was a rather busy time for Hughie's—a lot of johns took off from work early on Fridays so they could have a little...uh, companionship...before heading off to the suburbs for a weekend of Little League and barbecues with the wife and kids. And the hustlers were out in force, like sharks after chum. The variety, both in the johns and the hustlers, never ceased to amaze me. The only two major ways to tell them apart at times was by the way they were dressed and their degree of cool. Some surprisingly young good looking johns, and some surprisingly unattractive hustlers. Democracy in action.

I was on my second beer, having fended off two johns and one hustler, when Glen O'Banyon came through the door, dressed much like the last time I'd seen him at Hughie's, but this time with a Green Bay Packers jersey. If I'd never seen him before and were trying to figure out which side of Hughie's cultural divide he fell on, I'd have opted for the hustlers—despite the fact that he was a tad older than the oldest hustler in the place. He saw me, nodded, went to the bar for a drink, then came over to join me at one of the few clear areas along the wall.

I didn't waste any time in telling him about the twelve

obituary column listings, my discovery that five of the twelve were members of Rage, and my suspicion that Rage was probably involved, however unwittingly, in spreading the illness.

O'Banyon sighed, shook his head, and turned toward me, leaning against the wall on his left shoulder. "I got a call from a doctor friend in New York yesterday," he said. "Whatever it is, it's there...and, I understand, in San Francisco and Los Angeles. Only gays, and only gay men. And it's spreading. Fast."

"Jeezus!" I said. "And nobody knows what it is? How can that be?"

"Good question," O'Banyon said, taking a long swallow of his drink. "My friend mentioned something about a kind of cancer called 'Kaposi's Sarcoma', which he says is normally seen only in older men from certain areas of the Mediterranean. And pneumocystis, a strange organism that sometimes causes some kind of pneumonia."

"And it's spread by sex," I said.

O'Banyon shrugged. "They don't seem to know yet. He says it might be through using amyl, or...who knows."

"You've got to close Rage," I said.

O'Banyon looked at me for a good fifteen seconds, expressionless, before saying:

"I can't do that."

"I'm sorry, Glen, but why in hell not? Guys are dying! And if you don't close Rage, there'll be more."

Still looking at me, his lips formed a very small, sad smile, and shook his head again, very slowly. "Do you have any idea of the financial investment I have in Rage?" he asked. "And even if you're right, and it's spread by sex, do you really think closing Rage would stop it? The members would just go to another bath."

"Then close *all* the baths, for chrissake," I said, realizing immediately that that was never going to happen.

"On what grounds?" he asked. "Suspicion? Rumor? And

then everyone who goes to baths would go to the back-room bars, or the tearooms, or the parks," he said, logically. "Not to mention the financial shockwaves closing the baths would spread throughout the community—not just considering the losses to the owners. Did you realize, for example, that baths provide more than 25 percent of advertising revenues for gay newspapers? No, after talking with my friend in New York and listening to you just now, I'm afraid we've got something going on here that looks very much like it could be heading out of control, and frankly, it's scaring the shit out of me."

That was the first time I'd ever heard O'Banyon swear. But it was beginning to scare the shit out of me, too.

"What in the hell can we do?" I asked.

O'Banyon set his drink on the narrow ledge running the length of the wall, adjusted his baseball cap in an imaginary mirror, and picked up his glass again before saying: "Well, I've just been drawing up the papers for a new Gay Businessmen's League, and their first official meeting is next week. I'll bring the subject up before them to see if they have any ideas. Bart is out of town until the 19th, I think—I had a long talk with him the night before he left for Hawaii, by the way."

I'd been very curious as to whether there had been a confrontation between Rage's two remaining partners on the potential embezzlement issue, but hadn't wanted to mention it since it was, really, none of my business.

"Oh?" I said, noncommittally.

"Yes," he said. "I think we reached a...let's call it an understanding And you might be interested to know that part of that understanding involved selling Rage. When Kimmes determines the exact amount of the financial discrepancies, it was to have been taken out of Bart's half of the proceeds, and I doubt we'll be doing any more business together. Of course that was our agreement up until this little conversation we're having now. Now..." He drained his glass in one heads-back gulp. "...who knows?"

I shook my head. "Sorry," I said. "Lousy timing."

O'Banyon grinned. "Indeed," he said. "But until next week's meeting, what I will do is have Jim Hicks...you met him, didn't you?" I nodded. "...I'll have him have the staff start handing out condoms when members come through the door. If condoms can help prevent the clap and syphilis, they just might help against this new thing. And I'll have him post signs reminding the members to wear them. Most of them won't, of course. But if it can prevent just one member from getting sick, it'll be worth it."

* * *

O'Banyon was right, of course, about the economic loss to the community if the baths were closed—and the fact of the matter was that even if it was proven that whatever this thing was *was* spread through the baths, not very many bath owners would shut their own places down voluntarily. They'd have to be forcibly closed by law, and that, after Stonewall, would never be tolerated in a community just beginning to flex its muscles. Maybe, if it could be proven to be spread by sex, it might be another story.

But what if it wasn't spread by sex? I'd read a couple far-out theories that being gay was partly genetic. What if it were something in the genes? Unlikely, but...? Or if it were poppers? Or something in the lubricants commonly used for sex? I hadn't seen any lesbians' names in the obituaries...just guys.

Or how about some sort of fanatical right wing conspiracy? Or even a government plot? A sort of "Final Solution" to the "gay problem"?

Paranoia Alert! I told myself, and forced myself to take a couple deep breaths.

Face it, my calmer self observed: *the problem right now is that <u>nobody knows</u>! And until they do know, there's little point in jumping on your horse and riding madly off in all directions.*

After leaving O'Banyon at Hughie's, I went home, made

dinner and watched a little TV before changing clothes to make another round of the bars. This time, I told myself, I'd leave my gonads at home and concentrate on business. *Uh-huh.*

* * *

I worked my way all the way down one side of Arnwood and was making my way up the other—having hit six bars total and settling, after the second drink, for just a coke or a tonic-and-lime in each place. I'd seen nothing out of the ordinary, and talked to a couple of the bartenders in the quieter places—all of whom were apparently already on Jared's "contact" list. I was feeling pretty proud of my resolve when I walked into the Cove and spotted a tall, curly-haired redhead leaning up against the jukebox. We made eye contact and exchanged a Mona Lisa smile. *Down, boy, down!* I told myself. I deliberately tried to ignore him, walking to the far end of the bar after getting my drink and picking out a spot against the wall near the bathroom, where I could see just about the whole place. A few minutes later, the redhead came walking past me, I assumed to use the bathroom. Instead, he took an empty spot next to me, turned to lean his back against the wall and raised one leg to prop it against the wall. He didn't seem to even notice I was there until he took a sip of his beer, turned to me with a smile and said: "Say, do you smell owl feathers burning?"

I burst out laughing. "Can I use that one next time?" I asked. "It sure beats the hell out of 'come here often?'"

"Be my guest," he said. "It's great for separating the wheat from the chaff; if they look at you like you're crazy, they probably aren't worth going home with anyway."

He shifted his beer from his right hand to his left. "I'm Len," he said. "Len Stone," extending his now-free hand.

What about your resolve, Hardesty? my mind asked.

Fuck resolve, my crotch answered

"I'm Dick," I said, extending my hand. "Dick Hardesty."

* * *

I don't know...maybe it's because I'm a Scorpio, but I never cease to be amazed at how different the people I've gone to bed with are. I'm not talking strictly about sex, here—I'm talking more about the whole experience; the before and after as well as the during: how I *feel* about the person and the situation, and the balance between what's being given and what's being gotten. In a way, it's almost like music. A lot of the guys I've been with...most, probably, are TV commercial jingles; pleasant enough the first time, but one time is generally enough. Then there's the very rare type like Jared—a personification of the closing bars of "The 1812 Overture"—all cannons and fireworks and huge bells tolling and purely exciting and purely fantastic. Brad, from Rage, was like a good disco beat—lots of fun to dance to and always enjoyable, but you couldn't picture being around 24 hours a day. Toby? One of those songs you somehow triggers an almost visceral sense of something from your distant past that you can't quite remember.

And Len. Hard to pin down. A blend of old favorites and movie themes and an odd sense of ragtime and Sousa marches. Comfortable, like Toby, but somehow more...what...familiar? And then I realized that Len, though they looked nothing at all alike, reminded me very much of Chris, my ex.

Here we go again.

Anyway, we spent the night at my place. Saturday morning I made what Chris used to call a "Hardesty No Fault Breakfast"—coffee, toast, orange juice, bacon and scrambled eggs, and we ended up spending most of the day together, just bumming around. There was a street fair not too far from where he lived, so we went and wandered around, looking at the various artworks and crafts for sale and admiring the two-legged eye candy. Very pleasant day. Len had a company retirement dinner to go to that evening, but we exchanged numbers and promises to call, and I went home feeling not the least bit guilty about not having stuck by my resolve not to let pleasure interfere with business, but very glad I'd gone to the Cove.

* * *

Just as I was starting dinner, the phone rang—it was Len, just on his way to his banquet, telling me that he'd enjoyed our day together and hoping we could see each other again sometime. I echoed his sentiment, and suggested perhaps we could have dinner some night later in the week. He agreed, and I told him I'd call him Tuesday or Wednesday. I wondered, as I hung up, if he was just being a nice guy, or if maybe there might be a little interest there...or maybe both? We'd see.

I really didn't feel like making another bar tour that night, but didn't really want to stay home, either. So I decided to stop in at Ramón's and maybe talk with Bob for a while. Now that he was dating Mario, we didn't see as much of each other as we had previously, which was totally understandable.

I got to Ramón's around 10, and the place was typically weekend-crowded. Both Bob and Jimmy were working the bar. There was one stool empty at the far end of the bar and I zigzagged my way through the crowd to reach it. Jimmy, busily pouring drinks, saw me and gave a quick heads-up "Hi," which I returned with a small wave. Bob was too busy to even notice me, which of course I should have expected even before I left the apartment. I play some rather stupid games with myself at times.

After a few minutes, Jimmy came by for my drink order. "Too bad you weren't here last night," Jimmy said as he scooped some ice into a glass and reached for the bourbon.

"Oh? I missed something?" I asked.

Jimmy nodded, not looking up. "Your buddy Jared. He can be one scary dude when he's a mind to," he said. He put the drink on a napkin in front of me, and took my money.

"What happened?" I asked, genuinely curious.

"Tell you as soon as the rush dies down," Jimmy said, moving to the cash register. I knew Jared had a temper, and wondered what had apparently triggered it.

A couple guys I knew stopped by to say hi, and I waved at

a couple more, but I really wasn't in the mood for any serious cruising—which came as quite a surprise to my crotch *You're gettin' old, Hardesty*, it whispered, sarcastically

Jeezus, how many people do you know who have conversations with their crotch?

Jimmy found his way back to my end of the bar during a momentary lull—even Bob found a second to look my way and wave.

"So what happened?" I asked.

"The place was packed last night," Jimmy said, opening the beer cooler beneath the bar directly in front of me to check the supply. "Jared came in fairly early, and everything was pretty normal, when these three guys came in and came up to the bar next to him. I was working this end of the bar, so I caught most of what went on. They were having a good time, checking out the merchandise, and one of them spotted a guy over there against the wall." He nodded to an area in the vicinity of the jukebox. "'Jeez, look at that freak!' the one said. The guy he was talking about comes in every now and then. Nice guy when you get to know him. He has multiple sclerosis or cerebral palsy or something like that, and he has a hard time controlling his arms sometimes."

A customer signaled for service, and Jimmy pushed himself away from the bar and went over to take his order. I was getting that old mildly queasy feeling in the pit of my stomach. I was pretty sure I knew where Jimmy's story was going and I was *damned* sure I wasn't going to like it.

Jimmy took the guy's money, rang it up, handed him his change, then walked past me, out from behind the bar, and to the storeroom. A minute later he came back with a case of beer, which he opened and began to put into the cooler in front of me.

"Anyway," Jimmy said, picking up his story, "I saw Jared give the guy a really dirty look, but he didn't say anything. The guy didn't take the hint. 'What do you suppose is wrong with him?' he asked his buddies, referring to the guy against the wall.

His two friends tried to ignore him, but he kept it up. 'What a total spaz!' he said, laughing. His buddies didn't join in, and by now Jared was staring at him, hard.

"The guy against the wall was holding on to a beer, and his hand was shaking, and some of the beer sloshed out. The loudmouth thought that was really funny. '*Look* at that guy,' he said.

"At that point Jared stood up, tapped the loudmouth on the shoulder, and said, very calmly: 'What the fuck is wrong with you, you stupid sonofabitch? The guy can't help it. Drop it.'"

Another customer call drew Jimmy away again, and I sat there imagining the scene. I finished my drink and set it at Jimmy's edge of the bar for a refill. Jimmy came over to take the glass, put it in the sink, and grab a new one. When he came back, he said "Sorry...where was I? Oh, yeah. So as you know, Jared's a pretty imposing hunk of man, and when he stood up he towered over the other three guys. They all looked pretty impressed and the loudmouth got real serious real fast. 'You're right,' he said. 'I'm really sorry. I guess I can be a little insensitive at times.' Jared just nodded and sat back down. A minute or so later, he ordered a drink and got up to go to the bathroom.

"The three guys had been pretty quiet since their encounter with Jared, and the loudmouth said, very seriously: 'You know, that guy was right. I really should be more considerate. I think I'll go over and talk to that guy.' One of his buddies shook his head and said 'Bill...I don't think that's a very good idea. Just leave it alone.' But the loudmouth said 'No, no...I've got to start being more thoughtful of my fellow man,' and he picked up his drink and went across the bar.

"When Jared came back he sat down, then looked around and, seeing the loudmouth talking to the guy against the wall, started to get back up again, but one of the loudmouth's buddies stopped him. 'It's okay,' he said, 'Bill just went over to apologize.' Jared looked suspicious, but sat back down. He kept looking into the mirror to make sure the loudmouth wasn't pulling something, but he and the other guy were just talking."

Yet another customer call pulled Jimmy away again. I found myself so totally absorbed in Jimmy's story that I'd become completely oblivious to anything else going on around me. I don't think I even heard the jukebox, which is pretty hard to miss in a gay bar on a busy Saturday night. I knew there was more to Jimmy's story, and I found myself wishing he'd hurry the hell up and get back to tell me the rest of it.

After what seemed like an eternity, Jimmy found his way back to me.

"So," Jimmy said, "all goes well for maybe 20 minutes, with the loudmouth, Bill whoever, talking to the guy against the wall. Jared got up again for another bathroom call and this Bill character, glancing over and not seeing Jared, apparently thought he'd left. So he drags the guy he's talking to over to the bar and his buddies. I had a really bad feeling about it, so I tried to keep as close to them as I could.

"'Ted, Eric, I'd like you to meet Marshall,' this Bill guy said, very politely. The two guys shook hands with Marshall, and then that fucking asshole did it: 'His name is Marshall,' he said seriously, 'but I think we should call him Mr. Jiggles. Mr. Jiggles actually thinks he and I are going to go home together.' He burst out laughing, and his two friends just stood there looking shocked. This Bill guy turns to poor Marshall, who is suddenly pale as a ghost, and says 'Well, you can go back to your wall, now, Mr. Jiggles. It's been very nice talking with you. And try not to spill your beer all over the room on your way.' And he started laughing again. I was about ready to hop over the bar, but then I noticed that Jared had come up behind him. His two friends saw him and their eyes got wide, and when this Bill guy turns around, Jared reaches out with one hand, grabs him by the neck, and lifts him off the floor.

"Now, this Bill must weigh 165, but Jared picks him up like he's a broomstick. He could have snapped that guy's neck like a number two pencil, and I thought that he just might do that, right there in front of everybody. But instead, he turns around with the guy's feet still off the floor, swings him around like a rag-doll and starts walking him toward the door. The whole bar went deathly quiet, everyone just sort of frozen in mid motion, except for the guys in Jared's way, who just backed away without a word as Jared came through, holding this guy at arm's length like he's taking out a load of dirty diapers. And all the time he's talking to him real calm. 'You're a funny man, aren't you...Bill, is it? Really, really funny, *Bill*. And here's a joke I really hope you'll remember, *Bill*: ...if I ever see you again...and I do mean *ever*...anywhere, any time, you will be very, very, very sorry. So if you see me first, I suggest you start running. It won't do you any good, but you can try. Do we understand one another, *Bill*?'

"The guy couldn't talk with Jared's hand around his throat, so Jared just moved his wrist back and forth, making the guy's head nod. Somebody standing by the door opened it and held it open as Jared stopped just inside the doorway and flicked the guy out into the street, slamming him into a car at the curb. 'Good night, Bill,' Jared says, and turns around and goes back to his seat. The whole place went up for grabs, with everybody applauding and cheering and slapping Jared on the back. Bill's two buddies just sort of disappeared, and Jared bought Marshall a drink and left."

Jimmy grinned from ear to ear. "Boy, you couldn't *pay* to see a show like that!"

While I was deeply impressed by Jared's action, and proud of him for standing up for someone being mistreated, I had an overlaying, indescribable sense of dread. If the bar watcher had been there...

And then I felt a *real* wave of panic: what if the bar watcher *was* there? And even more chilling: *what if it was Jared?*

* * *

I finished my drink and left the bar shortly after hearing Jimmy's story of Jared's evening out. I was really troubled by it, and cursed myself for not having picked up a paper on Saturday. But just in case, I turned on the radio on my way home and tuned in to the news station. Nothing there, either, so I allowed myself to relax a little and criticized myself yet again for my tendency to paranoia.

Jared had a temper, sure, and he was big enough to do just about anything he set his mind to, physically. He'd had that run-in with Comstock; hell, so had I, though I stopped short of punching him. He'd been with me at Glitter the night before Richie Smith was found....*I don't like where this is going, Hardesty,* I thought. But I couldn't just shut it off. He'd been at the Hilltop the night the queens went over the bluff. He was really pissed when he heard what D'Allesandro had done to John Peterson. And, shit! He was in Venture the night Lynn Barnseth had the fight with George! And now last night, he'd been at Ramón's.

Relax, Hardesty, relax! I told myself. *You're getting way too paranoid over all this. What are the chances the bar watcher would have been in that one particular bar on that one particular night? Pretty damned remote!*

Unless...

"Okay," I said aloud, "drop it!"

Well, at least that Bill character, as Jimmy called him, was still alive.

For the moment, my mind said.

* * *

I didn't sleep all that well Saturday night, and was up by 7 a.m. The Sunday paper was outside the custodian's closet as always, and I brought it in to read with my coffee. I cursed myself for not having it delivered every day, but I'd grown so accustomed to picking one up on my way to the office....Of course that meant I usually missed Saturday's paper, and Saturday's was the one I most wanted to see. Press time, I knew, was 2 a.m., so there was an outside chance that if anything had happened late on Friday night, it might have happened too late to make Saturday's. But by Sunday, whatever might have happened Friday night would be old news. And I hadn't even listened to the news on Saturday except in the car on my way home from Ramón's. *Stupid, Hardesty, stupid!* Not much chance of there being anything new in there, but I automatically turned to page three, where last-minute local news usually showed up.

A domestic shooting; an apartment house fire, a bunch of teenagers injured when their van rolled on the way home from a beer party, a hit and run...

A hit and run? "Police are investigating the hit-and-run death of twenty-three year old William Hinson shortly after midnight Friday. The vehicle apparently involved was found abandoned six blocks away...."

CHAPTER 12

Lots of 'Williams' in this town, I told myself, trying to stay calm. *Lots of 'Williams.'* But I didn't buy it for a minute. *Nice try, Hardesty.*

I found myself reaching for the phone and dialing Jared's number without even stopping to think I might be getting him out of bed.

Luckily, he answered on the second ring. "Jared here."

"Jared!" I said, hoping I sounded cheerfully casual. "How've you been? I haven't seen much of you lately."

"You heard, obviously," he said, and I felt a chill down my spine.

"About...?" I asked, not knowing what else to say. If he referred to the hit and run...

"About my little run in with that creep at Ramón's Friday night."

Some relief, but still uneasy. "Yeah, that's why I called. Sorry I wasn't there to catch the show. Jimmy thinks he could have sold tickets for it."

"Well, yeah," Jared said. "That sonofabitch really pissed me off, treating that poor guy the way he did. He's just lucky I didn't break his neck right there."

"So who was the guy?" I asked, realizing Jared might know perfectly well what I was getting at. "Did you know him?"

If he caught it, he didn't let on; at least not at first. "Never saw him before, and plan to keep it that way. His name's Bill, according to one of his buddies, but..." He suddenly broke off in mid sentence and I could almost hear the thoughts falling into place in his head. "...Uh, Dick, are you telling me something here? You don't mean...?"

He knew.

"I'm not sure yet, but my gut tells me 'yes.'" I said. "There was a hit-and-run around midnight Friday night that killed a 23-year old guy named William Hinson. I'm going to have to check it out, but..." I wasn't quite sure how to phrase what I had to say next, so I just plunged in. "I'm going to ask you something I don't want you to take the wrong way, but I hope you were out in public somewhere with lots of people around at about midnight."

"Oh, *shit! Shit!*" he said, and I knew exactly what was going on in his mind. "No! I left the bar right after that run in—I wasn't in any mood to stick around a noisy bar. I went straight home—alone, damn it! Nobody saw me from the time I left the bar."

I decided we'd both better step back a pace or two. "Now let's not go jumping to conclusions just yet," I said, hoping I sounded a lot more encouraging than I felt. "Let me check it out first. There are a lot of 'Williams' out there...." It didn't sound any more convincing when I said it aloud. "But if I'm right that this 'William' was your buddy, 'Bill,' I think you can expect a visit from the police."

"Shit, Dick! What can I do? I don't have an alibi—who the hell ever thinks they're going to *need* one? And after what I said to the guy Friday night when I was throwing him out the door—everybody in the fucking place heard me, I'm sure—I can be in deep shit."

I suddenly realized that I was walking on very thin ice, here. While I simply could not believe that Jared could be capable of murder, I'd been wrong about people in the past. If he *was* the bar watcher, should I be talking to him like this?

"Uh, Jared," I said, deciding to go with my instincts, "it might get a lot worse."

Another pause, then: "What do you mean? How 'worse?'"

I told him of my arrangement with Lieutenant Richman, and that he knew quite a bit about the other murders, and that I'd promised not to keep anything from him. There was no way—especially if they did question Jared—that I could *not* tell him about Jared's having witnessed many of the incidents which led to the victims' deaths.

Jared was quiet again for a minute, then sighed. "Yeah, you're right, of course. Do what you have to do. But you *know* I didn't do it, don't you Dick?"

"Yeah, Jared," I said. "I know." And I really, really wanted to believe it. "But we're way ahead of ourselves here. This hit and run could be anybody. Let's wait and see what happens, okay?"

"Okay," Jared said.

"Okay," I echoed. "You just hang in there and don't worry about anything until it happens. Like I said, this could all be nothing. But I'll see what I can find out, and get back to you as soon as I know anything."

We left it there and I'd just hung up when the phone rang. I picked the receiver back up. "Dick Hardesty," I said.

"Hi, Dick. This is Toby." He didn't have to tell me.

"Toby," I said, "I'm glad you called. I wanted to call you last week, but I realized I don't have your number."

Toby sounded puzzled. "I'm sorry, Dick, I thought I'd told you—I don't have a phone. I don't talk to enough people to warrant the expense." There was only a short pause before he continued. "Anyway, I'm just on my way to the gym and wanted to call. I saw in the paper that the Chicago Symphony is coming to town and wondered if you maybe you'd like to see it with me?"

Despite my concerns about Jared and the maybe-new-victim in the case, I felt myself lightening up considerably.

"That's exactly why I wanted to call you," I said. "This one's on me, if you want to go."

"I'd love to," Toby said, sounding genuinely happy. "But I can buy my own ticket…" he added, as though he didn't want to impose on me.

"The hell you can," I said. "Let me call tomorrow and see what's available—can you call me tomorrow night after you get out of the gym?"

"Sure," he said, sounding little-boy happy. There was a

slight pause, and then he said: "You know, I went out and bought every Tchaikovsky record we listened to at your house? I love him. Wouldn't it be great if the whole world were as beautiful as his music?"

"Spoken like a true romantic," I said. "And I'm really glad you like him." I glanced at my watch. "I'd better let you get to the gym," I said. "Have a good time, and I'll talk to you tomorrow."

"It's a deal," Toby said. "And thanks. A lot. 'Bye."

As I hung up, I was aware once again of a very strange air of...what?...gentle sadness?... about Toby. He reminded me yet again of a little kid who wanted desperately to have people like him but didn't know how. I couldn't understand it, really. He was drop-dead gorgeous, sweet, gentle, kind. What could there possibly be *not* to like about him? So why did I sense this air of loneliness?

Big brother rides again.

Maybe. Or maybe I just attract mysterious people. A gift? Or something else?

* * *

Ramón's didn't open until 2 on Sunday, but on the outside chance that Jimmy might possibly know any of the three guys involved in the Jared incident Friday night, I called Bob Allen for Jimmy's phone number in hopes he might be home. Bob, however, wasn't. He was probably at Mario's or they were out to brunch or something. I left a message on his machine, and decided to call Ramón's after 2, in case either Bob or Jimmy were there.

The thought of brunch triggered one of my Hardesty-spur-of-the-moment urges, and I went into the bedroom to get my wallet. I found Len's number and, though I was sure he wouldn't be home, dialed his number.

"Hello?" a totally unfamiliar voice said after the third ring. *Oh, shit!* I thought. *He's got a lover! Or maybe it's last night's trick.*

"Uh, hi," I said, resisting the momentary urge to just hang up. "Is Len around?"

"Sure," the voice said, and there was a muffled "Len...phone."

Are you ever going to learn? my mind asked. *Think first, then act!* Well, it was too late now.

A moment later the sound of the receiver switching hands, then "Hi, this is Len."

"Len, hi," I said, feeling pretty awkward. "This is Dick Hardesty. I hope I'm not taking you away from something...."
Smooth one, Hardesty!

"Not at all," he said. "My roommate's just waiting for his lover to come over...he thought it was him calling when the phone rang."
Whew!

"Ah," I said, with my usual facile grasp of the language. "Well, I know this is really short notice, but I just had the urge to go out to brunch and wondered if you'd like to join me."

"Great!" he said. "I was just toying with the idea of brunch a few minutes ago. Where and when?"

"Well, there's Rasputin's, or Calypso's, or..."

"I'll leave it up to you."

"How about Calypso's? I'll call to see if we can get a table on the patio. And how about between 1:15 and 1:30?"

"Perfect. I'll see you there."

As soon as we said our good-byes I looked up Calypso's number, called, and asked for a patio table. The first opening they had was at 1:45, but I took it. Then I hung up the phone and headed for the shower.

* * *

I got to Calypso's at 1:05—a little late by my usual standards—and checked in with the maitre d'. Of course Len wasn't there yet—I didn't expect him to be. But when he wasn't there by 1:30 I was getting a little concerned. At 20 'til, the concern melted into becoming just a tad pissed. I remembered my college friend Alan who never, ever in all the time I knew him, was ever on time. I think it was one of the factors in our losing touch with one another. I didn't want another Alan in my life.

At 1:45, the maitre d' came over and said: "Your table's ready when you are," and I was about to tell him to cancel it when I saw Len's curly read hair approaching above the crowd of heads between me and the front door.

"Dick!" he said when he reached me, his face anxious; "I'm really sorry I'm late. I tried calling here to tell you, but they said there were too many people to take personal messages. I'm really sorry!"

The maitre d' was still standing there, menus in hand, looking impatient, so I just got off my bar stool, put my hand on Len's elbow, and said: "No problem...our table's ready."

There was no time to say anything before we'd sat down and the waiter had taken our drink order. Then Len said: "Right after I hung up from talking with you, I got a call from a friend of mine, Eric. He was telling me about having spent most of Saturday morning in the police station! The cops woke him up at 6:30 Saturday to tell him his car had been involved in a hit-and-run accident that had killed a guy. Eric didn't even know his car was gone! But then it turned out—and this I still can't quite believe—that the guy that got killed was the same guy Eric and some friend had been out with Friday night! When the cops found Eric knew the guy...Bill Hanson or Hinson or something like that...they hauled him down to the police station and questioned him for over two hours. But they finally let him go. He was terrified they were going to throw him in jail."

I just sat there, staring at him without saying a word even after he'd finished his story. He probably thought I was some sort of idiot or insensitive jerk.

Say something, stupid! my mind demanded.

Fortunately, at that moment the waiter came up with our

drinks.

"Are you ready to order?" he asked.

"Give us a minute," I said, and he left. Then I turned my full attention to Len.

"Jeez, Len, that's incredible," I said...but I knew that it wasn't. "You probably should have gone over to be with your friend—I'd have understood."

Len smiled and shook his head. "No, I wanted to come. Eric's okay. He's with his lover, anyway. Mark had stayed home Friday night with a cold, but at least he could give Eric an alibi—Eric had come home at 11:30 and I guess the accident was at around midnight. But my God, what incredible coincidences—his car getting stolen and then killing somebody he'd just been out with!"

"It's a pretty weird world," I said. "But I'm glad you came."

We looked at each other and Len blushed. "Me too," he said, and we picked up our menus.

* * *

Everything considered, it was a great brunch. I decided about ten minutes into it that I really *liked* Len. I really liked Jared and Toby, too, but that was different. Jared was a great guy, but the possibility of our ever being anything to one another other than what we already were had never crossed either of our minds. Toby? Well, I'd pretty much set up the parameters on that: Toby was my surrogate kid brother and pretty great sex; I just knew I wanted to be there for him if he ever *did* need protecting–and to maybe make him a little less ...lonely?

And then there was Len. Len was...well "comfortable" kept popping into my mind, and I know that could easily be misconstrued as 'damning with faint praise.' But I *like* comfortable, and if that made me a wimp in anyone's eyes, well that was their problem.

Okay, okay...I know: I said right at the start that I wasn't looking for Mr. Right, but I'd be just plain stupid if the right opportunity came along and I blew it (as it were). I *liked* being in a relationship when I was with Chris. I wasn't unhappy *not* being in one, but if the chance came along again....

We were finishing our coffee after the waiter had cleared the brunch dishes away, and while I'd very much hoped I'd leave myself alone and just let me enjoy myself, I couldn't resist bringing up the hit-and-run again.

"Len," I said, "I apologize...I really hate mixing business with pleasure but I may have told you I'm working on a case with about 300 different components, and I think this thing involving your friend Eric is part of it."

Len took a sip of his coffee and put his cup carefully in the center of his saucer.

He smiled. "Is there anything I can do to help you?" he asked. "I'd like that."

I returned his smile. "As a matter of fact, yes. Did Eric tell you about the dead guy's having gotten in an altercation earlier that night?"

Len looked at me as though I'd just pulled a rabbit out of a hat. "How did you know about that?" he asked.

"Long story," I said. "Did he say what happened afterwards?"

Len thought a minute, gently biting his lower lip. "He mentioned that he didn't like the guy that got killed...Bill whatever. Eric said he was a real asshole to some poor guy in some bar they'd gone to, and that some huge guy had literally thrown Bill out the door. A really big scene, I guess. Eric and his other friend sort of snuck out, and Eric just wanted to go home. But since they were all riding in Eric's car, Eric said he had to get home to see about Mark. His other friend was as pissed with Bill as Eric was and ready to call it a night, but Bill wanted to go to another bar and told Eric drop him off at the Pit Stop—I guess that was close to where he lived, and he said he'd walk home from there. So Eric left him off in front of the Pit Stop, took the other guy home, and then went home himself."

We were both quiet for a minute, and then I said: "This is an odd question, but I don't suppose Eric said anything about them being followed, did he?"

Len looked puzzled. "No, he didn't. Why might he think they were being followed?" he asked.

Because I'm pretty sure they were, I thought. "Just wondering," I said.

* * *

After brunch, when Len didn't express being in any particular hurry to be off somewhere else I suggested we take a ride to up to the Jessup Reservoir, about 20 miles outside of town. Not many people even knew about it, and even fewer went there, but it was a great area, mostly forested, with a nice walking trail that went all around the reservoir. Len thought it was a great idea—or was nice enough to say he did, so we left his car near Calypso's and drove on out.

I drove about halfway around the reservoir to a secluded area I'd found a couple years before. Luckily, there wasn't another car in the small parking area, and no one else in sight. It was a beautiful day—the kind where if you stood perfectly still, you could hear nothing but the soft murmur of the waves on the shore, and the wind talking to itself through the trees.

"Nice day," Len said.

"Very," I replied.

We came to a small trail that led off toward a rise overlooking the entire reservoir, and we followed it to the top. A couple large boulders provided a little semi-cave, and we sat at the entrance and looked out over the countryside. Not a single sign of civilization, or even a hint that we were not the only two people in the entire world.

"Did you ever have sex outdoors?" Len asked, totally out of the blue.

I grinned at him. "Uh huh. You?"

He blushed and shook his head.

"Ya' wanna?" I asked, unconsciously echoing Jared.

"Take a guess," he said, lying back on the long grass.

* * *

On the way back into town, I asked Len if he'd mind stopping off at Ramón's. While I really didn't want to get him involved in this whole tangled bar watcher mess, I also selfishly wanted to spend as much time with him as I could. He worked for an architectural consulting firm and had told me he had to leave town Tuesday for a week-long trip to Seattle on a company project.

We got to Ramón's around six. The place was relatively quiet, compared to what it had been Saturday night. Jimmy was on duty, somewhat to my surprise, and both Bob and Mario were sitting at the far end of the bar.

"Dick," Bob called when he saw us come in, waving us to him. Jimmy finished serving a customer and came down the bar to join us. I introduced Len, who got an appreciative once-over from Jimmy and a raised eyebrow nod of approval from Bob. Mario just grinned at me. Bob asked us what we'd like to drink, and Jimmy moved off to make them.

"I've been trying to get you on the phone all afternoon," Bob said, "but I see you've been busy." He grinned at Len, who blushed and grinned back.

I suddenly felt very guilty. "About Friday?" I said, and Bob nodded.

"They arrested Jared," Bob said, and I felt my heart fall through my stomach.

"*Shit!*" I said. "How the hell could they do that? They don't have a shred of evidence, other than his involvement in the tussle with that Hinson character."

"As you probably have noticed," Mario said, "the police don't always have to have a lot of evidence."

Jimmy returned with our drinks. Poor Len wasn't saying

anything—what could he say: he didn't know anything about what was going on. I put my arm on his shoulder so he wouldn't feel totally left out.

"It's okay, though," Jimmy—who had somehow apparently been able to keep track of the conversation even when he was halfway down the bar—said. "They let him go. He came by here about an hour ago, looking for you. They just held him at the station and gave him the third degree while they got a search warrant and went through his apartment. I don't think they found anything, but he says they made a mess of the place."

"The police called me at home around noon," Bob said, "wanting to know exactly what had happened Friday night—I wasn't here, so I didn't know anything except what Jimmy and some of the regulars told me Saturday. They wanted to talk to Jimmy, so I gave them his phone number."

"God, poor Jared," I said.

"'Poor' and 'Jared' are two words I'd never think of using in the same sentence," Jimmy said with a smile.

"Muscles are great to look at, but not always good to use," Mario observed, motioning to Jimmy for a refill for himself and Bob.

"You think Jared's home now?" I asked. "I should give him a call." Then, suddenly once again very conscious of my arm still around Len, I said: "I'm sorry, Len, I…" Len just smiled and slipped his hand down to my butt, which he gave a spread-fingered squeeze.

"Go call," he said, taking the drink out of my hand and putting it on the bar.

"You can use the phone in the office," Bob said getting up from his stool to walk me to the office door, which he unlocked with a key from the chain dangling from his belt loop.

Having let me in, Bob closed the door behind me and went back to the bar. I dialed Jared's number and let it ring four times. I was about ready to hang up when he answered.

"Jared!" I said. "Dick—are you okay?"

"Peachy," he said in a voice which left little doubt that

"peachy" didn't quite do it. "You should see this place, Dick!" he said, sounding more sad than anything else. "My thesis is scattered all over the fucking living room, my dresser drawers look like a family of raccoons had been in them, the closet's a total disaster...they even took the lid off the toilet tank and didn't bother to put it back. What a fucking bunch of idiots!"

"You want me to come over and help you clean up?" I asked.

"Nah, but thanks," he said. "I guess it could have been a lot worse...they didn't actually break anything."

I resisted sitting down at Bob's desk, since I didn't want to be gone from Len and the others...okay, mostly Len...too long. "So how does it stand with the police?" I asked.

"No idea," he said. "At least they let me go, and if they thought they had even a shred of something to really hang me on, they'd have done it. But they let me know in no uncertain terms that I'm still their odds-on favorite."

"Well," I said, "I'm just glad they let you go. And I suspect I'll be getting a call from Lieutenant Richman tomorrow, if there's not already one waiting for me when I get home—I'm down at Ramón's. But if I do hear from Richman, I'll let you know."

"Okay," he said. "I'd appreciate that. Now I'd better get back to this mess. Talk with you later."

We hung up and I returned to the others. Len didn't say a word; just smiled and handed me my drink.

* * *

When we left Ramón's, I had the distinct feeling that neither Len nor I wanted the day to end. I suggested that we stop somewhere for dinner, but Len shook his head.

"How about your place?" he asked. "I'm a pretty good cook."

"Great!" I said. "Shall we just leave your car at Calypso's and pick it up later?"

Len grinned. "No, I think I'd better pick it up now. We might not want to go out again later."

We stopped at a supermarket about two blocks from Calypso's for some steaks, salad fixings and, while I followed him around with the shopping cart, an assortment of exotic and mysterious—to me at any rate—things he very efficiently gathered together and for which he insisted on paying.

Comfortable. Why did that word always keep cropping up when I thought of Len or tried to describe our time together? Anyway, it was a "comfortable" evening in the very best sense of the word, and it reminded me of the best days of my relationship with Chris.

Though he didn't talk much about it, Len had mentioned that he'd been in a long-term relationship with a guy he adored, who had come home one night after four years to tell Len he'd found another lover. That had been two or three years before, but I sensed Len still hadn't gotten over it and sometimes in the dark I thought I could see the flicker of flame from a torch Len still carried for the guy, reflected in his eyes.

I talked him into spending the night, and we even slept—when we finally got to sleep—in my favorite together-position that Chris liked to call "spoons."

Comfortable. And very, very nice.

* * *

Sure enough, when I checked my messages upon arriving at the office Monday morning there was a call from Lieutenant Richman, which I returned immediately. This time it wasn't a request to meet him privately at Sandler's for breakfast. This was a summons to his office—politely phrased, but unmistakably a summons. I told him I would come right down.

I was reminded, as I walked into police headquarters annex of the City Building, of how one of the reasons I'd joined the Navy was because I thought sailors looked hot in their blue uniforms. That was before I was put on a carrier with 3,000 other guys and learned that 3,000 sailors all in one place are just so much blue. I was revising my cop fantasies on the same basis as I wove my way through a lobby full of police.

I gave my name to the officer at the desk in front of the elevators, and told him Lt. Richman was expecting me. To my considerable surprise, he merely waved me toward the elevators. Richman's office was on the 17th floor, and I wandered down the hallways until I found a door marked "Lt. M. Richman" and knocked.

"Come," I heard Richman's voice say. Under the circumstances, I would have preferred him to say "Enter."

I walked in to find Richman seated in one of the two chairs flanking and facing the desk, behind which sat a very large, very once-blond, very once-handsome man who for some odd reason I thought looked like he might, in his younger days, have been a poster boy for the Hitler Jungend.

Richman got up to shake my hand, then turned to the man behind the desk, who also rose.

"Dick Hardesty, Captain Karl Offermann" Richman said by way of introduction, and Offermann leaned slightly forward to shake hands. He must have been about 6' 5" and I felt like one of the members of the Lollipop Guild. Richman motioned me to the other chair, and the three of us sat down. "Captain Offermann is head of our homicide division," Richman said, as though I hadn't already guessed. I didn't imagine Richman would have given up his desk for someone who did not considerably outrank him. I'd seen Offermann's name in the papers on numerous occasions, but don't think I'd ever seen a photo of him.

After a rather awkward moment of silence, Lt. Richman, said: "In light of the most recent...incident...Captain Offermann feels that it is time that Homicide stepped in to take over the entire investigation, but I asked him to listen to you first. We need to know everything you know before we can determine how to proceed. I've kept Captain Offermann appraised of our...understanding, and he has been supportive of it. However, things seem to be getting out of control. So why don't you start from the beginning?"

I'd known this moment was inevitable, so I'd prepared for it as best I could. "All right, gentlemen," I said. "But since I have more theories and speculations than hard facts, I ask that you bear with me."

I then proceeded to tell them everything from my first meeting with Comstock to Jared's arrest, of course leaving out anything not directly related to the case. They listened impassively, and when I'd finished, Richman looked at Offermann, who in turn looked at me and said: "You and this Martinson, are...close...friends?"

Gee, that was subtle, I thought, and wondered if he'd heard a word I'd said. "We're friends, yes," I said, "but not in the way I think you're implying. As I told you, Jared's been very helpful in providing me with information I might otherwise not have come by. His job gives him access to very wide circle of contacts in the bar scene."

"And you think these deaths are directly linked to what goes on in homosexual bars?" he half-asked, have stated.

Excuse me? I thought. *Where in the hell did that come from? What have I just been saying these past twenty minutes?*

I wasn't quite sure yet whether Offermann's decidedly homophobic implications meant he was definitely anti-gay or just playing his Head-of-the-Homicide-Division role. Either way, I wasn't going to have any misunderstandings as to where my loyalties lay. "I don't think this has anything to do with 'what goes on in homosexual bars,'" I said. "There aren't any generalizations involved: these are isolated, specific incidents which are not typical of anything or anyone. It would be grossly unfair to try to paint the entire gay bar scene with the same brush. We're talking here of one individual who, when he observes someone being callously or deliberately cruel, takes it upon himself to makes sure that it doesn't happen again."

Offermann gave me a very small, Mona Lisa smile. "You

almost sound like you approve of the killings."

I shook my head. "No, I do not. Gratuitous cruelty is inexcusable, but it doesn't warrant a death sentence."

"You've linked each of the deaths to a specific incident in a bar," Offermann said watching me closely, "except for Comstock. Was he involved in one of these bar incidents?"

"Not that I'm aware of," I said. "But I'm convinced that he was the trigger for everything that's followed. I'm positive that it was Comstock's arbitrarily exclusionary membership policy for Rage that led to his death. He was a first-class asshole who had absolutely no regard for anything or anyone other than himself. That his refusal to let anyone who didn't fit his arbitrary standards of physical attractiveness become members was humiliating to them didn't phase him in the least. I think that, having killed Comstock, the murderer felt empowered to take on others he perceived as being in Comstock's mold. As I've indicated, every single subsequent victim, from everything I have been able to learn about them, seems to have been, like Comstock, a thoroughly rotten excuse for a human being."

"Well, I hope you don't mind my saying so, Mr. Hardesty," Offermann said, "but I really don't think 'gratuitous cruelty' is much of a motive for one murder, let alone...how many do you say there have been so far?...Seven? Human beings are notoriously cruel to one another—if they weren't, I wouldn't have a job. Why is this guy only killing homosexuals—especially if he's homosexual himself?"

"It isn't so hard to understand," I said. "The killer is undoubtedly used to being a target for bigotry, hatred, and intolerance from straights—that's just the way life is when you're gay, but I suspect he can't stand the idea of gays acting that way toward one another. It may not be logical, but I'm sure you've noticed that murderers often have their own logic."

Offermann sat quietly for a moment, then said: "So why are you convinced your friend Martinson is not the one doing the killing?"

I shrugged, and avoided bringing up the obvious fact that

if they had a shred of solid evidence against Jared, he'd be in jail now. "I admit that the fact of Jared's being my friend might be an influencing factor," I said, "but it's not a major one. If I were to guess—and I'm not trying to play armchair psychologist here—I would say the killer is someone far less sure of himself than Jared, and has probably been exposed to a lot more intolerance and hatred than I can imagine Jared ever having been. He's quite likely someone who is or considers himself to be physically unattractive; he may very well have been refused a membership to Rage, which could have lit the fuse to this whole thing,"

Offermann sat back in his—Richman's—chair and pursed his lips. He hadn't taken his eyes off me for more than an instant since I'd started talking.

Finally, his lips unpursed and he said: "And if we were to...request...that you back away from the case and let the police handle it from here?"

I'd been expecting that one, too.

"With all due respect, Captain," I said, "I think that would be a very bad idea. I will, of course, if you make it more than a request; and I might consider it if your police force included some openly gay officers who could pick it up from here. But right now, I'm the only one in this building who not only knows what's going on, but who knows his way around the gay community. I've done nothing to impede your investigation, and I assume from my being here that you haven't gotten any closer to finding the murderer than I have. The difference between us is that I can go places and find out things you can't, and that I sense I'm getting close. And when I find him, I promise you he's all yours."

Richman and Offermann looked at one another again, and Offermann got up from his/Richman's chair. Richman and I followed suit.

"Well thank you for coming in, Mr. Hardesty," Offermann said. "We'll be in touch with you shortly."

"Thank you, Captain," I said, taking his extended hand.

"And thank you, Lieutenant, for your support." Richman and I shook hands, and I turned and left the office without looking back.

* * *

Actually, it had gone rather well, I thought. No rubber hoses or brass knuckles were brought out, and I was able to keep from telling more than I wanted to tell. I'd tried to diffuse the fact of Jared's presence at so many of the scenes by the fact that I myself had witnessed two of them. And they had not asked who had hired me—I assumed it hadn't been difficult for Richman to figure out, since it was O'Banyon who had put me in touch with him in the first place, and he had undoubtedly told Offermann—so O'Banyon's name never came up.

But as soon as I got back to the office, I called O'Banyon's office and was lucky to find him in. I told him everything that had happened from Friday night on. And before we hung up, I asked him to remember, at the Businessmen's League meeting, to bring up the question of the mysterious deaths. He said it was top on his agenda, and I felt a little guilty about pushing him on it. But I knew it was important that someone start taking action on this thing.

I next called Jared and left a message on his machine asking him to call me later at home.

And then I called the Civic Arts Center for tickets for Toby and me for the Chicago Symphony. I managed to get two in the front mezzanine for Saturday night. I was really pleased, for Toby's sake as well as my own. And I noticed the minute I thought that last sentence that I thought of Len, and felt the slightest twinge of...guilt?

Jeezus, Hardesty! my mind said, contemptuously.

Well, I realized that I was in fact juggling three—what did Blanche Dubois call them?... "gentlemen callers"—all at the same time: Jared, Toby, and Len. And I was a lousy juggler.

* * *

I'd just returned from the kitchen after smelling the meatloaf burning—which to me was an indication that it was done—and removing it from the oven to the counter to cool for a moment when the phone rang. It was Len, calling to thank me again for the weekend, and to say goodbye until he returned from his business trip the following Sunday evening. I told him to take care of himself and to have a good time, and that I'd look forward to hearing from him when he returned. I did not tell him that I would miss him, but I knew I would.

Hardesty, you're hopeless! my mind said. It was right.

Dinner over, I was stacking the dishes in the sink and trying to find a convenient excuse for not washing them right then when the phone rang again, providing the perfect out.

"Dick Hardesty," I said, wiping my hands on the dishtowel I'd grabbed before moving into the living room.

"Dick, it's Jared," the voice said.

"Jared! Glad you called." I then proceeded to tell him of my meeting with Richman and Offermann, and my feeling that he was probably more a token suspect than a real one. I was sure by this time they had done a fingerprint check of the steering wheel of the car involved in Hinson's death, and obviously Jared's weren't there or they'd have yanked him in immediately. He seemed relieved.

"I'm sorry about yesterday," I said. "I really should have come over to help you straighten the place out, but I was with someone."

"Toby?" Jared asked.

I was surprised to feel my face get warm. "No," I said. "Len. Len Stone. I don't think you've met him."

"No grass growing under your feet," Jared said. "But I sort of thought you and Toby were an item."

Again, the warm face. "Not really," I said. "He's a great guy, but..."

"Yeah," Jared said, "I've been there...not with Toby, of

course, but..."

"So tell me," I said, switching subjects with my usual whiplash speed, "did you notice anything unusual in Ramón's—anybody paying particular attention to what was going on? Anybody different, or..."

"Hell," Jared laughed, "*everybody* was paying attention. And as for who was there, the usual mix of regulars and guys I'd never seen before; and Toby."

"Toby?" I asked.

"Yeah," Jared said. "I wasn't going to mention him if I thought you might be unhappy to know he was there, but since you've got a new one on the line...But I think he might already have left by the time the fun started...I don't remember seeing him during or afterwards—of course I didn't see anything 'during;' just that asshole's face." I heard the sound of a doorbell in the background. "Pizza's here," Jared said.

"Okay, I'll let you go," I said. "Let's get together next week sometime."

"Sure. I'll give you a call."

We hung up, and I suddenly felt oddly queasy. Then I realized why. Jared had been right: I *was* unhappy to hear that Toby had been at Ramón's Friday night.

And I don't think it had anything to do with jealousy.

CHAPTER 13

Hardesty, you need a vacation, I told myself. A little healthy paranoia is good for the soul, but...

So Toby was at Ramón's. Are you <u>sure</u> *what you're feeling isn't just good old Scorpio jealousy? Just a little bit? I mean, here you are, alpha stud, and one of your harem is off straying.* Oh, God, even *I* couldn't buy that one. But Toby as a murder suspect? No way. The worst thing I'd ever heard him say about another human being was when he referred to the fact that D'Allesandro 'wasn't a very nice man.' Hardly the kind of uncontrolled rage that might lead to murder. Toby was the kind of guy who'd let a mosquito bite him rather than swat it. I'd seen a lot of things in Toby, but never anything that hinted at even so much as a temper—unlike Jared, unfortunately. Anyway, Jared said he'd left by the time the tussle started. And how about Len, while I was at it? What did I know of him? He could very well have been in every single one of those bars—maybe wearing a fright wig and a false nose. But Len not being allowed into Rage? Or Toby? Hardly.

And exactly what was there about me that insisted I had to already know the killer? Umpteen gazillion gays in this town, and I personally know the murderer? More than a tad unlikely.

How about O'Banyon? How about Bart Giacomino? How about Jared's pizza delivery boy? No, he wouldn't count...I didn't know him.

No, I told myself, the murderer is some sad, strange little man who no one ever notices, standing quietly against the wall, in the shadows, watching and dreaming. *Shit!* I *did* feel sorry for the guy.

And even as I felt sorry for him, I knew that one night I would be in a bar, and some asshole would be honing his craft, and I would see the sad little man and see him watching, and

I would follow him when he left the bar, and...

There were times—rare times—when I really didn't like my job.

* * *

Tuesday morning I did my dreaded going-through-the-paper routine, hoping I wouldn't find anything, and noting three new listings in the obituary column of young, single men, dead much, much too young of "complications" and "long illnesses"and not a single banner headline screaming: *"Something's KILLING These Men!"*

Just before leaving the office for lunch, I got a phone call from Lieutenant Richman. He'd had a long talk with Captain Offermann after I'd left (*Surprise!* I thought) and decided they'd let me continue on the case, on condition that I did nothing to jeopardize the police investigation (I'd seen very little evidence that there was a police investigation going on, but I didn't bring that point up to Richman.) I of course agreed, having already done so when he and I had our first conversation, and I also redundantly agreed to keep him posted on anything I found out.

Whew! Off the hook! I thought as I hung up the phone.

I next called Bob Allen to ask him for Jimmy's home phone number. I wanted Jimmy, if he could, to give me the names of everyone he could remember having been in the bar Friday night at the time of the ruckus. I was determined to contact every single one of them to see if any of them may have noticed anyone acting strangely, or if they'd remembered anyone following Hinson's two friends out of the bar. While I was at it, I asked him to ask Mario if he could do the same thing for the night Lynn Barnseth did his little number with George at Venture.

Of course, I realized how difficult this would be. I was in Venture with Toby, standing about four feet from George when that particular incident took place, and I couldn't remember anyone I knew being there. Other than Mario, of course...and Jared. I'd have to remember to ask Jared, too.

I don't know why I hadn't thought of this approach before. It would involve a hell of a lot of time and undoubtedly take me on 400 different wild goose chases, but by this point I was willing to try anything, no matter how much effort it took.

* * *

Tuesday night at around nine I was home going over the list of names I'd picked up from Jimmy that afternoon, looking up phone numbers, when the phone rang.

"Dick, hi!" I recognized Toby's voice immediately and realized I'd forgotten completely that he was going to call about the symphony tickets. "I just got out of the gym," he said, "and thought I'd give you a call before I headed home."

"Glad you did, Toby," I said. "I was able to get two pretty good tickets for Saturday night, if that's okay with you."

"That's great!" Toby said, and he sounded genuinely pleased. "I'm really looking forward to it! I've been listening to my new records nearly every night since I got them."

I was once more aware of what an odd mixture Toby was. On the one hand, he was Mr. Calm-and-Composed. On the other, he reminded me of a little boy who'd never lost his sense of the wonder at discovering new things.

"I'm glad," I said. "I know you'll like the symphony. Why don't I pick you up at your place? There's no point in our taking two cars."

There was a slight pause, and then a rather hesitant: "Oh...uh...okay. That'd be fine, if you're sure it won't be a bother. I live at 247 Cloverland—do you think you can find it again?"

I remembered from having driven him home that first night we spent together. It was in what used to be known as a 'working class' neighborhood, now in slow but irreversible decline. Tenements, flats, a few single-family houses holding on without much hope for gentrification or renewal.

"Yeah, I can find it easy enough," I said. Then I had a spur of the minute thought which my mind somehow told me wasn't quite as spur of the minute as I'd imagined.

"Tell you what," I said, "I know you don't like restaurants, but Warman Park's just a block away from the Civic Arts...what do you say we have a sort of picnic dinner before the performance? You can bring whatever you like, and I'll bring something for me, and a bottle of vintage cranberry juice for both of us. We can relax and have a chance to talk a little."

Again a slight pause. Then: "Sure. Why not? It'll be fun. I like picnics."

"Great!" I said. "I'll pick you up about...6:15? That should give us plenty of time."

"Okay," he said, "that sounds good. I'll see you at 6:15 Saturday, then."

* * *

I spent most of the remainder of the week contacting everyone I could find who had been in either Venture or Ramón's on the night of the incidents. When I ran out of them, I'd start on the Hilltop and Faces. I decided to concentrate on the smaller bars—Glitter would be next to impossible given its sheer size and the number of guys there at any one time, but I asked everyone I called if they might have been at Glitter the night Richie Smith threw his fit, just in case. I ran into four guys on the Ramón's list who had been at Venture the night Barnseth did his number, and two who had been at Glitter and Venture on the right nights, and one who'd been at Venture and the Hilltop. Nobody could tell me a thing.

By the time Saturday rolled around, I was ready for a break. I had one of those secretary's spiral notebooks filled with names, and names the names had given me, and little arrows and scrawls and circles from one to the other, and...

I went to the store for the week's groceries and picked up

stuff for a couple sandwiches for me, plus a large bottle of cranberry juice and some fruit. By five o'clock I was all ready to go and had everything in the cooler I'd dug out of the storeroom after having all but forgotten about it for a couple years. I tried to time it so I wouldn't be too early, but found myself turning down the 200 block of Cloverland at about five after six.

To my surprise, Toby was standing on the sidewalk by the curb, like a kid waiting for the school bus. He had a sport jacket over one arm, and a brown paper bag in the other hand. Whatever he had in the bag could not been one tenth as delicious as he looked. God, he was beautiful!

I pulled up to the curb, and he got in. "I would have come in for you," I said.

He smiled and turned to put his paper bag and sport jacket in the back seat next to the cooler. "I know," he said, "but parking can be a problem and I didn't want to put you to any extra trouble."

He was wearing a white shirt open at the collar, showing off his tan to full advantage, and his little silver chain only added to the overall effect.

"I wasn't quite sure what to wear to a symphony," he said. "I've got a tie in my jacket if I need it."

"You look fine just the way you are," I said, and I meant it.

* * *

We parked in the public garage under the west side of Warman Park, and took our bag and cooler up to the surface, emerging about 300 feet from the central fountain. There were quite a few people who'd obviously had the same idea as we did, but it wasn't crowded by a long shot, and we easily found a picnic table.

Toby, it seems, took most of his meals in liquid form. He had two small thermoses of I-couldn't-guess-what, a small plastic bag of some sort of cracker, a banana, a peach, and an apple. Oh, and a small bottle of assorted pills and capsules which he washed down with the contents of one of the thermoses. I'd made two bologna/summer sausage/ American cheese sandwiches (lots of mayo and mustard) and had brought a couple apples, oranges, and the bottle of cranberry juice, which had barely fit in the cooler. Luckily, I did not forget the paper cups.

It was a beautiful afternoon with relatively little traffic on the surrounding streets. We were close enough to the fountain to be able to appreciate the soothing sounds of falling water. The sky was a crisp, sharp, no-nonsense blue with only an occasional cumulus cloud drifting lazily overhead, trolling its shadow lightly across the ground.

"You know, Toby," I said when I felt the time was right, "it occurred to me the other day that we've seen each quite a few times now, and I don't even know your last name."

Toby gave me one of those Toby smiles. "Brown," he said. "Toby Brown. Did you know Brown is the most common last name in America?"

No, I didn't, and I shook my head. When he didn't volunteer any more information I pushed ahead, hoping I didn't come across as actually pushing. "And I don't know very much about *you*, actually. Where you're from, your family, stuff like that."

He smiled again. "Does it matter?" he asked, calmly.

I felt my face flushing slightly and hoped it was all on the inside. "No," I stammered; "not really...I didn't mean to pry."

Still smiling, Toby reached across the table and took my hand. "I'm sorry," he said; "I just try not to think about my past very much if I can avoid it. I'm a farm boy, as I think I told you once. My family was about as poor as you can get and still make do. My dad and mom worked like dogs trying to make a living off the farm, but they never quite did. And then when they..." he paused for only a heartbeat, but it could have been a full minute..."died, I picked up and left. They were the only things that held me there."

I sensed again that the topic of his family was a painful one for him, so I thought it best to change the subject. "So how do you like city life, now that you've been here awhile?"

"I'm not sure I like it," he said. "As a matter of fact, I've been thinking of leaving. I've got some business back home I've got to take care of and then...I don't know."

I was both surprised and sorry to hear him say that he was thinking of moving—I'd just gotten to know him and automatically assumed he'd become a part of my life. But before I could say anything, he continued talking. "But I'm glad I moved here," he said. "I've learned a lot about people, and about being gay. And if I hadn't have moved here, I wouldn't be here now, going to the Chicago Symphony with you. You don't know how much it means to have a real friend."

I don't know why, but that really got to me and made me oddly...well, sad. I'd always been blessed with close friends: to imagine being without them.... "Thanks, Toby," I said. "I'm really glad we met. But I would think you'd have more friends than you could handle."

That small smile again. "When I first got here, I met lots of people—they'd all come up to me and smile and flatter me and tell me how great I was, and here I am a kid from a wide spot in the road—what did I know? So then they'd take me home and after they got what they wanted, I'd never see them again. Nobody here wants friends...all they want is sex. After a while I just gave up trying—until I saw you at Glitter."

"Then why did you disappear that night?" I asked.

Toby shrugged. "Because I saw you were with someone. No point in my sticking around."

I shook my head. "I know there are a lot of shits out there, Toby, but there are some nice guys, too. Don't give up too quickly."

I decided a subject change might be in order. "Jared mentioned he saw you at Ramón's the other night—did you catch the action? I understand it was quite a production."

Toby's face lost the smile completely. "Yes," he said. "I was there. Your friend Jared's the big one, right? The one you were with that night at Glitter? I've never officially met him, but he was very nice to do what he did. That guy he threw out of the bar was...not nice. How can gays treat each other like that? Don't we get enough of that from straights?"

"No argument there," I said. "Did you know the guy who caused the trouble was killed later that night? A hit-and-run."

"Really?" Toby asked in a tone implying complete disinterest. "I guess some people do get what they deserve."

I glanced at my watch and noticed that it was nearly 7:25. "Wow," I said; "we'd better get going—we have to run this stuff back to the car."

We picked up all our garbage and Toby walked it over to a nearby trash receptacle while I put his thermoses back into his paper bag, and closed the lid on my cooler. We vectored in on the parking garage entrance, found the car, and locked everything in the trunk, then headed for the Civic Arts Center.

* * *

The symphony was wonderful, and Toby was totally enthralled. I could almost feel him absorbing every note of music as though he were a very large sponge. When the concert ended, with the 1812 Overture, it looked as though he were close to tears. (Yeah—like I wasn't.)

As we rose from our seats and made our way down our row to the aisle, shoulders touching, arms at our sides, Toby moved his hand slightly forward to grab mine. "Thank you, Dick," he said. "That was probably one of the most wonderful experiences I've ever had in my whole life." And it made me oddly sad to realize that he truly meant it.

Ah, Toby, I thought.

We didn't talk much on the way back to the car...Toby was still on cloud nine. He'd picked up three programs from seats we passed on our way out, in addition to his own, apparently so that in case he wore one of them out from looking at it, he'd have spares.

You're a good kid, Toby Brown, I thought.

As we pulled out of the parking garage and onto the street, Toby broke his silence to say: "Would you like to stop somewhere for a drink, Dick? I really don't want the night to end just yet."

"Sure," I said. "Anyplace special?"

"There's a place not too far from here—The Stardust, I think it's called. I always thought it was kind of a fru-fru name for a gay bar, but we can try it if you'd like."

"Sure," I said. I'd been there a couple of times, and Toby was right about the fru-fru—it catered to the sort of piss-elegant clientele Chris always referred to as the "ribbon clerk crowd." I don't think I'd care to go in there if I were out by myself cruising, but with Toby with me I didn't mind.

We found a parking place not too far away, and walked in to find the place only about half full. Everyone stopped whatever they were doing to check us out and I heard someone at the end of the bar say "Oh, *Mary!*" when Toby, who'd been behind me, stepped around to my side.

We took two stools fairly close to the door and ordered a cranberry juice, rocks, and a whiskey old fashioned, sweet. A few minutes later, the door opened and a good looking guy built like a truck driver strode in, looking pretty much out of place. He was wearing what looked like a silk referee's shirt, with wide white and black stripes, and tight black pants that displayed a noticeable bulge. He started to walk past us and then suddenly stopped in front of us: "Hey, Toby! How's it hangin'?"

"Fine, Stan. How's it with you?"

"Not bad. Not bad," he said striking a West Side Story Jets pose, and adjusted his crotch. On a closer look, I'd judge the bulge was probably two pairs of rolled-up socks. He stood there until Toby said: "Oh, yeah...Dick, this is Stan. Stan, Dick."

We shook hands and he looked me over carefully from head to foot, his jaw moving slowly back and forth as he chewed his gum, like he was inspecting a motorcycle someone was trying to sell. Toby just looked at him, impassively, until Stan said: "Well, I just come in to see if my boy Stevie's here. If he ain't, I'm heading out to Thorson's Woods to pick up a little action."

But he continued to stand there until Toby said: "See you later, Stan."

Stan took the hint. "Yeah, see ya later." and moved about five stools down the bar.

"Not one of your favorite people, I gather," I said.

Toby shrugged. "We work together," he said. "I try to avoid him whenever I can, but he's always hitting on me. That's bad enough, but somebody told me he has a lover. He shouldn't do that."

I shrugged. "Maybe they have an open relationship."

Toby looked at me with a raised eyebrow.

"Well, it happens," I said.

"Not with me, it doesn't," he said.

The door opened again and a young guy came in, noticed Stan, and turned to go.

Too late. "Hey, there you are, sweetcakes!" Stan called. "Come on over here."

The young man...Stevie?... straightened himself up, turned, and walked reluctantly over to Stan.

"I told you I didn't want to see you anymore," the young man said quietly.

"Why, fer chrissakes?" Stan asked, reaching out to take hold of Stevie's sleeve with one hand while pulling out the barstool next to him with the other. Stevie plunked himself down.

"Because you've got a lover," the younger man said. "And you used me to rub his nose in the fact that you don't give a shit for him. And for you to take me home and not even tell me he was there! That was mean, Stan; really mean."

Stan leaned closer. "That fat old fart's not my lover, baby," Stan said. "I told you that. I just let him *think* he is. He's a fat, ugly old queen. If he's stupid enough to think that anybody might actually be able to *love* him, that's his problem. I let him blow me a couple times a month, if I feel like it, and he thinks that's love. But he pays. He's almost out of money now, and when it's gone, *I'm* gone." Stan laughed, as if he found the idea very funny. Stevie did not join in. I looked at Toby, who was staring into his cranberry juice, completely expressionless. I wanted to suggest that we leave, but didn't.

"You're sick, you know that?" Stevie said.

Stan leaned closer, though he didn't lower his volume. Others in the bar were beginning to notice, surreptitiously, and I unconsciously began to watch them. I'd never done that before, and wondered why the hell I hadn't. There were two guys I definitely recognized...another one, I was pretty sure I'd seen in Venture, though I couldn't remember when. A couple others looked familiar. The rest I didn't recognize, but that didn't mean anything. And there was one small man I couldn't see clearly, standing against he wall in the shadows.

"Sick, huh?" Stan was saying. "Well, I'm healthy enough to give you a two hour pony ride whenever you want it, right, Stevie? You sure like that pony, don't you, baby? It's all yours."

Stevie got up from his stool. "I've got to go," he said, but Stan grabbed him by the arm and pulled him back down. Stevie got up again, and Stan reached out for him again. I looked around for the bartender, but he'd apparently gone to the storeroom for something. Everyone else in the place seemed to be studiously pretending they weren't watching and listening to every word. That's when I got off of my own stool and walked over to stand between Stan and Stevie.

"He said he's got to go," I said. "So let him go."

Stan looked up at me in surprise and his jaw stopped moving in mid-chew. He let go of the younger man's arm, to Stevie's obvious relief. Stevie shot me a quick glance and then turned to stare at Stan for a second, but didn't say anything, then turned and walked out the door.

Stan seemed unconcerned, his jaws moving again and his eyes moving up and down my body. "You're a tough one, aren't you?" he asked, not belligerently. I just turned and started back to my stool.

"You want t' dump pretty boy there, I can show you what a *real* man can do for you...or maybe a three-way?"

I ignored him and sat back down, turning my attention to Toby, who was still staring into his cranberry juice. "I'm sorry, Toby," I said.

Toby turned to me with a soft smile that reminded me of the smile John Peterson had given me—that painting of a saint I'd seen somewhere, and said: "I wasn't paying attention. I was listening to music in my head."

I put my hand on his shoulder. "Maybe we should go," I said.

"We don't have to," he said. "Not yet. I'm not going to have somebody like that spoil a great night." He smiled. "And it has been great."

I let myself relax a bit. "Yeah, it has," I said. But I tried to keep one eye on the door to see who came in or left—especially who left.

A few minutes later, I felt Stan standing behind us. Toby and I both turned slightly to face him.

"You two take it easy," Stan said. "I'm off to the woods for a little huntin'—lot of wild ass out there, just waitin' for a blast from Stan's big gun." He laughed, and walked out the door.

I kept my eye on the door, but no one followed him out, and I was relieved until I looked around the bar again. The little man against the wall was gone. The back door to the bar was just swinging shut. *Shit!* I wanted to get up and follow him, but I couldn't. Toby didn't know anything about what was going on and I couldn't spring it on him now.

"You know," Toby said, apparently unaware of my being distracted, "when I was a kid, I used to go hunting with my dad. Not for fun, but because we really needed the meat for food. I hated it! Every single time I had to shoot some poor animal, it tore me apart. But like I said, it wasn't a matter of choice. We did what we had to do. I did it, but I never liked it."

I thought again of what a rough life Toby must have had

as a kid. I wished I had known him then.

Noticing that I'd finished my old fashioned, Toby drained his cranberry juice and said: "Maybe we should go...it's getting late."

We left the bar and started walking back to the car.

"Would you like to come over for a while?" I asked.

Toby smiled. "I'd like to Dick, but...can we take a rain check? I'm still hearing the music and I want to hold on to it as long as I can. You'd be too much of a...distraction, if you know what I mean," he said, and his smile turned into a sexily wicked grin.

I returned his grin. "I'll have to admit, I'd sure do my best," I said.

* * *

I dropped Toby off in front of his place and headed home. I was about six blocks from Toby's when whatever had been simmering in the back of my mind since we'd left the bar suddenly bubbled to the surface: *Thorson's Woods!*

Thorson's Woods was a notorious cruising area. Technically, it was a city park, and it spread over the slopes of the same range of foothills that, about a mile to the north, turned into the bluff the two queens had sailed off in the classic Packard. Stan had told the whole fucking bar that he was going to Thorson's Woods! And the guy in the shadows had left the bar right after Stan!

I knew it was just a hunch—the chance that the bar watcher had been in the Stardust at that exact time was incalculably remote, but what if he *had* been there? If he had, he'd definitely have heard Stan wave his First Class Prick credentials in front of the entire world. Stan may not yet have become a World Class Prick like D'Allesandro or Comstock, but from his little display at the bar, he was rising fast in the ranks. How could anyone be so deliberately mean spirited toward someone who loved him, for whatever the reason? *Everybody* is worthy of being loved—it doesn't matter what you look like, or what you weigh, or how much hair you have, or how old you are....We all deserve to be loved.

Yes, Dick, we know, my mind said, not unkindly.

I made a quick and totally illegal U-turn and headed for Riverside Drive. I could tell when I reached the edge of the Woods because suddenly both sides of Riverside were sprinkled with parked cars. I found a parking place near one of the primary walking trails and got out. The Woods was crisscrossed with trails, but there were a few that were particularly popular for their accessibility to totally secluded areas. I headed up the main trail, then took one of the branches that led to the most popular cruising spots. Though it was well after midnight by now, and there were no streetlights, it was a fairly bright night, and I could easily make out forms standing by the edge of the trail, or lounging up against trees. The lights from cigarettes dotted the night like fireflies.

Though I could see forms, faces were another matter. Shit! Any one of them could have been the guy from the bar. Stan, I was pretty sure, I'd be able to spot from that shirt—those black and white stripes would stand out like neon lights even in this light. On a hunch, I took a side trail that led to the highest point in the Woods. Not so many guys here—a lot never bothered to come this far. But I knew there was an area up there called "the grotto" which attracted those into group sex...and Stan struck me as being a group sex kind of guy.

The path was steep and rocky, so I had to watch my step, particularly in the darker areas where trees blocked out what light there was. I reached the grotto to find maybe three or four guys there, busily engaged in the activities that had drawn them there. One guy, on his knees in front of another, noticed me and stopped what he was doing long enough to motion me over to join them. I didn't see Stan among the participants, so I managed to resist my crotch's suggestion that I take him up on his offer. I just waved and turned back down the hill.

I was just turning a small bend in the path when I saw,

coming up the hill, someone in a white-and-black shirt that stood out clearly even in the low light. I knew who was wearing it.

I stepped quickly off the path, where I could watch him but he couldn't see me. And then I noticed there was someone else coming up the path behind him. *Looks like things are picking up at the grotto*, I told myself. The guy behind Stan was closing the gap between them, and I suddenly got a strange feeling in my stomach. Stan gave no indication he knew the guy was there. They weren't close enough for me to make out faces or much detail, but then I saw the guy behind Stan stop, bend over, and pick up what appeared to be a very large rock.

Jeezus! I thought. I didn't move a muscle until I was sure I knew what the guy had in mind. He moved up quickly toward Stan, who was apparently so focused on getting down to business at the grotto that he still didn't know there was anyone behind him. The guy was only about five feet behind Stan, now, and I saw him raise the rock over his head with both hands.

I jumped out into the path and yelled *"HEY!"* then took off running—or as close to running as the trail would allow—straight for Stan, who just stood there, probably startled out of his gourd. The guy behind him dropped the rock, turned, and ran back down the hill.

I reached Stan, who was still just standing there like a deer caught in the headlights, completely blocking the path, forcing me to almost come to a dead stop. "Move!" I said, reaching out to grab him by the shoulders and practically throw him out of the way. He stumbled into the underbrush and I continued down the twisting path. I could catch only occasional glimpses of the guy ahead of me, moving fast. When he reached a point where three trails came together, he suddenly darted off into the woods. He turned his head slightly to look back at me, and ran into a low-hanging branch of a pine tree, which caught him and spun him around, hard. But he regained his balance and continued running, disappearing into the woods. *Damn!*

When I got to the point where he'd entered the woods, I

realized that he could have quickly backtracked to any one of the three trails. I chose one at random, and continued running.

Nothing. More guys along the trail as I neared the bottom of the hill, and I hadn't had a good enough look at him, other than as a running figure, to be able to even know if he was one of the guys I passed.

Totally frustrated, but pretty sure the guy wouldn't make another move on Stan that night, I found my way to my car and drove home.

* * *

I had the dream again—one I'd had several times in the past few weeks: being in a crowded, dark bar where I couldn't make out faces, or features...just eyes.

I woke up around 7:30 and without giving it much conscious thought got dressed and headed out to my car. No shower, no coffee, just the knowledge that I had to return to the Woods—I had no idea why.

Riverside was all but empty. There were maybe three or four cars parked along the entire stretch of the Woods. I pulled up close to the trail from which I'd emerged not all that long ago and retraced my steps as best I could to where the three trails met. I had a very strange feeling and still had no idea what it was. But there was a familiar tightness in my stomach.

I tried to pick the exact spot where I'd seen the guy run into the woods, and managed to pick out what I thought was the pine tree he'd smacked into. I walked slowly toward it, trying to retrace his steps. Why? What the hell was I looking for? Footprints? Dick Hardesty, Boy Deerstalker. I walked directly toward the tree, as the guy had run to it, and tried to pick out the limb that had caught him.

So now what, Nattie Bumpo? I asked myself.

My eyes dropped to the ground beneath the tree and were caught by a brief glint of something. Bending down, I pushed aside some loose pine needles and picked up a thin silver chain.

CHAPTER 14

I've done some pretty stupid things in my life, but I realize that what I did after picking up the chain was without a doubt right there at the very top of the list.

I put the chain in my pocket and opened the car door. How had I gotten from the tree to the car? I couldn't tell you. I was suddenly aware that my mind had been a total blank between those two actions. I wasn't thinking anything, I wasn't feeling anything—how I even managed to walk across the street to the car without being hit I couldn't tell you, other than it was a Sunday morning and there wasn't much traffic.

Back in reality and seated in my car, I was still numb and operating pretty much on autopilot. When I felt I was at least sufficiently together to be able to drive without getting myself into an accident, I started the car, checked the rear-view mirror for oncoming traffic, and pulled out into the street.

I didn't tell myself where I was going until I pulled up in front of 247 Cloverland. I parked, got out of the car, and went to the door. For a relatively small building, it had a lot of tenants, according to the mailboxes in the small entry. I found one that said "T. Brown, 218" and walked up the stairs and down the hall to the door marked 218. I knocked, and there was no answer, but I could hear the soft sounds of music. Francesca di Rimini. I knocked again.

"Toby," I said, "it's Dick."

A moment later I heard a security lock being turned, and the door opened.

I had been dreading actually facing him. I know I should have called the police immediately. But I also knew—or hoped to hell I knew—that Toby would never hurt me. And when I saw the look on his face, any possible concern I might have had for my own safety vanished. His eyes were red, and I'm sure he hadn't slept.

"Hi, Dick," he said, his voice oddly flat. "Come on in."

I entered his tiny apartment and noticed a couple cardboard boxes on the small couch and another on the coffee table and could see, through the open bedroom door, two suitcases on the oddly slanted bed.

I reached into my pocket and took out the chain. "You dropped this," I said. "I know how much it means to you."

Toby looked at me and his eyes filled with tears, which ran down either side of his nose and onto his upper lip. He reached out with an open hand and I dropped the chain into it.

"Thank you, Dick," he said softly, the tears still running down his face. He made a quick scooping swipe with the back of his free hand from the bottom of his chin to under his nose, to catch them. Don't ask me why, but I wanted more than anything in the world to be the big brother I'd thought of myself as being, to reach out and grab him and hug him and tell him it would be all right. But I wasn't, I didn't, and it wouldn't.

"It's over," I said.

Toby nodded. "I know," he said. "That's why I was leaving today. I can't stay here anymore. I was going to call you before I left, though, to say goodbye and thank you for being my friend." He looked at me, very seriously, his eyes searching my face. "Are you still my friend, Dick?" he asked.

Still his friend? my mind yelled. *He's killed seven people and almost killed an eighth! Are you his friend???*

"Yes, Toby, I'm your friend," I said, and I meant it.

What a poor fucking excuse you are for a P.I. my mind said, disgustedly.

Toby tried to smile, then looked around and said "Can we sit for a minute?"

"Sure," I said. I realized I was a lot more calm than I had a right to be, but aside from being calm, I was indescribably sad. There was so much I wanted to know and so much I realized now I didn't really need to be told; that I already knew.

As Toby bent over to move the open cardboard box from

the couch to the coffee table, I saw a framed photo. As we sat, I instinctively reached into the box and took it out. It was a black and white photograph of two dorky-looking teenagers, smiling into the camera with their arms around each other's shoulders. One of them was enormously overweight, the other not as grossly fat, but obviously probably about 50 pounds overweight.

"That's J.J.," Toby said, tapping the glass over the grossly overweight figure on the left. "My best friend."

"And the..." I started to say, then nearly bit my tongue when I realized who it was.

"That's me," Toby said. "I weighed 230 pounds when I was sixteen years old."

I shook my head. "It must have been really hard for you," I said.

Toby gave me the merest shadow of a smile. "You have no idea," he said. "I'm pretty sure if I go to hell when I die, it can't be much worse than being fat and ugly and gay in a small farm town. The adults never said much, because they liked and respected my folks—but the kids! Oh, God, the kids. Especially two of the local jocks who thought the bigger the bully you could be, the bigger the man you were." He was silent for a moment, then said, matter-of-factly: "They killed my folks."

I'm sure my incomprehension was written all over my face. "You don't mean literally, I hope?" I managed to say, fully aware of how stupid a question it was.

Toby shrugged. "They weren't arrested for it, if that's what you mean," he said. "It was never proved. But the night my folks died, I was supposed to go to some school thing. We had an old beat-up pickup truck that my dad and I managed to keep running with wires and tape. But I got sick while I was coming home from school that night, and went right to bed. My folks decided to go into town to return some canning supplies my mom had borrowed." He gently chewed his lower lip for a moment or two, remembering. "They never came home," he said. "They went off a bridge halfway to town. They said it was an accident, but it wasn't. I know those two jocks were responsible. They saw the pickup, thought it was me going to the school thing, and ran it off the road. They'd done it to me before. But this time it wasn't me."

What could I say? Apparently, Toby didn't expect a response. He was caught up in his story, and I was equally caught up in hearing it.

"So I went to stay with relatives in Georgia and decided I'd had enough of being the ugly fat kid. I started working out, and changed my diet, and slowly but surely I changed myself over.

"I kept in touch with J.J., of course, and convinced him that he should do what I did. And he tried; he really tried, and he lost 125 pounds himself. When I moved here, I had J.J. come out for a visit. He looked great—we almost didn't recognize one another after having been friends for nearly 20 years. He hadn't gotten to where he wanted to be yet, but he was really looking good and starting to feel good about himself for the first time in his life."

He stopped talking for a moment, and reached out and took my hand. "Am I talking too much, Dick?" he asked.

I squeezed his hand. "No, Toby, you're not. Don't stop."

He sighed. "It's my fault, really. We'd both realized we were gay about the time we turned 14, but we were too good friends to do anything about it with each other. We just looked and dreamed and pretended we weren't fat and ugly—kind of hard to do when you're reminded every day. But at least we had each other.

"So anyway, when he came out to visit, Rage had just opened up and I thought I'd let J.J. see what the gay community had to offer. So I took him down to Rage. I didn't know you had to be a member, but when I asked about joining, the clerk called that Comstock guy out, and he told us that I could join, but that J.J. couldn't because he wasn't attractive enough! My God, Dick! Can you imagine? Can you imagine what that did to J.J.?"

I could, indeed, and suddenly wondered if he and his friend had been the ones Jared had mentioned seeing his first night at Rage.

"J.J.'d never been anywhere where there were other gays," Toby continued. "I guess from what I'd told him he expected that since we'd all lived with prejudice and hatred all our lives, we'd all be like one big loving family. Comstock took care of that with one sentence. It told J.J. that no matter what he did or how hard he worked, people would always hate him... even what I'd told him so often were 'his own' people. And he just wasn't the same after that. I told him he should move out here with me, but he said he wanted to go back home, where at least he knew who hated him.

"That's when I started sending those notes to Comstock. And then I got a letter from J.J.'s mom telling me that J.J. had died. He'd gone out rabbit hunting by his farm and apparently tripped and his gun went off. I know that's not what happened, but I hope his folks don't."

He sighed and released my hand.

"I slashed the top and the tires on Comstock's car on my way to work one morning. And when I got home that night, I got the letter from J.J.'s mom. So I went back that night and killed Comstock. Found his keys and let myself in and went into his office. I took a handkerchief out of my pocket and picked up the letter opener, and when he came in, I stabbed him. And you know what, Dick?" He looked at me and I found myself shaking my head. "When I used to have to shoot animals, I'd feel terrible about it. But when I killed Comstock, I didn't feel a thing. I was just taking out the garbage."

I was sitting right beside him, but I was terribly aware, from the impassive look on his face and the hollow tone of his voice, that Toby was completely, utterly alone.

What's happening to you, Hardesty? my mind demanded, sincerely shocked. *This guy kills people and you* _agree_ *with him?*

Toby sighed again and went on talking. "And then the night

I saw you in Glitter, that Richie character treated that poor older guy with such contempt, such disrespect; such *meanness*, I knew in his heart he was just like Comstock. And I realized that I didn't have to just stand back and watch that kind of thing anymore. So I followed him home and went into his garage—he was pretty drunk, because he just sat in his car for awhile—and when he got out of his car, I just pushed him really hard and he fell forward and hit his head on the door stoop. So I went and turned the engine of his car back on, pressed the door close button, and went out of the garage while it was closing."

He looked at me again. "Do you want me to go on?" he asked. I shook my head—I'd heard enough. I didn't need the details.

Toby smiled a strange, sad smile. "And not once did I care," he said. "Not once did I feel that I'd done something bad. When I'd kill a deer, my dad would say: 'You've got to do what you've got to do, boy.' And he was right."

"Where is the gun you used for the two queens and D'Allesandro?" I asked.

Toby shrugged. "I got rid of it last night after I left Thorson's Woods," he said. "It was an old hunting rifle I'd brought from home. It could never be traced, and it's somewhere no one will ever find it."

I took a very deep breath and turned to face him full-on. "You've got to turn yourself in, Toby," I said.

"Am I'm crazy, Dick?" he asked, his eyes searching my face for…what?…reassurance?

I shook my head again. "No, Toby, I don't think you're crazy. But killing is killing, no matter how solid the motives may be."

Thinking of Toby spending the rest of his life in prison tore my heart out, but I knew that was what had to be. Thank God we don't have capital punishment in this state!

"I'll go with you to the police, if you'll let me," I said.

Toby smiled again, a really warm smile that only made me

feel worse about this whole fucking mess—if that were possible!

"I wish everyone were as nice as you, Dick," he said. "You know, none of those men had to die. All they had to do was be nice. Is that so hard?"

He got up from the couch and put the picture of himself and J.J. back in the box.

"Do you mind if I finish packing first, Dick?" he asked. "I don't have much, but somebody has to do it."

"Would you like me to keep it for you?" I asked.

"Would you?" he asked. "That would be wonderful. I don't know when I'll be able to have it again, but it would be nice to know it's all safe."

My God, Hardesty! What in the hell are you doing? my mind demanded again. *This guy kills people!*

"I've just got a few more things to put away," Toby said, once again the calm, in control Toby I'd first met. He went into the bedroom, then to the bathroom, which I could also see from the open bedroom door. I watched him put toilet articles into a dopp kit and then return to the bedroom.

I suddenly realized I had a terrific headache—no morning coffee, partly; stress mostly. "Do you have an aspirin by any chance?" I asked.

Toby turned to me. "Sure," he said, and turned again to reach into his dopp kit, coming up with a small bottle of aspirin. "I think there are some glasses in the kitchen cupboard."

"Don't bother," I said, getting up to join him in the bedroom. "I'm an old hand-scooper."

He opened the bottle and tapped two aspirin into my hand.

"Thanks," I said, and moved past him into the bathroom.

Watch out, you fucking idiot! my mind screamed. *You can't be dumb enough to turn your back on him!?!*

My mind could scream at me all it wanted to: if I knew anything in my life, I knew Toby could never—would never—hurt me. I looked into the medicine cabinet mirror and saw him bending over one of his suitcases, putting things away as I turned on the water, cupped my hand under the flow to fill it with water, popped the aspirin into my mouth with my free hand, and bent over the sink to drink.

I smelled something very strange and started to stand up. As I did so, I looked in the mirror to see Toby standing directly behind me.

Oh, shit! I thought as I spun around just in time to feel a wet cloth being pressed over my nose and mouth, and then I don't remember anything else.

* * *

The first thing I realized when I woke up was that I couldn't see, and I couldn't move my hands or feet. Then I realized that was because I was bound and gagged with duct tape, and shut inside Toby's closet. I'm not sure how long it took me to extricate myself—maybe half an hour. He'd also moved the dresser *and* the bed in front of the door, which took another five or ten minutes to work out of the way enough so I could get out. The apartment was empty. The boxes gone, the suitcases gone, Toby gone.

In the living room, on the coffee table, was a note.

Dick:

I'm so very sorry I had to do that...I hope you weren't too uncomfortable. It was just some chloroform I'd taken from the hospital when I worked there.

You'll be fine.

I'm sorry I couldn't go with you —I have some unfinished business to take care of at home first. I'll never forget you, and I will miss you. Please remember me as I will remember you—as a friend.

Toby

* * *

The puzzle was finished—at least insofar as that every piece I had was finally in place. But the picture wasn't complete: there were a couple large empty spaces. Some were easy to guess what was missing: the embezzlement issue would somehow be worked out between O'Banyon and Giacomino; whatever the solution to that one might be was up to them.

What O'Banyon would be able to do—or what I might be somehow able to do—about this new, frightening shadow falling over the gay community was a large hole over which hung an ominous question mark.

And how O'Banyon would react to all this as far as my contract went—if he'd want to honor it or not under the circumstances—I neither knew or really cared. I'd call him and the police immediately, of course.

My own future as a private investigator was also in question: when the police learned that I'd tried to bring Toby in on my own without calling them immediately, they might well want to yank my license—and I couldn't blame them. However, I told myself, the fact remained that there was not one single piece of solid evidence to link Toby to the murders. Even Toby's chain wouldn't do it if I'd given it to them—no crime had been committed: Stan was still alive and free to continue being a despicable son-of-a-bitch—he didn't even know he'd been in danger. No, I imagined they'd probably just be pretty pissed at me for awhile.

I had no idea where Toby was heading—he had never said. A small farm community is all I knew, and how many of those are around? And as he had pointed out, his last name is the most common in the U.S. His accent could have been almost anything, including Canadian. I had no idea even of what kind of car he drove, or where it might be licensed. But I did know what he was going to do when he got there.

And there would be a dramatic drop in the murder rate among the local gay community's asshole population, which part of me still could not see as something less than a pity. But the police would be happy to know that even if Toby were to keep on doing what he had been doing, it would be someone else's problem.

I just hoped that Toby, wherever he ended up, would be able to find some degree of happiness and love. As for myself, well, I had a really good feeling about Len. We'd have to see where that led. And if it didn't go anywhere at all, I knew that Jared would always be around to offer some occasional kink and comfort.

And finally, I wished there were some way to remind everyone out there in darkened bars everywhere to just be a little more kind to one another. Someone may be watching.

I got up from the couch, left the apartment, and headed for a telephone.

THE END

The Bar Watcher
by Dorien Grey   Copyright 2001